Timon of Athens

Sweet Cherry

Publishing

Published by Sweet Cherry Publishing Limited
Unit E, Vulcan Business Complex,
Vulcan Road,
Leicester, LE5 3EB,
United Kingdom

First published in the USA in 2013
ISBN: 978-1-78226-080-6

©Macaw Books

Title: Timon of Athens
North American Edition

Text & Illustration by Macaw Books 2013

www.sweetcherrypublishing.com

Printed and bound by Wai Man Book Binding (China) Ltd. Kowloon, H.K.

~About~ *Shakespeare*

William Shakespeare, regarded as the greatest writer in the English language, was born in Stratford-upon-Avon in Warwickshire, England (around April 23, 1564). He was the third of eight children born to John and Mary Shakespeare.

Shakespeare was a poet, playwright, and dramatist. He is often known as England's national poet and the "Bard of Avon." Thirty-eight plays, 154 sonnets, two long narrative poems, and several other poems are attributed to him. Shakespeare's plays have been translated into every major existent language and are performed more often than those of any other playwright.

Timon: Timon is a wealthy man in Athens who likes to throw lavish feasts for his friends and send them gifts. But when he goes bankrupt, everyone deserts him. Then he goes into the forest, hating humanity.

Flavius: He is the loyal servant of Timon. He repeatedly tries to warn his master not to spend so much money, but his words fall on deaf ears. He even goes in search of Timon in the forest but is sent back by Timon with harsh words.

Ventidius: He is a young Athenian whom Timon helped to get out of

prison. However, he refuses to help Timon when Timon goes bankrupt.

Alcibiades: He is a soldier who has raised an army to destroy Athens. He meets Timon in the forest, who supports Alcibiades. In a way, Alcibiades tries to right the wrong that has been done to Timon.

Timon of Athens

Once upon a time, there was a lord in Athens by the name of Timon. Though he was very wealthy, Timon had a tendency to spend much more

than he actually had. He would not spend much of it on himself, but rather would spend his fortune on all kinds of people—be it the poor people of the city or even other wealthy lords like himself. His house would always be open to everyone and grand meals would always be prepared for anyone who might want to visit at any time of the day. Even the rich people of the town would deflate their egos and go to Timon for a feast. There was not a

single person on the streets of Athens who had not been under the patronage of the great Timon.

He would commission unworthy poets, buy paintings from painters that were not being sold to anyone else in the city and persuade jewelers to sell him high-priced stones that no one else could buy. Anything and everything which required his wealth to help another person was done and he cast no distinction between anybody.

A large number
of people who lived as
Timon's dependents were
actually young men from
rich households who
had been thrown into
prison by their creditors
for the nonpayment
of loans, and Timon
would immediately get
them out of jail. One
such spendthrift was a
man called Ventidius,
for whom Timon
had recently paid a
huge sum to absolve
him of his debts.

But Timon did not
realize that all these men

were interested in was his wealth, not his companionship. They would all cherish the moment when Timon took a fancy to anything that belonged to them, for they would then charge him an exorbitant amount for the item. Some people would even

send him things that
he had commented
on some time ago.
They knew that
Timon would accept their gifts
and return their "generosity"
with a more expensive gift
or, in most cases, money.

But it was not that Timon
only spent his wealth on such
people. He would also act as
a philanthropist in noble and
praiseworthy acts. For instance,
one day his servant came to
him and declared that he
had fallen in love with a rich
Athenian's daughter. However,

he knew he could never express
his love for her because of his
poor and pitiable condition.
Timon immediately gave the
servant a huge amount
of money, making
him rich beyond
his wildest dreams
and enabling

him to marry the love of his
life. However, such acts were
few in number, as most of

the people who fed off his wealth were spendthrifts who managed to increase their own fortunes by misleading the noble Timon.

Timon never considered that his wealth might soon be gone due to how much he was spending. His steward, Flavius, a rather honest fellow, would

often try to bring it to his master's
attention, but Timon would
always succeed in changing the
topic to something more frivolous.
He paid no heed to his steward's
genuine words, but rather doted
on the false exaggerations of
his flatterers. Every night, when
the rooms of his house were

full of freeloaders,
drinking his
wine like water,
Flavius would
retire to a solitary
corner and cry his heart out
over his master's foolish ways.

But one day, Timon was
forced to face reality. He ordered

Flavius to sell some more of his land to meet his payments, only for Flavius to inform him that most of the land he owned was either already sold or had been forfeited. What he had at that moment was not even worth a third of the debts he had incurred. Timon tried to

explain to him that he
had lands from Athens
to Lacedaemon, but
Flavius only replied, "O
my good Lord, the world
is but a world, and has
bounds; were it all yours
to give in a breath, how
quickly were it gone!"

But Timon managed
to console the weeping
Flavius by telling him
that all was not lost.
After all, he had not
made unwise decisions
regarding his expenses
but had spent the money
on his friends, who would
now surely take care of

him. He sent Flavius to the houses of various lords who had once been the recipients of Timon's generosity and asked them to lend him money. He also sent his noble steward to the house of Ventidius, the young man whom he had rescued from prison, to ask for the return of the money he had paid previously. After all, Ventidius's father had died recently, leaving his son ample wealth. Timon was confident

that when his friends received
the message, they would open
their coffers and pay him up to
five hundred times the amount
of money he had asked for.

Flavius first arrived at
the house of Lord Lucullus,
a wealthy man who had been
feasting off Timon his whole life.
He had long been dreaming of

a silver cup, and the minute he
was told that Timon's servant
had called upon him, he thought
his dream had come true and
that Timon must have sent him
the silver cup he had cherished
for so long. But when he heard

the true nature of Flavius's visit,
he at once made a song and
dance about how he had always
warned Timon of his spending
habits. He had supposedly come
to dinner many a time with the
request that such dinners should

not be had, as they would one day come back to haunt Timon. And of course, when he could not conclude his argument at these dinners, he would come back for breakfast and lunch the following day and continue with his speech. Finally, he ended

his whole soliloquy by trying to bribe Flavius, so that the honest steward could go home and tell his master that he had not been able to meet Lucullus at home.

There was little success at the house of Lord Lucius, who still lay in bed after the hearty dinner he had consumed at

Timon's house the night before. When he heard the news and realized that the winds had changed, he lost no time in crying over Timon's fate. However, he had made a rather hefty purchase the day before, and was now

in no position to
repay his generous
friend and pull
him out of the dire
straits he was in. He
kept up the pretense
of crying and rebuking himself
for not being able
to help a friend
who had always
showered him with
gifts and affection.

It was the same
story throughout
the city of Athens.
Every house
Flavius went to
came up with the
same story—they

wanted to help their friend,
but for some reason or other
they were unable to. Even the
ungrateful Ventidius refused to
pay the money his friend had
so generously given him to get

him out of prison, even though
he now had plenty to do so.

Timon's house, once a place
where everybody would stop
and go inside, had now become
somewhere people would just
walk past, perhaps even run,
in the event that Timon might

spot them and come out to ask
for money. The only people
who came to visit Timon now
were his coldhearted creditors,
who would thrust bills before
him and ask him to pay the
amounts requested. Timon's
house was now like a prison,
a place he could neither stay

in nor leave until his
dues had been paid.

However, there was
the last act of the setting
sun that had to be carried
out. All the lords who
were avoiding Timon
like the plague were
suddenly bewildered to
find themselves invited to
a feast at his house. They
all thought that he had
merely pretended to be
poor to test their love for
him. But they were happy
that Timon was now back
to his old self and soon
they would be able to rip

him off like they had done
so many times before.

So, when the
declared date arrived,
all the lords and ladies,
dressed in their finery,
made their way to
Timon's house to partake
in the festivities. When
they arrived, they saw

45

that everything was back to
normal and it was as if Timon
had never been poor at all. They
all wondered how a poor man
had been able to arrange such
a gala feast when
suddenly, the food

appeared. Alas, all
that was being
served was smoke

and lukewarm water. It was
Timon's way of showing his
"friends" what their friendship
was all about. Before the guests
realized what was happening,
Timon started to throw the
water at them, abusing them.
The guests left without another
word. Some lost portions of
their gowns, some ladies

even lost their jewelry,
but no one dared
to stay there for a
minute longer. There
was no knowing
what this madman
would do next!

That was the last
time they ever saw
Timon. He headed into
the forests beyond the
city walls, where he
found the wild beasts
more grateful than the
people he had given all
his wealth to. He wished
that all the houses he
could see on the horizon
would fall, leaving those

men to the same fate to which
he was now consigned. He ate
the wild roots in the forest and

drank from the streams
that nature provided.

One day, as he was
trying to dig up some
wild roots for his meal, his
spade struck something. It
was a huge chest of gold,
perhaps left there by some
robber who could not
make it back to retrieve
it and was now perhaps
rotting in prison. It was
now in Timon's possession.

Had Timon been
the Timon of old, he
would be pleased he
now had enough gold
to buy his friends again. But the
very sight of the gold disgusted

him, and he was about to bury the chest when he decided he could use it for something worthwhile.

A group of Athenian soldiers, under the leadership of General Alcibiades, had been camping near the edge of the forest. They too had faced ingratitude from

the people of the city, whom they
had defended with their lives,
and were about to march into
the city to fight the ungrateful
senators. Timon took the gold
to Alcibiades and asked him to
pay all his soldiers. All he asked
in return was that they attack

the city and kill its inhabitants,
not leaving a single soul alive
at the end of their
conquest. Timon
truly hated all
Athenians and
mankind in general.

One day, as Timon lay in
the forest, completely naked—for
he had lost all his clothes—he
saw a man standing near him,
looking on respectfully. It was
his old steward, Flavius, whose
love for his master had made him

come to the forest
looking for him.
But Timon felt that
since Flavius was a
human being, he must
also be a traitor and the tears
that he cried were false. Flavius
tried to prove to his master that

he was not like the men who had
deserted him when he needed
them the most, and he was able
to convince Timon that there
was at least one honest man left
in the world. But since he was
in the garb of a man and part
of mankind, Timon had to ask

him to leave. And that was the last that Timon saw of Flavius.

But now the Athenians thought of Timon again, because besides being the friend that he was, he had also been the general of the army, the only man who could resist the attacks of the murderous Alcibiades. His men had stormed the city and were destroying everything like wild boars. A group of senators went to the forest in search of Timon, to beg him to save them. When they found him, they tried everything they could to get Timon to agree. They promised him riches, nobility, dignities, retribution for past injuries,

everything. But Timon, the man-hater that he was, could not care less. There was no way he would ever go back to save mankind.

However, just as the weeping senators were about to leave, Timon turned to them and said that there was only one way in which the Athenians could save themselves from the

cruelty of Alcibiades. He mentioned that there was a huge tree in front of his cave, which he was about to cut down. He asked the Athenians to go to the tree and hang themselves from it. That was the only way they could save themselves from the wrath of Alcibiades!

Soon thereafter, whenever someone walked by the sea coast near the city, they would see a grave there with an epitaph that read: *While he lived, he hated all living men, and while dying, wished a plague might consume all left!* Timon of Athens lived the rest of his life as the man-hater he had become. And what better place for his burial than the sea, so that the waters could cry for him forever!

About the Author

MOHAMED LARBI BOUGUERRA works at the Alliance for a Responsible, Plural and United World, where he is in charge of the Water Programme. He was previously Professor of Science at Tunis University, and Associate Director of Research at the French National Centre for Scientific Research (CNRS).

Zed Books wishes to express its appreciation to the Alliance of Independent Publishers for its support in the publication of this book.

The Alliance of Independent Publishers is a non-profit-making association governed by French legislation, set up in spring 2002 on the initiative of a small group of book professionals. By gradually setting up an international network of publishers, working independently of the major publishing groups, who meet regularly and work together on publishing projects, the Alliance of Independent Publishers is contributing to the circulation of ideas and the building of an international civil society.

Water under Threat

Mohamed Larbi Bouguerra

Translated by Patrick Camiller

White Lotus
Bangkok

Fernwood Publishing
Nova Scotia

Books for Change
Bangalore

SIRD
Kuala Lumpur

David Philip
Cape Town

ZED BOOKS
London & New York

Water under Threat was first published as *Les batailles de l'eau*
by Les Éditions de l'Atelier in 2003

This English translation was first published in 2006 by

In Burma, Cambodia, Laos, Thailand and Vietnam:
White Lotus Co. Ltd, GPO Box 1141, Bangkok 10501, Thailand

In Canada: Fernwood Publishing Ltd, 32 Oceanvista Lane
Site 2A, Box 5, Black Point, NS B0J 1B0

In India: Books for Change, 139 Richmond Road, Bangalore 560 025

In Malaysia: Strategic Information Research Development (SIRD),
No. 11/4E, Petaling Jaya, 46200 Selangor

In Southern Africa: David Philip (an imprint of New Africa Books),
99 Garfield Road, Claremont 7700, South Africa

In the rest of the world: Zed Books Ltd, 7 Cynthia Street, London N1 9JF, UK,
and Room 400, 175 Fifth Avenue, New York, NY 10010, USA
www.zedbooks.co.uk

Copyright © Mohamed Larbi Bouguerra 2006
English translation © Patrick Camiller 2006

Designed and typeset in Monotype Janson
by illuminati, Grosmont, www.illuminatibooks.co.uk
Cover designed by Andrew Corbett
Printed and bound in Malta by Gutenberg Press Ltd

Distributed in the USA exclusively by Palgrave Macmillan, a division of
St Martin's Press, LLC, 175 Fifth Avenue, New York, NY 10010

A catalogue record for this book is available from the British Library
Library of Congress Cataloging-in-Publication Data available
Library and Archives Canada Cataloguing in Publication Data

    Bouguerra, Mohamed Larbi, 1936–
       Water under threat / Larbi Bouguerra.
    Includes index.
    Translation of: Les batailles de l'eau.
    ISBN 1-55266-202-0
      1. Water-supply. 2. Water use. 3. Water-supply—Management.
    I. Title.
    HD1691.B6813 2006   333.91   C2006-902032-9

ISBN 1 84277 704 1 Hb
ISBN 1 84277 705 X Pb
ISBN 978 1 84277 704 6 Hb
ISBN 978 1 84277 705 3 Pb

Contents

Introduction

I was born in the medina of Bizerte, in the far north of Tunisia, and spent my early childhood in a house without running water. Before the Second World War, such a luxury existed only in the European Bijouville district, even though the whole town had the benefit of a system of drains.

In fact, people nearby thought of our house as rather posh, for it had both a shared well (which made relations with our neighbours easier) and a rainwater tank. During the summer, my mother regularly asked female relatives and neighbours to come and help her clean out the tank. First they washed their woollen mattresses with the water left at the bottom: none was ever wasted. Then they carefully sealed any cracks and whitewashed it, and burned some incense to the sound of ululations that were supposed to attract friendly spirits. The work ended in a festive atmosphere over a good meal. I was always told that this tank maintenance would ward off what we quite often saw around us: cases of typhoid and people with yellow eyes and skin, indicating hepatitis due to contaminated water. This was how I first became aware of the importance of water for human health. No one in our local area would have refused water to a neighbour, or even to a passer-by or stranger. It was always thought of as a vital substance to be shared with others, not as private property.

The *kuttab* (Koranic school) where I learned to read and write – which contains the tomb of one of the town's saints – stood opposite a magnificent large public fountain, donated by a Jew, on whose marble plaque one could read a text in Hebrew characters. From this I learned that water crossed the religious divisions in the town of my birth. I also knew that, during periods of drought, people went to Koudiat hill at the edge of town and offered special prayers for rain. In my own neighbourhood, children made their contribution to these prayers by creating a vaguely feminine scarecrow out of reeds and rags, *Um Tango* (Mother Tango), which they carried from house to house chanting 'Um Tango asks God for rain, asks God to sprinkle her'. In reply, women came to their doorstep and threw a little water on the scarecrow, at the same time offering the children a few sweets. Undoubtedly it was all a remnant of some pagan ritual, in a country that had been Muslim for more than a thousand years.

Subsequently, in my professional life, I have worked for a long time on the analysis of organic pollutants, especially pesticides in water, and most recently the Fondation pour le progrès de l'homme has given me the opportunity to work in this field at an international level. Here I shall present the lessons I have drawn from these experiences, although I know full well that no book can ever offer a complete picture of such a vast topic. Many of the examples I give show that this precious resource has the capacity to sow discord, in an increasingly large number of industrialized countries as well as in others. Since 11 September 2001 water has been seen as an Achilles heel of developed societies: it is the source of numerous fears and worries, and receives the attention of a whole army of security guards in the United States and elsewhere. In France, the Vigipirate Plan contains provisions to protect the water supply from attack by increasing the quantity of chlorine.

Clearly, at local, regional and international levels, water is the critical natural resource that can create either problems or opportunities for cooperation. This is why, in the first part of the book, I lay great stress on the symbolism of water, on the fact that the water cycle ties us all to one another as well as to Mother Nature (as the Native Americans say). I emphasize its presence in our imagination, our language and metaphors, our ways of life, and the history of our countries and their civilizations. Along the way, I also show that science does not know everything about this little tri-atomic molecule, that we still have things to learn about it. Water imparts a lesson in modesty to human beings.

On this planet that cosmonauts see as blue, water is a finite quantity that is very unevenly distributed: we need only compare the share that falls to Iceland with that of Djibouti or Kuwait! But, on top of these physical limits, Malthusian economists turn a blind eye to the forced competition for water among the main sectors of the economy – agriculture, industry, tourism – just as they turn a blind eye to the huge international disparities in water consumption and the way in which this precious resource is mismanaged in many countries.

The example of Algeria is instructive in this respect, for although they have a scarcity of water the Algerian people suffer just as much from bureaucracy and a tormenting lack of political will over the decades to tackle the problem. Technology has a role to play, of course, but solutions can come only from a responsible leadership and a will to work together to overcome the customary divisions. Hatred, injustice and contempt for others have to be set aside and replaced with cooperation, dialogue and solidarity. Otherwise, there is a danger that there will not be enough water to quench the fires of civil and international conflict over water. But we should be wary of hasty conclusions and undue pessimism: there can be successes in the management of water when men and women take their destiny in their hands, or when they fuse traditional wisdom with scientific knowledge about the soil and plants; examples abound from Niger (where women help the desert to blossom) through Burkina Faso to Rajasthan. In the developed countries, the struggles of civil society to preserve water as a common good of humanity are starting to bear fruit and have placed the whole issue on the agenda of international organizations. They have also raised public awareness of its importance in industrial societies, and often have placed the water merchants on the defensive by exposing their machinations and seeking legal redress.

I have further tried to show that, at the dawn of the new century, pollution is a major and insidious threat to this vital resource that serves to make it more scarce; a contaminated aquifer has to be written off for a very long time. Take, for example, the 2-million-year-old fossil aquifer in Saudi Arabia, which has now been contaminated by the fuels and other products used by US aircraft during the first Gulf war. The new factor arising from globalization is that this threat does not spare either the North or the South, even if the minority who consume 80 per cent of the world's resources have many more ways of temporarily staving off the danger. On this point I have deliberately piled up the examples and the statistics, as I have the feeling that the evidence is known only to specialists. And, to paraphrase Nobel prizewinner Erwin Schrödinger, what use is knowledge that experts mutter among themselves? 'A curse on science that is of no use to men', says the Arab proverb.

These various types of pollution of the world's water place a question mark over affluent lifestyles, breakneck industrialization, intensive agriculture and animal farming, and the ever greater use of chemicals for skin care and anti-ageing creams, pharmaceuticals, automobile plastics, furniture and clothing. To a greater or lesser degree, all these products end up in the hydrosphere: a small waterway near London carries no less than an annual average of 100 kilos of acetylsalicyclic acid (better known as aspirin), which cannot be eliminated by a water treatment plant. Without wishing to don Elijah's mantle, I would argue that a drastic change in lifestyles is bound to come, and that we should hope it comes sooner rather than later. We cannot keep trying to control the nitrate or pesticide levels in the water without doing anything to stop the pollution at source. Even if it is true that political time does not coincide with ecological time, we should remember Bossuet's warning against 'being distressed by the effects while putting up with the causes'. That is very short-sighted politics.

The measures taken will allow us to gauge the extent to which there is a water crisis. Too many individuals and pressure groups have an interest in waving the spectre of crisis and, like the arsonist fireman, being the first to propose solutions, the people behind the pollution of our water supply are often the same as those with a stake in denitrification plants. Once again, we must avoid cut-and-dried proposals. According to a report dated April 2003, per capita water consumption in the OECD countries has fallen 11 per cent since 1980, but a great deal still remains to be done: measures to reduce pollution, to protect aquifers and to end the agricultural subsidies in the North that are ruining the peasantry in the South. Moreover, we learn from the same report that agriculture in the OECD countries consumes 45 per cent of fresh water.

Neoliberal globalization demands that water management should be handed over to private firms, allowing for regular price rises and opaque business deals, and that international financial organizations should exert pressure on the governments of heavily indebted countries to surrender control of their national water systems. I give many examples of this too, so that the reader can see it is a question of solid facts, not an ideological *parti pris*.

The media regularly cover new conflicts or health disasters due to strains on the water supply, flooding, drought, deforestation or climate change. International conferences follow one another at a steady pace, the most recent being the Earth Summit in 2002 in Johannesburg, which concluded that anyone living on $2 a day was well-off, and that the task by 2015 was to halve the percentage of human beings without access to drinking water or basic sanitation. I show below that contaminated water kills 6,000 children a day: to picture what this means, imagine that fifteen Boeings crash into the sea every day – and that the evening news does not breathe a word about them! Clearly the issue of water represents a major challenge to humanity, at the levels of ethics, justice and solidarity.

But water conflicts are increasing in the USA, where individual states are savaging one another in the courts over this or that river and even invoking a charter granted by Charles I in 1632. In another federal state, the Indian Union, the victims of water shortage are numbered by the million, and in Madhya Pradesh armed guards escort water trucks to prevent thirsty crowds from waylaying them. In the Middle East, where the Palestinians are still victims of injustice, a curfew may be imposed for weeks in a town where the water supply has been zealously destroyed by the army of occupation, and where the Palestinians, since 1967, have had access to water only with the goodwill of Israeli military governors.

Water is first and foremost a political–ethical issue, and no other deserves greater attention on the part of humanity. It is decisive for world peace and the future of all living things. That is the message of this book.

Finally, I owe a debt of gratitude to the Charles-Léopold Mayer Foundation; to Gustavo Marin and Michel Sauquet, who gave me the opportunity to study the issue of water in the world; to Bernard Stéphan, Les Éditions de l'Atelier; and to Zed Books and the other publishers who were kind enough to include this book in the Global Issues series.

PART I

A symbol and a source of fascination
for artists and scientists

I

Unparalleled symbolism

> If you split the heart of a single drop of water,
> One hundred pure oceans flow forth.
>
> *Mahmud Shabestri, fourteenth-century Sufi poet*

Water is rarely out of the political headlines. From the Johannesburg Earth Summit (September 2002) through the World Water Forum in Kyoto (March 2003) to the G8 meeting in Evian (May 2003), it has become one of the main issues in the global debate about the future conditions of human existence. And the rallies of the political and financial establishment are matched by the counter-forums of the alter-globalization movement, as in Florence in March 2003 or Annemasse in May 2003. Newspapers, magazines and television channels rival one another in presenting special issues and discussion evenings on the *water crisis*, while multinational corporations, international organizations and registered associations also regularly debate the question. Economics, ecology, climate change, technologies, commodification of water, deforestation, contamination are the most frequently mentioned topics, and everyone involved seems to have a special interest to defend. But it is necessary to ask the right questions!

The quantity of water on earth is finite. This is the first inescapable physical reality. Moreover, we are all part and parcel of the global water cycle, which links us, through blood, spinal fluid and primeval amniotic fluid, to the earth and the whole biosphere.

Curiously, only a few theologians and philosophers occasionally venture to address the symbolism of water that is present in the most diverse cultures. In the East, for instance, water engages the spiritual dimension of our being and leads on to the mystery of the universe. In China, peasant opposition to the huge Three Gorges dam (which began to fill up in June 2003) had its roots in the fact that the project made it impossible for them to be buried alongside their ancestors in the family cemetery.

Faced with those who know the price of everything and the value of nothing, it seems useful to show at the outset that water is not an ordinary element, still less a commodity. It enters into the constitution of our beliefs and ideologies, impregnating our reasoning, vocabulary and imagination as much as it does our body cells – not to speak of its huge role in the history of human societies both past and present.

As we shall see in the case of Cochabamba, in Bolivia, tragic misunderstandings may result from passing over the cultural and symbolic dimension of water. Besides, is not the Celtic cult of water and sacred fountains still alive in the heart of Europe, in Brittany? And, across the seas, do not Africans and indigenous Americans use the same metaphors and recognize the same ties to Mother Nature? All are essentially expressing what we owe to water, to the biosphere: quite simply, life itself! 'Water', wrote the French philosopher Gaston Bachelard, 'is an organ of the world.'

The question of water cannot be dealt with in a purely technical framework. Indeed, overweening technological or scientistic attitudes have caused untold damage throughout the world: Nature, rivers and ecosystems cannot be squeezed indefinitely into a casing made of concrete, reinforced cement and asphalt, any more than forests can continue to be felled without endangering our own existence. To mark the human need for nature, as well as to underline the danger of human depredations, Quebec has decided to create a national park to protect its only remaining unspoiled river: the Moisie.

While water policy is duty-bound to ensure that it is economically viable, it must equally incorporate the need for social solidarity, cooperation with countries lacking water resources of their own, ecological responsibility, and respect for the needs of future generations and other living beings that share the planet with us. This being so, any approach that relegates the symbolic dimension of water to the museum of antiquities, or that treats water merely as a raw material for other uses, threatens to open a gap of mutual incomprehension and rejection among the world's peoples. And that can only make our world more dangerous still.

Only a universal, humanist approach to water resources allows us to grasp their exceptional importance for our survival on earth. Such an approach will also demonstrate the absurdity of those views which seek to subordinate water either to the logic of the market or to the most unbridled technical applications. This is what we shall try to show in the present chapter.

Water, the driving force of Nature

Thales of Miletus, one of the Seven Sages of ancient Greece, wrote in the sixth century BC: 'Water is the origin and the basis of all things.' This powerful conception of water as the fundamental element came to him when he was looking for a causal link between marine fossils imprisoned in the rock of a hill and the sea that had probably once been their home. For other Greek thinkers, such as Heraclitus, Pythagoras, Empedocles and Democritus, all matter consisted of four basic elements: earth, air, fire and water. But, with Newton's alchemical speculations, water again took pride of place, without competitor. During the Renaissance, Leonardo da Vinci held that water was 'the driving force of Nature'. And, more recently, Bachelard underlined the 'fine pleonasm of pure water' when he wrote: 'Water is an organ of the world, a nutrient of flowing phenomena, the vegetating element, the element that makes things shine, the substance of tears.'

Egypt provides us with the archetypal example of water as a miraculous creator, which we should constantly bear in mind when considering its contribution to life. Egypt, 'the gift of the Nile': Herodotus, to whom this formula is often attributed, himself tells us that he borrowed it from one of his Greek predecessors, most probably Hecatæus of Miletus. But it had previously been applied only to the Delta; the great merit of Herodotus was to realize that it was true of the whole of Egypt. Of course, as a great Egyptologist has written, the Nile's importance for 'the existence of Egypt is a truth too obvious and long-established to require demonstration'. All human, animal and plant life there depends on the Nile's water and flood silt, whose coincidence in time with the greatest heat (June to October) is not the least of the miracles. Each year (before the building of the Aswan dam), the Nile waters covered a narrow strip of living land: some 30,000 square kilometres useful to man, over a length of 1,000 kilometres as the crow flies, but much more if we take into account that the valley line is far from straight. An Egyptologist has pointed out:

> In Upper Egypt it almost never rains; the whole of agriculture
> is based on a canal system from which water is constantly drawn
> with the help of balancing poles (*shaduf*) or ox-driven wheels
> with buckets (*sakiya*). This system has hardly changed in any
> fundamental way since antiquity: the *sakiya* continues to squeak
> as it did thousands of years ago.... Since it is enough to stir with
> a wooden hoe the silt left by the Nile floods, an iron plough

has no reason for existence in Egypt. People can rely on two, sometimes three harvests a year. The ancient division of the year into three seasons – the flood *akhet* (summer–autumn), the *peret* opening and growth (winter–spring) and the *shemu* harvest (spring–summer) – still corresponds to the present climate.[1]

Agricultural techniques, arts, beliefs and lifestyles: everything bears the mark of the river. In fact the 160-million-year-old Nile – which only recently in geological time decided to flow into the Mediterranean rather than the Indian Ocean – is as much the result as the agent of geology, climate and history, of the politics and economics of Africa's peoples.[2] For, without the Nile ribbon, there would have been no pyramids, no cotton and no fellahs. For the ancient Egyptians, the Nile was God. Through the festival of Sham el Nessim, the only one jointly celebrated by Copts and Muslims, contemporary Egypt shows that it has not completely forgotten the old pagan rites in homage to its Eternal River, as the great poet Shawki called the Nile.[3]

The perennial miracle of water merrily crossed the centuries, with their changing beliefs, so that life could continue as before.

Cosmogonies and religions

In Egypt as elsewhere, since the dawn of time, water has been an element charged with symbols and meanings, in all religions and beliefs. The archaeological site of El Guettar, in Tunisia, has revealed what is probably the oldest religious construction in the world: a 'Musterian' monument (45,000 BC), erected to keep a spring in existence. In Europe, Cimbre tribes honoured the Rhône river as a god. And all the ancient civilizations of Mesopotamia had a water-based cosmogony and revered the Tigris and Euphrates as manifestations of the divinity. In Sumer, on the banks of the Euphrates, excavations have uncovered traces of an

important city founded in the fourth millennium BC, which had a
port and a major sanctuary dedicated to the god Enki, the lord of
rain and fertilizing water.[4] It was in Babylon – or, more precisely,
Sumer – that the Ancients situated one of the Seven Wonders of
the World, the Hanging Gardens, which they attributed to the
legendary Semiramis; it bore witness to the exceptional harness-
ing of water which that civilization achieved. For the Ancient
Egyptians, the source of all life, human and divine, was the mass
of primeval water that they personified by the name of Nu. It was
the source of the two holy rivers: the life-giving Nile, and the
sky that supported the ship of Ra, the Sun god.[5] The birthplace
of Ra is a lotus emerging from the water, at the dawn of the
world. Each year, on 19 July, when the Nile floods brought the
first 'water of renewal', the star Sothis (Sirius or the Dog Star),
an incarnation of the goddess Isis, rose above the horizon at the
same time as the sun. It was a remarkable coincidence observed
by Egyptian astronomers, but one that occurs only at the latitude
of Memphis–Heliopolis! In any event, the Nile and the heavens
were in harmony with each other, so how could there be any doubt
about the divine nature of the river? The period of its flooding – 19
to 21 July – marked the New Year for ordinary Egyptians, and the
regularity of the event provided the basis for the so-called Sothic
calendar. The Book of Genesis, for its part, situates the Garden
of Eden between two rivers, the Tigris and the Euphrates, where
water flowed in abundance; God had a garden there, the earthly
paradise, where Adam and Eve were meant to live.

   In Greco-Latin mythology, Poseidon (in Greece) or Neptune
(in Rome) ruled over the seas and oceans, where sirens lived and
acted as tools of the gods, as we can see from the adventures
of Odysseus and his son Telemachus. According to Hesiod, the
first woman, Pandora, received life from Hephaistos, who formed
her out of earth and water to become the instrument of divine
vengeance. Thus, water infuses earth with life: it is life itself

for the Greeks, the great potters of antiquity, who knew that it enabled craftsmen to mould and work on clay. What could be more logical than to imagine that the gods did the same, by creating with water and earth. The soul was like clay: water could make it bend and yield. Gaston Bachelard could write in *L'eau et les rêves*: 'An excess of water makes the soul soft, affable, smooth, sociable, ready to yield.'

For the Jews, God made the first man by mixing earth and water. As to the Chinese, they held water in awe: was their country not a land of drought and floods? Around 250 BC the Middle Empire deified Li Bing, governor of what is now Szechuan province, a genius in the field of hydraulics who built the first dam on the Minjiang, a tributary of the Yangtse. He also invented a system of canals which, when open, permitted irrigation and, when closed, kept flood water under control. Long before the famous *zouave* soldier was erected at the Pont de l'Alma in Paris, Li Bing placed three human statues in the river to keep a watch on tides: if their feet were visible, it meant drought and the dam gates were opened; if their shoulders were under water, it meant flooding and the gates were shut. From that point on, there was constant progress in human control over water, and the Chinese put in place sophisticated systems of bamboo pipes to irrigate the fields and supply the towns (Hangzhu in 1089, Canton in 1096). It was also water that permitted the Chinese to discover salt as long ago as 6000 BC, when crystals appeared following summer evaporation at Lake Yuncheng.[6] According to tradition, water, salt and soya were sufficient for a wise man to keep himself alive.

Water was scarce, precious and unpredictable from Attica to the Peloponnese, from Thrace to Arcadia. It inspired fear and respect. For some it had fantastic origins, such as the Hippocrene, that fountain which sprang from the rock on Mount Helicon, where Pegasus, the legendary winged horse symbolizing poetic inspiration, struck the ground with its hoof. The muses gathered there, and poets drew its water to enhance their powers. Nymphs, fairies, sylphids and naiads inhabited the lakes, rivers and ponds of ancient Greece. Respect or even worship for them was imperative when man used the waters, drew on their riches or sought their favours. As we have seen, the Cimbre venerated the Rhône as a god. And, at Hadrian's second-century aqueduct at Carthage, part of which is still in use today, imposing ruins remain of a temple to the protective divinity of springs and fountains. As to the goddess Aphrodite, we know that she was born from the froth of the waves fertilized by the blood of Uranus. Hesiod, the shepherd-poet on the slopes of Helicon, who had such a deep feeling for Nature, wrote 800 years before the Christian era: 'Never urinate at the mouth of rivers flowing into the sea: take care to avoid it.' Or again: 'Do not satisfy your other needs there either: that would be no less baneful' – for it would be an outrage to Mother Nature, as Bachelard puts it. Similarly, at a distance of many centuries, an authentic hadith of the Prophet Mohammed says: 'No Muslim shall urinate in stagnant water.' And, in the same spirit, another hadith teaches: 'Beware of the three curses: do not defecate in water, on the road or in shadow.'[7] This respect for water and public health appears to be universal: the Orang Rimba, who have lived for 4,000 years in the jungles of Sumatra, take great care of river water, forbidding people to defecate in it or to use soap or other detergents whose lather might 'defile' it. The intrusion of 'civilization' has brought its share of settlers, industrial plantations and forest devastation, the rivers have been filled in and changed into tarmac roads for the transportation of timber, and water pollution has spread gastroenteritis and strange infections that the medicine men no longer know how to treat. All this threatens the short-term survival of the Orang Rimba.[8]

In the Harappan civilization, which flourished between 3000 and 1500 BC in what is now Pakistan and western India, this respect for water was evident in the widespread use of wooden toilet seats built into the external walls of houses and linked to a sophisticated sewerage system.[9]

Among the Altiplano Indians, the creative gods were thought to emerge from Lake Titicaca, while for the Aztecs the place of genesis was the springs they worshipped under the name *pacarina*. The Incas, for whom water was a gift from Heaven, accomplished major hydraulic works whose traces can still be seen today; canals, dams and aqueducts were constructed through a system of periodic *mita*, or collective corvées, that the population performed in return for a regular water supply. In his *Conquest of New Spain*, Bernal Díaz gave an eyewitness account of the Aztecs' fascinating mastery of horticulture, especially around Lake Tenochitlán, the site of present-day Mexico City. Their sumptuous floating gardens greatly impressed Cortés himself, and Díaz was quite astounded by their consummate art in arranging waterfalls and reservoirs. In 1521, however, the Spanish destroyed the gardens during their siege of the city on water, and went on to drain the lake and thereby destroy forever the thriving garden culture. Was this a sign of things to come? Aztec poetry highlighted the beauty of the floral fleet and rightly stressed that we humans blossom for only a short time.

The Mapucho Indians, for their part, venerated the magnificent system of lakes in Patagonia – Nahuel Huapí, Huechulafquen and so on – set like a jewel among the high volcanic peaks of the *cordillera*. Alas, the bloody Conquest of the Desert, led by Argentinean war minister Julio Roca in the late nineteenth century, scattered the population and its culture and ended the ancestral respect for water. The mysterious disappearance of the Maya civilization in Yucatán between 800 and 900 AD is thought to have been due to drought, since agriculture in that chalky region was completely dependent upon rainfall. On 14 March 2003 *Science* published the work of a team of paleoclimatologists which provided evidence in favour of this hypothesis thanks to variations in the waterborne deposits of titanium. Natural science and history have thus come together at last to provide the 'key' to the disappearance of the Mayas: shortage of water and lasting drought.

In ancient Hindu literature, the oldest of the Veda, the *Rig-Veda*, sings: 'Oh, waters, it is you who bring the strength of life', while the *Satapatha Brahma* says: 'In the beginning, only the waters and the ocean existed.' The Ganges, the most venerated of India's rivers, is the object of fervent worship every twelve years, when the Ganga Kumbha Mela festival draws 30 million pilgrims to its banks, from Benares to Allahabad – the largest human gathering on earth, whose high point is ritual bathing in Prayaga (Allahabad), at the confluence of the Ganges and the Yamuna and Saraswati rivers. Haridwar – where the Ganges, having completed its journey down from the Himalayas, enters and brings new life to the central plains of India – is considered a holy site. And Indra, an ancient divinity going back to Vedic times, is considered the 'king of the gods': he represents the energy driving all beings and is symbolized by rain.

A symbolically charged element

The many religious meanings of water are ambiguous and mysterious, but they involve a consistent reference to the origins of human life in its cleansing, purifying, transcendent properties. In the three great monotheisms, Moses, Jesus and Mohammed perform miracles linked to water. The element has always fascinated men and women; to produce, transform or cross it has always appeared supernatural. The Bible records the Flood and reports many a tragedy associated with water. But the theme of the Flood also appears in the oldest-known epic, the epic of Gilgamesh, which recounts how God punished Mesopotamia by means of water – and similar stories are to be found in many pagan cultures of the North and among the indigenous peoples of the Americas. Christians use water for baptism, and in the Gospel according to St John (3:23) we read that 'John also baptised at Ennon, near Salim, because there was much water' in the Jordan. The same gospel often makes direct, material mention of water, in a highly symbolic sense (as in the washing of the feet and the miraculous conversion of water into wine at Cana, or in Jesus' conversation with the Samaritan woman near Jacob's well). The passages that strike us most, however, are those where the element serves as a symbol for something else. On one occasion, Jesus associates it with faith and sincerity: 'If someone is thirsty, let him come to me and drink – he who believes in me'; for, as the Scriptures say, 'Streams of living water shall flow from his breast.' And, on another, he says: 'I am the bread of life: he who comes to me shall no longer be hungry, and he who believes in me shall no longer be thirsty.' By contrast, the Book of Revelations speaks of an 'angel of water' who 'empties his bowl into the rivers and watersprings and they also turned into blood, just as had the sea'.

Far from such considerations, Voltaire wrote in his character-istically mischievous manner: 'At last the bourgeoisie has begun to suspect that it was not St Genevieve who gave or halted the rains but God himself who decided what the elements should do.' But Corneille, closer to tradition, made his hero Polyeucte say: 'Baptism ... washes away our crimes in health-giving water.' Bossuet used a water metaphor in his *Funeral Orations* to underline the transience of humankind's stay on earth: 'We are all as flowing waters.' Pierre Cauchon, the presiding judge, condemned Joan of Arc to 'the bread of suffering and the waters of anguish'. And the Mandeans of Basra, in Iraq, who see John the Baptist as the true messiah, baptise themselves in water every day.

It is often forgotten that the sacred precinct of the Kaaba, in Mecca, contains the well of Zemzem.[10] Until recently, every *haji* (pilgrim) had to drink a mouthful of its holy water, as the prophets Abraham and Mohammed once did, and also had to take home a little vial to add to the water in which he would be washed after death – for the popular belief was that the well was directly linked to paradise. It is also forgotten that the term *sharia*, which now simply means 'law', once designated 'the law of water' – striking proof of the ancient codification of matters relating to water among the Arabs.

To enter a mosque after having had sexual relations, a Muslim man or woman must wash from head to toe and therefore, in most cases, visit a hammam. At the height of Baghdad's splendour, in 1993, there were 1,500 such establishments in the city and every prosperous member of the community had a bath in his own home. The hammam thus became a distinctive component of the oriental city. In *Islam and Muslim Art*, the art historian Alexandre Papadopoulo writes:

> The word *hammam* has become so acclimated in France as to earn the distinction of an entry in the *Petit Larousse....* [Yet] such comfort and luxuriousness were incomprehensible to a people [the Arabs] for whom ... water [was] too scarce to be wasted. True, Muhammad had decreed five obligatory ablutions before praying so as to enter into a state of purity, but in practice the believers in the desert were permitted to make do with a few precious drops.

Papadopoulo shows how the hammam, inherited from the Greco-Roman baths, worked a transformation of the Arabs, who launched themselves, with the success that we know, on the conquest of the world. Although the Prophet and his companions did not know 'the pleasures of water', their discovery

> must have come to the new masters of the world as an extra-ordinary revelation. Besides the hygienic and curative virtues, the Muslims could attribute to it a religious significance all their own in which the baths were deemed the most convenient way of washing away all the defilements of the flesh so as to be in a state of purity when the time came to pray.

The Islamic specialist William Marçais, quoted by Papadopoulo, notes that this ritual use of water would influence the architecture of the Muslim city:

> The public bath proved to be the suitable place for proceeding with the major ablution ... that does away with the defilement left by the sexual act. And for that reason it gradually became a kind of annex to the mosque. It was under cover of this ritual utilization that it ... came to earn a worthy place among the essential institutions of the Muslim city.[11]

Finally, we learn from Papadopoulo:

> The role of the public bathhouse in Muslim social life grew to be almost as important as that of the mosque and libraries.... It became one of the main places for social encounters, a place for hygiene and ritual purification, but also for relaxation and conversation. Such a city as Damascus had fifty-two hammams in the twelfth century.[12]

The pleasure-loving Flaubert visited a hammam on a visit to Egypt and described his plunge into the delights of the Orient: 'I was alone at the rear of the steam room.... Hot water was running all around.... It was most voluptuous and gently melancholic to bathe in this way.' And Théophile Gautier went even further: 'What an exquisite pleasure to abandon yourself to its slabs..., your limbs dulled, amid a perfumed steam cloud beneath a rain of rose and benzoin.'

The Jewish Torah orders ritual purification: for seven days after the end of their menstrual period, and for six weeks before giving birth, women are supposed to cleanse themselves by following the ritual of the Tahara. At nightfall, 'impure' women must go to the special *mikveh* baths.[13]

For the Koran, water is the purifying element par excellence, both of the body and of the spirit: 'When He covers you with torpor, with safety coming from Him, brings down water from heaven to purify you, to dispel on you the stain of Satan' (Sura VIII, v. 11). Does not the holy book of Islam spell out the unique role of water as the source of life: 'And we have created every living thing based on water' (Sura XXI, v. 30), or, more clearly still: 'He who created man from water' (Sura XXV, v. 54)? Indeed, water is the origin of animal life: 'God created every animal on the basis of water' (Sura XXIV, v. 45). Nor can there be any plant life, and therefore food, without this key element: 'He who brings down water from heaven, with which we make all kinds of vegetation emerge, makes the greenery and diverse grains appear, the palm tree with its clusters jutting from its spathes, and the gardens of vines, olive and pomegranate trees' (Sura VI, v. 99). In the Mary Sura (XIX, v. 24), the newly born Jesus turns to his mother and consoles her: 'Do not be sad! Your Lord has placed a stream [the child with an extraordinary destiny] at your feet.' A number of hadiths also underline the special character of water: for example, the one entitled 'To be a believer is to be clean', or 'Nothing is more pleasing to God than to give water to him who asks for it.'

On street corners everywhere from Kuwait to Casablanca, one often comes across *sabils*: fountains, earthenware jugs and other (now often refrigerated) receptacles that devout donors, including a considerable number of women, have placed there for the use of passers-by. Islam even prescribes a *haq al shafa* (*shirb*) – a 'right to quench one's thirst' – for everyone without exception, even the worst of enemies.

To give water has always meant recognizing the social bond as non-exclusive; it is the act of humanity, the human gesture par excellence. The expression of charity urged by Islam became a duty for anyone responsible for the fate of a town – the emir and, by extension, the state – and this has posed quite a few problems for politicians. In Saudi Arabia, water is virtually free – but its cost price is a state secret!

In Arabic, *shafa* means not only 'to quench one's thirst' but also 'to cure' or 'to restore or recover one's health'; there could scarcely be a clearer indication of the virtues of this vital liquid. In the Koran there are sixty-three occurrences of the word 'water' (*m'a* – interestingly, the shortest word in the Arabic language), and for Islam happiness is to be found where there is water. 'God guides by their very faith those who have believed and who have performed beneficial works. Beneath them, streams flow into the gardens of happiness' (Sura X, v. 9). This is a recurrent theme, for we read in Sura XXII, v. 23: 'God allows those who have believed and performed beneficial works to enter the gardens beneath which the streams flow.' If the text evokes paradise as a garden with flowing streams, this must mean that the idea of the garden needed a context in which water was scarce. As in the Prophet's Arabian desert, it is where water is scarce that it is most strongly associated with life. The same Sura (XXII, v. 20) also shows that Allah may use boiling water to punish infidels. But Sura VII tells us that no punishment can compare to water deprivation – even in the afterlife. Moreover, the Koranic paradise is adorned with a river whose water is particularly sweet: the River Kawthar (Arabic for 'nectar'), while rain in the Holy Book often looks fateful as it beats down.

The Kawthar has nothing in common with the Styx of Greek mythology. The winding Styx encompasses Hell, but its dark icy waters have magic properties: Thetis dips Achilles in them to make him invulnerable. How mysterious is this combination of quite different properties that popular beliefs have given to water!

Islam's emphasis on the cleansing role of water applies to the soul as well as to the body. The ablutions required before each of the day's five prayers are the key to the purity of soul that comes through prayer. So, we can see that Islam makes no rigid distinction between body and spirit: they are two complementary and intertwined elements. The injunction to wash reappears in a number of circumstances: when one is in a rage, when one comes into contact with a corpse or is involved in transporting it, when one recites from the Koran or the hadiths, when one attends a course in religious knowledge, when one enters a mosque, when one calls others to prayer, when one preaches, and when one visits a cemetery.[14]

An object of fascination for artists, poets and writers

Water, the great purifier, has also always been a conveyor and mediator of the deepest human feelings. In Upper Egypt a love song has been found from the Middle Empire (1500–1000 BC): 'I wished to go down to the water to bathe before you. I let you see my beauty in a tunic of transparent linen, impregnated with fragrant essences, my hair crowned with rushes.... Oh, my hero, my beloved, come and look at me.' And, echoing this several centuries later, Venus Anadyomene emerging from the waves and twisting her hair became the unparalleled masterpiece of the Alexandrine painter Apelles, recognized as such by countless generations.

Poets and writers have always been inspired by water, in all cultures and all latitudes. The theme of water, of the lake associated with woman, love and separation, is also found in many literatures: in China, for example, the beloved woman has a voice 'as pure as a trickle of water' and 'eyes as clear as spring water'. The contemporary novelist François Cheng, in his Ming-era story of Platonic love *L'Éternité n'est pas de trop*,[15] puts into the mouth of its hero, Dao-sheng: 'When I reached the banks of the Yangtse, my heart leapt as I watched the waves. All I had to do was cross them to reach ... the person in my thoughts.' In this fine novel, water occupies a prime position: the author gives us invaluable information about its symbolic significance, its ruthless control by the central authorities, its perception by ordinary Chinese, and its economic or even ludic importance in the Middle Empire, as well as in the seventeenth century when the Jesuits arrived:

> Around the time of the Qing-ming festival, the heavens gener-ously granted the peasants' wish and provided rain in abundance. The terrace rice fields, gazing at the troop of passing clouds, everywhere sparkled with emerald. With the arrival of summer, the hopes of a good harvest turned into a near-certainty.

Cheng then describes the dragon-boat race on the Yellow River that marks the high point of the celebrations, the enthusiasm of the crowd, and the thoughts that the spectacle inspires in Dao-sheng:

> He sees himself again on the broken dykes, among the convicts trying to fill them in. Their bare torsos form a pathetic rampart against the onslaught of the waves, which are fiercer than wild-cats on the loose. How often has a non-swimmer been carried away like a heap of straw? These descendants of the Dragon, long turned into peasant farmers, are no longer capable of putting together imaginative games. But their fate still depends as much as before on the watery element. Do they not spend the whole year waiting for the precious liquid, which likes to play the game of life and death with them? When there is enough of it, water brings them happiness. When there is too much or too little, it causes drought or flooding. It has become a capricious deity that men venerate with love and fear.

The novelist then evokes the disgrace and exile of Qu Yuan, 'China's first celebrated poet', and concludes in the purest of Asian traditions: 'By throwing himself into the Milo river, he performed the sacrificial gesture that renews through water the marriage of Earth and Heaven.' In Chinese cosmogony, water engages the spiritual dimension of Being, opening onto and transfiguring the mystery of the universe.

All around the world, literature has always dealt with the joys and dramas of water. Jean Giono, for example, who lyrically sings of his childhood Durance in southern France, has masterfully described in *Colline* the fierce struggle for water, the deserted villages, the torn families, the hatreds and the deaths that can result from the drying up of a spring. Guy de Maupassant, who visited the Algerian south in 1888, noted that water was 'the main reason for the quarrelling and animosity' among tribes.[16]

In his *Correspondance*, Gustave Flaubert paints a picture of the Nile at Elephant Island, near Aswan, and as always his artist's eye proves more revealing than that of the expert: 'The Nile is as flat as a river of steel.' In March 1850 he wrote to a poet friend who had said that the Nile 'roamed' its banks:

> There is no better term that is either broader or more accurate. It is a funny and magnificent river, more like an ocean than anything else.[17] Sand banks stretch ashore as far as the eye can see, furrowed by the wind like beaches at the sea. It has such proportions that you cannot tell the direction of the current. Often you think you are on a closed lake.

This testimony gives us some idea of the damage that 'modernity' has inflicted on the Nile, through the construction of factories and farms along its banks. 'The Nile is a cesspool', wrote one former Egyptian minister. But it is not the only river to suffer from pollution. The Cuban writer Pedro Juan Gutiérrez has this to say about the rivers of his own country, which are a long way from the postcards and paradisiacal beaches of the tourist industry: 'As a kid, I thought all rivers were made of shit. The first time I saw one with flowing water, I couldn't believe my eyes and asked where they'd put the shit and mud for it to be so clean.' According to Avital Gazit from Tel Aviv University, children in Israel who are asked what a river is reply: 'It's a canal that stinks when you pass along it.'

Literature again. On a trip to Algeria in 1888, Guy de Maupassant was struck by the beauty of the 'magnificent' palm trees: those 'guardians of life, protectors of strength and vigour, are constantly dipping their feet in water, while their brow bathes in fire.' The writer from Normandy fell under the spell of Bou-Saada oasis, 'one of the most charming in Algeria', and was thrilled by the 'miracle' of water 'kept in large tanks like gas in our own countries'. For him, 'the Bou-Saada valley carrying the river to the gardens is as wonderful as a dream landscape', yet 'when you leave the oasis…, the desert lies in wait, the yellow parched desert, which at the garden gates suddenly gulps it down into its sterile sands.'[18] But the oasis has powerful allies against the desert: Saharan legend tells us that, long before the arrival of Islam and its monotheism, Shehili (the sirocco, the god of hot winds) constantly unleashed its fury against Waha (the oasis), daughter of Ounihil (god of the waters), and that Waha found refuge with Safi (god of the sands), who covered her with his burnous cloak.

Water also features prominently in a number of Maupassant's short stories. Clear and light? For the writer it can also be heavy and troubling. In his story 'On the Water', for example, the river is the only hero and testifies to his fascination with the element.

Nor have painters lagged behind in this respect. From Botticelli's 'Birth of Venus' through Canaletto's paintings of Venice to Floris Francesco's 'Susanna Bathing', water has given inspiration to artists in every epoch. John Constable (1776–1837), who never left his home country yet greatly influenced the French Barbizon School, found his inspiration on the banks of the River Stour: 'I associate my carefree childhood', he writes, 'with everything to be found on the banks of the Stour. It is they which made me a painter, and I am grateful to them for it.' His first very large canvas, 'Flatford Mill on the River Stour', attaches great importance to water, and in 'The Leaping Horse', a fine composition from 1825 in which he draws precisely the canalized river as it bridges the old watercourse, now the only spillway, the painter performs the work of a historian by showing us the hydraulic techniques of his age. Water is an ever-recurring theme in his paintings. He knew how to depict it in a way that left no one indifferent, placing it at the centre of human activity and lyrically bringing out its power and energy. With all the colours of his magnificent palette, Constable endeavoured to convey what he called 'the chiaroscuro of nature'.[19]

The global water cycle and the biosphere: a strong link

These artistic evocations of water underline the fact that we are all an integral part of the 'global water cycle'. The water cycle is to the biosphere what the circulation of blood is to the living organism. In the ninth century, the Brethren of Purity, a group of Muslim scholars based in Basra, described the water cycle in their famous *Encyclopedia*, and the concept was later refined, in the thirteenth century, by the geographer Al Quazwini.

Water is life – and therefore, unlike oil, irreplaceable. Water, according to the Dogon people of Mali, is inhabited by Nommo, a spirit with great and mysterious powers whom human beings hold in absolute reverence, for he can decide to send either rain and prosperity or, if people somehow neglect to worship him, drought and poverty. Perhaps it is Nommo who manifests himself in Cameroon, where Lake Nyos and Lake Monoun are to be found. For Africa has the dubious privilege of these two 'killer lakes', which in the 1980s caused some 1,800 deaths: alone among the world's 'crater lakes', as geologists call them, they have deadly build-ups of carbon dioxide and hydrogen sulphide that can lead to catastrophic eruptions.

The great historian of Africa, Joseph Ki-Zerbo from Burkina Faso, writes:

> In my mother tongue, it is said that there are more than croco-
> diles in water. This refers to the complex nature of reality, not

only because a thousand less spectacular animals live in it, but also because water affects things over and above what is visible: for example, life.... Water is ever present in myths of the origins of life, in Africa and elsewhere. Let us recall the Dogon Water God: 'The vital force of earth is water. God kneaded earth with water, and he also made blood out of water. There is this force even in stone.' The various peoples' myths of the origins of life are often associated with water, rivers, lakes and wells. In ancient Ghana, the legend of Wagadu speaks of a totemic ancestor of the royal family, the Serpent God, to whom people offered sacrifices and who guarded a well and ensured fertility. His extermination will mark the onset of drought. These first episodes in the life of various peoples are marked by the crossing of rivers in miraculous circumstances.... Thus, when the Baoule migrated from Ashanti (Ghana) to their present home in Ivory Coast, they had to cross the Comoé river. Similarly, the first kings of Ségou derived their name (Coulibaly) from the fact that, when halted by a river on their flight from their enemies, a giant silurid is supposed to have positioned itself so that the fugitives could use it as a bridge from one bank to the other, without a dugout ('couloubaly' in the Bambara language). In Africa such legends reflect verifiable facts, in so far as Saharization or water shortage underlines the importance of this element. Water enters into the relationship of ecological, economic, social and political forces, as a medium active within the three realms (animal, vegetable and mineral) that creates the space–times which form the models, if not the structural moulds, of historical development. For example, where aridity is the prevailing condition, camels are introduced and give rise to an original social-historical system. Sutton has described the 'aquatic civilizations' of prehistoric East Africa, but the dynamic of water may lead to regression.[20]

Ki-Zerbo explains that the Iron Age civilization based on wood, and therefore on the presence of water, accelerated deforestation, and that forest regions with high rainfall were home to the tsetse fly. This was an obstacle to the breeding of horses and the use of cavalry – hence the limited expansion of the empires of the time.

In West Africa, most of the commercial and political metro-
polises are situated where desert meets savannah and a natural
change of loads takes place on the caravan routes: Oualâta,
Timbuktu, Kounbisale, Gao. And all the rivers or lakes, adjoin-
ing this watery frontier in the south, powerfully underline the
potential of this region, the programmed cradle of the kingdoms
from the Sénégal to the Nile, by way of the Niger loop, the
Benue and Lake Chad.[21]

Ki-Zerbo concludes:

There is a kind of hydrotropism of power, in which the iso-
hyete[22] is an indicator and even a generator of power. It is also at
this interface that the areas of rift and conflict are found between
nomads and the settled population. The tendency of the groundwater to decline is a major infrastructural climatic ally for the
nomadic groups.... Oases and wells mark out the caravan routes,
and further south, according to the tales of European travellers,
a public water service used to be perfectly organized for jour-
neys in Benin and Congo. But, over and above this operational
aspect, as if echoing the myths of the origins of life, there is the
idea that all these elements are too precious to be the object of
ordinary transactions. They have to meet people's needs and
demands, especially those of strangers. A stranger means water,
it is said.[23]

In Africa, in the Sahel, guests and strangers are always politely
welcomed with an offer of water. In the dark continent, water may
also serve as a bearer of conviviality, or even of an ecumenical
spirit. In the Banco forest near Abidjan, for instance, the river
is used for Christian baptism as well as for ceremonial worship
among animists. One tribe with more than a million members, in
Limpopo province in South Africa, holds water in such reverence
that it has a powerful Queen of the Rains to control the elements,
although she must not allow herself to be seen, even by Nelson
Mandela!

The Zairean theologian Okavu Ekanga writes that, for Africans, nothing depends on the human will: 'It is Heaven or God who gives the rain and hail', for 'it is Heaven that creates the rain and hail'; 'you have to wait to receive everything'. The same author quotes an impressive series of African proverbs and aphorisms, the one more delightful than the next, in which water often provides the material for comparison. Thus, to suggest that someone's bad behaviour tarnishes the reputation of his or her parents and his whole lineage, people might say in a sententious tone: 'A dirty back brings shame downstream.' Or, to underline responsibility for everyone's actions and their future impact: 'If you look at the filth upstream, will you have the courage to drink the water?' Or again, to express legendary African hospitality, and to say that all men are just passengers on the frail barque of the world: 'A stranger is like a puddle of rainwater. It evaporates' – that is, it will rejoin the eternal water cycle and return to nature. In the same register, the well-known French urban theorist Pierre Merlin writes: 'The black man is very concrete, deeply assimilated into nature, the rain, water, earth, grass, trees, the moon, the sea.... Each of these elements of nature is intimately bound up with the invisible world, with universal transcendence.'[24]

Is this a universal idea, applicable to man's relations everywhere with nature, and especially with water? In 1854 the famous Chief Seattle, replying to the US president's offer to buy his ancestral lands, stated his belief that everything in the universe was linked to everything else, in the way that blood links a family together: 'The earth is the mother of the red man.... The rivers are our brothers, they quench our thirst.... This shining water that moves in the streams and rivers is not just water but the blood of our ancestors.' In the arid far west of Colorado, the Anasazi Indians built extraordinary hanging villages on the cliffs, immortalized in John Ford's *Stagecoach*; they danced there with snakes to make the rains fall. Still today, Hopi rainmakers dance with the same kind of reptiles, just an hour's flight from Las Vegas and its obscene water orgies![25] On the two sides of the ocean, Africans and Native Americans use the same metaphors and recognize the same bonds with Mother Nature: all tell of the things they owe to water, and of how men should be grateful to it for their very life.

Finally, we should recall that the natives of the New World had acquired deep knowledge of their environment and its most secret resources, as we can see from the example of the saguaro cactus (*Carnegia giganta*). This plant is especially well adapted to the desert: it can do without water for more than three years at a time, while continuing to blossom and bear fruit. Out of its fruits the Indians have made wine and various preserves. In periods of drought, they used to draw water from its stem and branches, for the plant secretes a waxy substance that prevents evaporation. It would be within the capacities of contemporary science to confer this genetic property on food plants in parts of the South without a large supply of water. But whether there is a will to do this for impecunious Third World nations is quite another matter.

Water, cities and architecture

The symbolism of water, so present in ancestral cultures, has also found its way into the most modern societies. In April 2003 the Holy See officially took a clear position on a highly sensitive political issue when it declared that water was a common human good and should remain under public control. In May 1999 a pastoral letter issued by Roman Catholic bishops in the Columbia basin area underlined the importance of the river, which had been subjected to a number of controversial schemes in recent years. For these churchmen, the Columbia is a 'driving force in the spiritual life of the region' and should not be seen only as a 'beast of burden for its economy'.[26] Water is universally associated with the idea of power and energy, but it should nevertheless be treated with care. As people say in Mali, 'It is water that sustains man.'

The most modern societies feel instinctively that their life depends on water, even if, in the big cities, it is most often invisible, canalized, tamed and domesticated. City-dwellers are setting out to rediscover it, with a sense of nostalgia. Their demand is so strong that, in Paris, the mayor has made it part of his programme to increase public awareness of the covered Bièvre that winds its way through the capital.

All around the world, the high and mighty have used water to add lustre to their rule and to perpetuate their glory. Today in the Arab world, especially (but not only) in the most arid countries, fountains of various kinds are a common way of displaying the largesse and munificence of the existing regime.[27] The aim is to reproduce, with some taste and accuracy, the royal *almunya* (country residence) in Toledo and its famous Noria that the sovereign could reach by boat. 'An ingenious system channelled water to the top of the cupola in the Noria,' wrote one chronicler, 'so that as it flowed along the walls it enveloped the royal refuge with a curtain of coolness.... The sky seemed bathed in dewdrops. The fountain lions opened their huge mouths to pour forth unlimited water.'[28]

All rulers, and especially all Arab potentates, dream of reproducing the rustic beauty of Mohamed V's fourteenth-century fountain with twelve lions in the Alhambra in Granada: 'the acme of refinement of a refined art'; 'an oasis of prayer, with the 124 palm trees of its columns around what was an image of paradise, a garden with four rivers'.[29] They also dream of reproducing the Generalife in Granada, its fragrant gardens with clear water, and its basin courtyard planted with myrtles and flowers through which a fountain-lined canal lazily flows. They all dream of Toledo, which 'God has protected like a fiancée by encircling it with a river [the Tagus] similar to the Milky Way'. Does not the imagination of writers, painters and historians continue to be excited by any mention of the Hanging Gardens of Babylon? Do not the Grandes Eaux festivities, each August at Versailles, recall to wondering crowds the Sun King and the splendours of his court? Is not the Trevi fountain in Rome, the masterpiece of Nicola Salvi (1697–1751), not a veritable triumph of rocks and water? Does not Hokusai's 'The Wave', aka 'The Breaking Wave Off Kanagawa', take one's breath away with its realism, power and energy? Has not the Alexandrine bas-relief of the Hellenistic era – which depicts children playing in the water and marsh vegetation of the Delta, beside a majestic old man representing the Nile – spread the idea of the personification of rivers?

Besides, water often seals the fate of a town. Why did the rather unimportant Gharnâta (Granada) become the capital of the Zirids, a city where music, literature and science were valued as in few other states at the time? The memoirs of Emir Abdallah (r. 1073–1090), the last of the dynasty, contain the answer: 'The Arabs became absorbed in contemplation of this magnificent plain furrowed with watercourses and covered with trees. They admired the mountain that is now the city of Granada, and its situation captivated them.' Hyderabad, now India's fourth largest city and capital of the South, sprang up in the late sixteenth century because of a shortage of water, when Sultan Mohammed Quli – who lived in the famous Golconda Fort, stocked with tonnes of diamonds – had the idea of establishing himself on the banks of the Musi river to overcome this recurrent problem. The city became a legendary bastion of Indo-Islamic civilization: 'A stranger only gradually discovers this secret world where water gushes from the fountains.... It is a calm universe, where time seems to stand still.'[30] At Isfahan in Iran, the eighteenth-century bridge-dam of Khadju still testifies to Persian architectural genius and the refined artistic taste of the Safavid dynasty. Referring to the magnificent Shah's mosque in Isfahan, one historian wrote:

'The immense role of water: the ground has become a mirror, reflecting and reduplicating this shell; we have a sense of being at the centre of a marvellous world.'

André Gide knew no more beautiful or 'harmonious' city than St Petersburg, and praised its 'marriage of stone, metal and water'.[31] But if water embellishes a city, it can also help to make it ugly and tell us things about how it is run and maintained. Thus *Newsweek* journalist Barbie Nadeau, visiting Rome in the summer of 2002, claimed that the Eternal City had lost much of its attraction for tourists and that, while they should continue to admire its monuments, they should avoid the Tiber. For 'it was a sewer of dead fish, killed by no one knows quite what. The stench still lingers and the embankments shimmer with an oily residue, festooned with dead carp and eels. ... If a river is a city's symbolic lifeline, Rome is in trouble.'[32]

The Indian ecologist Anil Agarwal pointed out, in one of the sensational editorials of which he knows the secret, that the city of Edo (Tokyo) had not needed Roman-style aqueducts to meet its water needs, since the Japanese had used dry excrement to fertilize their harvests, whereas the Tiber had been one big sewer. In the 1870s the authorities canalized the Tiber to check the spread of cholera, but this did not prevent devastating floods. In the New World the Olmsted brothers built more than 300 kilometres of boulevards and flowery banks along the rerouted Los Angeles river, but in canalizing and impoverishing the riverbed they created highly monotonous landscapes. There too, however, Nature was not to be bullied, and phenomenal floods were recorded in 1938 in the great Californian metropolis. Faced with such events, the only solution is to plan and coordinate all activities that have an impact on area development. After the disastrous flooding of Prague, which had been foreseen seven years earlier, a Czech newpaper wrote: 'The once-in-a-hundred-years flood is a natural phenomenon which, in its scale and functioning, escapes all control.'[33] Waterways must also be respected as ecosystems, for they are essential elements linking nature and the landscape.

For ordinary mortals, water is an element with many mysterious properties. One interesting historical case in point is witchcraft laws, which specified that anyone who managed to cross a river before the devil would escape his clutches! In Tunisia people still throw water on the footsteps of those leaving on a journey, so that it will pass without trouble and they will return to their nearest and dearest. And in Palestine people sprinkle with water the bedroom to be used by newly-weds, so that it will bring them happiness and prosperity. A Tuareg proverb advises: 'Man, drink water to make yourself beautiful!' Truly, water holds great power and mystery in the collective imagination.

To master nature: what a pretension! In the twenty-first century, humanity does not succeed in mastering water, nor in accurately predicting the temper of the element it has raised to the level of the gods – a god to which human sacrifices were once offered up, as in the Scandinavian countries. Science, for its part, has not understood everything about this little molecule, which accompanies men and women throughout their lives, and without which they would not exist. Indeed, water imparts to scientists a necessary lesson in humility.

Science and water:
research continues

Knowledge is a legacy for humanity.

Louis Pasteur

That I am of the earth my feet know perfectly,
and my blood is part of the sea.

D.H. Lawrence

Hydrogen, one of the constituents of water, is the simplest, lightest and most easily spread element in the universe. It is also the primal substance in modern cosmology. After the hypothetical Big Bang, which remains swathed in quantum uncertainty, the universe emerged as a mass of fire, radiation and hydrogen. Oxygen was then synthesized in the stars, which took shape at a later time. Earth resulted from the nuclear fusion and synthesis that followed the Big Bang, as did its primal volcanic atmosphere made up of many different elements as well as water vapour. The word 'hydrogen' comes from the Greek and means 'maker of water'.

As the planet cooled, this vapour condensed into the saltwater of the oceans and seas, the freshwater of the lakes, rivers and underground sources, and the snow and ice on mountaintops, even (as with Kilimanjaro) in tropical lands. The oceans formed in a huge, awesome deluge, in comparison with which the biblical version seems like a little spring storm.[1] The universe still bears traces of this cosmic origin of water. Apart from Earth – where, uniquely in the solar system, the precious substance exists in the three states of matter – the Moon, the planet Mars and Jupiter's moon Europa show the presence of water. Information gathered from space probes leads us to believe that there is ice on the Moon and liquid water beneath the icy surface of Europa.

A banal substance?

Water is the commonest substance on Earth and the most characteristic of the blue planet. In fact, the scientific notion of an element is descended from Thales' theory that water is the supreme element at the origin of all things. In 1864, in his in-augural course at the Collège de France, the renowned chemist Marcellin Berthelot taught that 'All living beings, vegetable and animal, are essentially made up of the four elementary bodies: carbon, hydrogen, oxygen and nitrogen.... Living beings consist of carbon combined with three gases that are the elements of water and the elements of air.'

It is true that, before Berthelot, the French chemist Proust had been the first to demonstrate the constancy of the composition of water, whatever its origin. Lavoisier achieved the synthesis of water in 1785 – a feat which, in addition to its great scientific inter-est, had repercussions on other planes. For it helped to slough off the faded metaphysical finery and gave birth to modern chemistry, by definitively refuting the theory of a special fluid, phlogiston, supposedly inherent in all bodies and productive of combustion at the moment of its departure from them. Thanks to Proust's work and Lavoisier's synthesis, it was placed beyond doubt that water was a combination of two odourless, colourless and tasteless gases. In fact, liquid water is the most extraordinary substance we know, unusual in all its physical–chemical properties. It has a unique capacity to exist, under normal conditions of temperature and pressure, in the three states of matter: gas, liquid and solid. This is the result of its peculiar chemical structure, which is still not fully understood. One thing we do know is that, thanks to the intermolecular hydrogen bond, water can absorb large quantities of heat before letting its molecules vaporize; this is why the oceans are capable of affecting the climate through the alternate absorption and release of heat in the different seasons. In the liquid state, the hydrogen bond creates the surface tension that allows water molecules to stick to one another and to support heavy objects, apparently defying the laws of gravity.[2] Unusually, in the solid state, intermolecular hydrogen bonds stretch to give greater volume but less density[3] to ice – which means that it is actually lighter than liquid water. The physical–chemical properties of water, compared with other hydrides in column VI of the periodic table of elements, have the peculiarity that, whereas SH_2 (hydrogen sulphide) is gaseous under normal conditions (like H_2Se and H_2Te) and smells of rotten eggs, water has a high boiling point and, as everyone knows, is odourless. If H_2O were gaseous like the others, life would never have appeared on Earth. The ability of water to give life, as well as its ability to preserve and dissolve, are therefore nothing short of miraculous. In fact, the miracle has a name: the hydrogen bond, which means that the water molecule could be written: $(H_2O)_n$.

As many cosmogonies claim, life began in ocean water for the most common cellular organisms. These filtered the most dangerous solar radiation but brought about marine photosynthesis, which in turn led to the formation of atmospheric oxygen and the protective ozone shield that permitted life to appear on Earth. Water thus determined not only the structure of biomacromolecules (proteins) but also their biological function.

If water permits life, this is especially due to a number of chemical and physical–chemical phenomena through which it surrounds and coats the other components of life, hydrolysing them and transporting them in a 'hydrated' form. Thus, water acts on rocks and dissolves their nutrients, which then percolate through the soil to nourish plants before returning to the sea either directly or in the hydrological cycle (evaporation and condensation) driven by solar energy. Without water, there would be no plants and therefore no photosynthesis. It was the magnificent work of the physicist Martin Kamen (1913–2002) which confirmed that all the oxygen released during photosynthesis comes not from carbonic gas – as it had long been thought – but from water. How much progress has been made since the days when Robert Boyle, the seventeenth-century English chemist, believed in the transmutation of matter! Seeing plants absorb moisture, he even thought that water could transform itself into flowers, leaves and fruits!

Water forms 75 per cent of the human body[4] and controls our internal temperature, as it does the Earth's climate. The body of an adult weighing 80 kg contains 50 to 60 litres of water. Our life, like that of plants and animals, is dependent on the biological functions of water, which dissolves and transports food and fuel (energy) through our organism and our metabolic tracts; it purifies our cells, ridding them of waste and filling our whole system with spinal to amniotic fluid. In a close, permanent and profound manner, water binds us to one another and to our origins, since human blood contains water and salts in the same proportions as the primeval ocean in which life first developed. It is often wondered whether life exists on other planets, and the cinema and comic books have made us familiar with little green men from Mars. But if water were detected everywhere in the cosmos, that would not mean there was life. On Mars, for instance, where water exists at the poles, it is in the form of ice. And, for there to be life, water must be in the liquid state, which – so far as we know – is alone capable of dissolving nutrients, carrying them to cells and ridding these of metabolites and waste. Not all hope is lost for Mars, however, as some probes have suggested that there might be liquid water beneath its surface. On 20 February 2003, *Nature* published an article by an American specialist who, having studied the pictures of ravines and channels sent back by Odyssey, concluded that the red planet passes through a climatic cycle lasting 100,000 years. At the beginning of the cycle, snow falls and forms ice flows and snow drifts. Then, under the heat of the sun, the snow begins to melt from the bottom up, and the resulting water erodes mountainsides and hollows out ravines over a period that may last as long as 5,000 years. The layer of snow above the liquid prevents it from immediately evaporating, so that snow proves to be a 'miniature greenhouse' providing a 'wonderful habitat for life'. It is possible, then, that life will be found in the form of microorganisms, but probably not in the form of little green men. Too bad for the science-fiction authors. In any event, in May and June 2003, NASA launched two special robots towards Mars, to clear away any doubt on the matter.

Recent scientific findings

Science does not know everything about the tri-atomic molecule: the *aqua simplex* of the alchemists is continuing to reveal its secrets with considerable parsimony. The structure of the water adsorbed by metals is not well understood, in spite of its great economic importance for the phenomena of catalysis or corrosion. The calculations of American experts in the field have given us a better grasp of the difficulties.[5] Moreover, in March 2002, after six years of work on a supercomputer, researchers at the University of Nagoya in Japan discovered how the disorderly state of liquid water passes into the organized structure of ice. Since the volume of water increases by 10 per cent when it freezes – which is harmful to living cells – researcher Iwao Ohmine concludes: 'It is of the greatest interest to know whether amorphous ice rather than crystallized ice can be obtained in the ambient conditions.... If it can, the freezing techniques currently in use ... could change spectacularly.'[6] We can see the practical interest of this type of research into the water molecule and its metamorphoses: body organs, for instance, might be frozen without damage to the integrity of their cells.

In June 2002 a research team led by David Quéré at the Collège de France discovered that, on a suitable surface, drops of water could rebound like springs without splashing. We know that water does not wet the feathers of a duck or the leaves of a lotus, but French researchers have now discovered that the rather surprising behaviour of water might allow us to develop new materials that never get wet – for example, a permanently dry glass. For when a drop of water strikes a certain surface, part of it splashes but the rest remains on the surface and slips to the side. By contrast, a drop that falls on a hydrophobic surface like wax does not spread out and is virtually spherical. Using high-speed photography (10,000 frames a second) and a particular hydrophobic surface, David Quéré and his team have shown that drops may change shape and bounce back in a spectacular manner, more like a spring or a ball than a liquid. This creates real opportunities for the creation of permanently dry hydrophobic surfaces, and indeed Quéré is currently holding talks with a major French manufacturer of flat glass, with the aim of developing new car windscreens. Such research also helps us understand the impact of raindrops on motorway asphalt and the manner in which they wend their way towards groundwater.

As we can see, water has not ceased to arouse human curiosity and to surprise researchers, but some of its surprises may be, to say the least, highly disagreeable. Take, for example, the sinister revelations concerning the underground nuclear waste dump that the US authorities plan to build beneath the volcanic Yucca Mountain, in the Nevada desert.[7] In the opinion of experts, the main way in which radioactive waste could escape would be through the seeping of rainwater from the peaks to the subsoil. In fact, rainwater flows regularly at the edge of the waste dump, feeding wells and appearing on the surface in the form of springs. It is calculated that it would take between 9,000 and 80,000 years for water actually to reach the accessible environment. In 1996 the Energy Department declared that it would take 50 years to reach groundwater level, 400 metres beneath the dump, but researchers have found cracks in the rock that offer it a much faster passage. In 1997 traces of chlorine 36 were detected in a tunnel that had been dug to explore the mountain, and, as this element is artificial, its presence means that fission products resulting from nuclear explosions – the first of which date back to 1944 – have already penetrated the rock and reached a depth of more than 240 metres. We know that the underground water free of tritium (or chlorine 36) dates from before 1944, since these radioactive elements can come only from the atmospheric nuclear tests that began in that year. Of course, the Yucca waste is packed in containers, but the Energy Department has constantly argued (and the Nuclear Waste Policy Act has actually legislated) that 'the site's geology [should] form the primary isolation barrier' of radioactive material. This allows the State of Nevada, in conflict with the federal government, to ask the courts to rule that the Yucca Mountain cannot serve for millennia as a dump for radioactive waste – since the routes taken by the water are unpredictable, and it retains traces of our depredations and misdeeds in relation to our environment.

In spite of all our serious efforts, with the most sophisticated instruments and the most rigorous methodology, science and scientists continue to make mistakes. In France, in 1988, there was the famous affair of *water memory*: infinite dilution of a solution of antibodies, which nevertheless seemed to remain biologically active. In 1966 a Soviet scientist[8] supposedly discovered an 'abnormal', 'polymerized' form of water, which was the subject of hundreds of articles; only in 1971 was it realized that it was normal water contaminated by sweat, and a few years later the researchers retracted their previous findings.[9]

It has been established that the chemical composition of water is essential for the quality of food: cheese producers know this as well as bakers or pastry-makers. Every beer-lover knows the distinctive tastes and flavours of the famous Dublin stout, London bitter or Czech Pilsner; in fact, it is the composition of the water – 90 per cent of the total ingredients – which makes the difference. Today brewers treat the water and de-ionize it, to remove certain elements such as calcium, phosphorus or salt so that it reacts in the required way with the malt or barley. The chemical composition of water has also been decisive in the take-off and development of certain industries: the action of local waters, on wool and leather respectively, led to the flourishing of tapestry in Aubisson and leather-tanning in Fez (where the tenth- to thirteenth-century Almoravid supply system is still in use). Similarly, the retting, braking and combing of flax or hemp largely depend on the properties of the water used for the purpose.

Water quality has thus been a major factor in the fortunes of various regions and given them their distinctive economic character – not without repercussions, of course, for both the landscape and society.

Finally, we should note that opal, 'the queen of precious stones', is nothing other than hydrated silica – that is, sand and water. It is formed at low temperatures when underground water washes the silica from the soil, then evaporates and abandons it. The Romans saw this as a guarantee of happiness, while the Arabs placed opal in paradise; some even endow it with magical properties and use it to make prophecies. The precious stone may 'self-destruct' if it loses its water, following the gradual spread of tiny cracks across its surface, but synthetic opals, made in France by Pierre Gilson since 1974, do not have this drawback, as they do not contain any water.

Although science does not yet know everything about *aqua simplex*, it has high hopes that the little molecule might one day solve the energy crisis, mitigate the greenhouse effect and help to offset global warming.

Already, car engines are running in California on electricity internally generated by hydrogen. The gas can be obtained through electrolysis of water, and it can thus enable a battery to function that produces energy by reforming the water molecule. Automobile manufacturers are currently experimenting with this process on numerous prototypes. But even greater benefits are possible. For hydrogen has the interesting characteristic that, when burned, it causes the opposite reaction to the decomposition of water, yielding not only water but a release of heat (exothermic reaction). Automobile-makers are working on hydrogen-fuelled engines and foresee that one day the gas will make oil obsolete, together with its pollution and its wars. There is an obvious problem that the breaking down of water into oxygen and hydrogen requires as much energy as the amount obtained through combustion of the resulting hydrogen. But, to get round this 'thermodynamic' difficulty, experts are working flat out on catalysers able to lower the energy barrier of the water breakdown process, so that hydrogen can be produced at a lower cost. Chemists at Tokyo University have developed a lanthanum-boosted catalyser that breaks down water under the impact of ultraviolet radiation: it requires that the oxygen and hydrogen should not be produced at the same place, since then the water molecule would reform and the whole operation would fail. Lanthanum boosting, which involves creating crystalline particles of a sufficient size, enables the surface of the catalyser to achieve this result with a significant yield of hydrogen, so that the water breakdown becomes faster than the water synthesis. A lot still needs to be done, but Japanese researchers are confident that they have found a way of moving towards a hydrogen economy – thanks to the water molecule.[10] So water, which made it possible for life to appear on Earth, may possibly free our planet from the clutches of carbonic gas and spare us a death through global warming, of which summer 2003 gave us a terrible and violent foretaste.[11]

Finally, we should stress the key role of engineering sciences in making available hitherto unsuspected water resources for agriculture, industry and domestic consumption, as well as the hydraulic energy to obtain iron in abundance and to gain access to the mechanical world. Watt's development of the steam engine meant that it was water which underpinned the triumph of mechanization and the Industrial Revolution. It is true that humans were playing the sorcerer's apprentice. In one recent book we read: 'Our access to fresh clean water has been radically transformed by interventions … dams, storages, diversions, overuse and pollution.' These interventions have encouraged people to settle in places they would not otherwise have chosen – Las Vegas, parts of the Netherlands, the Bangladeshi capital Dhaka, southern Australia, to give just a few examples – in a way that is not sustainable in the long term, so that huge engineering projects that began amid environmental ignorance in the early twentieth century are ending amid a full-blown environmental crisis.[12]

PART II

Water as a political issue

3

The problem of distribution and management

> Water, like a skin
> That no one can wound.
>
> *Paul Éluard*

Water has existed on Earth in finite quantities virtually since it first appeared in the cosmos. This is a physical fact. Were it distributed evenly on the planet, the existing quantity would be enough to meet the needs of a population ten times larger than today's. But water is not evenly distributed on the planet – far from it. Whereas in Iceland each person has available 600,000 cubic metres a year, the corresponding figure for Kuwait is a mere 75 cubic metres. Rainfall, too, presents a huge diversity: at one extreme, in northern Chile, it almost never rains; at the other, tropical forest and cold peaks condense clouds and attract as much as 2,400 mm a year.

A highly uneven distribution

In fact, twenty-three countries possess two-thirds of global water resources, the main ones being the fourteen-nation EU plus Brazil, Canada, the USA, India, Indonesia and Russia. Asia is home to 60 per cent of humanity but only 36 per cent of the world's water, against 8 per cent and 15 per cent respectively for North and Central America. India, whose population comes just behind China's, has only 4 per cent of this planetary resource, while the Arab countries, representing 10.3 per cent of land surface and 4.5 per cent of the world's population, have only 0.43 per cent of recoverable water and receive only 2 per cent of global rainfall. For the six member states of the Gulf Cooperation Council, the shortfall of water in relation to needs is of the order of 15 billion cubic metres.

Despite these figures, however, India as a whole is not short of water: it is capable of feeding all its children, even when the monsoon is disappointing. The difficulties stem from the fact that the subcontinent receives its water during the four months of monsoon, and that some regions are much less favoured than others. There is also a major problem of mismanagement, since Indian canals lose 70 per cent of their water before it can reach the consumer.

China, with 22 per cent of the world's population, has only 8 per cent of its water, and the resulting shortages, which affect 60 million Chinese, cause the peasantry to embark on 'raids' – veritable revolts – in search of arable land. The authorities thought the water problems could be solved through growth, but they have lost on both counts: environmental degradation and resource depletion are costing the country 8 to 12 per cent of its GDP.[1] In August 2001 the Chinese vice-premier told *Le Monde* that water shortages are a serious obstacle to future development. In February 2003 the government announced a vast programme to divert the great rivers to the thirsty northern plains, where anarchic industrialization has drawn excessively on the existing groundwater. The first phase of this plan is due to end in 2010, with an expected investment of $19 billion. For the moment, out of a total of 668 towns, 400 face water shortages; millions of Chinese are drinking polluted water, and even official sources mention reports of peasant riots in the countryside over water issues.[2]

There are many problems connected with the supply of water, since the planet's resources take the form of drinking water, freshwater, salt water (98 per cent of the world total), groundwater – even flowing 'blue' water (of rivers) and 'green' evaporation water that feeds the main biomes of the temperate and tropical zones. Renewable resources meet 85 per cent of our water needs and are powerfully affected by human activities: acid rain, for instance, influences the composition of 20,000 Canadian lakes. Water is expected to be a much more worrying issue than food or energy in the twenty-first century,[3] and Terence Corcoran, Toronto editor of the *Financial Times*, sees it as 'the oil of the twenty-first century'. But such predictions are not shared by everyone; the Indian ecologist Anil Agarwal even claimed in The Hague, in March 2000, that 'there is no scarcity of water', and that the solution lies in an end to the mismanagement of resources. We must keep a cool head, for scarcity is a social relation to things, not one of their intrinsic qualities, but we should also note that capitalism can function only on the basis of scarcity. We therefore need to be very cautious when speaking of a water crisis, and always try to discover who stands to gain from crisis.

In many countries, moreover, spatial and temporal disparities are often at the origin of crises and conflicts. The four Gulf states – Bahrain, Kuwait, Saudi Arabia and the United Arab Emirates – have so little fresh water that they have to derive 75 per cent of their total through desalination and long-distance transportation, whose high total cost, as we have seen, remains a state secret. Before the oil boom, Kuwait imported water from Iran on a flotilla of boats,[4] while Bahrain is so short of fresh water that desalination is the only way of meeting people's needs. In Saudi Arabia, where oil means that energy is cheap and plentiful, 70 per cent of drinking water is similarly processed from the sea. Desalination is still too costly and unsuitable for the great majority of countries in a state of hydric stress, and it is obviously not feasible in landlocked countries such as Mali, Chad or Niger. President Kennedy used to say that the country which developed a good desalination process would derive a much longer-lasting benefit from it than a country which wanted to be number one in space. In the United States itself, Texas, California and Florida see two major advantages in the desalination projects they are developing for the near future: first, of course, the technology is not affected by periods of drought; and second, it is perfectly reliable – unless the seawater is polluted by hydrocarbons. Soon the largest desalination plant in the Western hemisphere will come into operation in Tampa, Florida,[5] producing 25 million gallons of drinking water a day, or 10 per cent of the city's requirement. It will use the reverse osmosis procedure, which forces seawater through a membrane under very high pressure, but this means that for each litre of drinking water there will be a litre of brine. With recent technological advances, this process has become less and less costly and more and more efficient – hence its great attraction. But it still remains very expensive in energy terms.

Specialists point out that, at least in the United States, the cost of desalination should be set against what would have been needed to build new wells and dams, reservoirs and recycling plants. For environmentalists, however, desalination does not have the same attractions: on the coast each unit must be flanked by an ugly and polluting electric power station, and the large quantities of discarded brine have a negative impact on the marine ecosystem. Some theorists have proposed the idea of 'virtual water' for countries in deficit. The argument is that, since food imports are ultimately nothing other than water imports in disguise, such countries should leave the production of food to others and, in the spirit of free trade, rely on high technology to generate the foreign currency to pay for it, thereby automatically reducing the amount of water needed locally. The problem is, however, that a less water-intensive agriculture may still increase agricultural and food dependence on the big agribusiness corporations. In Israel, where farmers enjoy preferential rates, voices are being raised against the excessive use of water by agriculture (86 per cent of total consumption) in relation to its small share of GNP (1.8 per cent); these protests are a new departure, since Israeli leaders, for propaganda reasons, long praised the success of national agriculture in 'making deserts bloom', and farmers used and misused water with establishment approval. Now this false rhetoric has had its day. In April 2002 Christian Salmon, executive director of the International Parliament of Writers, following a visit to the martyred town of Jenin and occupied Palestine, described as follows the devastation caused by the Zionist soldiery: 'In the area around the settlements, they destroy houses, pull down olive trees, raze orange orchards to improve "visibility"! … Already in the 1950s they planted forests of fir trees to erase the traces of Palestinian villages.'[6] Speaking of the moving frontiers that the Israeli authorities are now establishing, Salmon adds: 'The creeping frontier: encircle the villages, the watering places.'

Rainfall is an important source of water, but the total that falls from the skies is not an infallible indicator. As the geographer Jean Despois puts it: 'Average rainfall figures, however important they may be, are still abstractions: plants and animals, agriculture and animal husbandry live not on averages but on realities…. Harvests and pastures depend on the distribution of rainfall; it is that which determines people's happiness or unhappiness.' And he concludes: 'When the earth is thirsty, the fellah is hungry.'[7]

Precious traditional techniques

What counts most is the temporal distribution of rainfall.[8] In Tunisia, the dry cultivation of cereals (wheat and barley) corresponds quite precisely to the 400 mm isohyet and the limits of regular drainage to the sea. In the sandy terrain around the Gulf of Gabes, 'occult precipitation' – that is, the direct fixing of water vapour by the soil – is equivalent to several millimetres of rain. But in Morocco, the humidity of the ocean is such that it makes cultivation profitable around the 300 mm isohyet. In North Africa, torrential rains – more than 30 mm in twenty-four hours – are largely lost to agriculture. In the Sahel–Sudanese zone, rain falls at most for four to six months of the year, and then mostly in the form of storms; the sun rapidly evaporates any water that remains on the surface. For the peasantry, then, the problem is how to capture and keep the water so that it can be useful for agriculture. The *zaï*, especially widespread in Burkina Faso, has been developed through the ages as one of the best solutions.[9]

This method involves the preparation of unused land very early in the dry season, by digging basins 20–40 cm wide by 10–15 cm deep in staggered rows (every 80 to 100 cm) and shifting the earth further down to hold back the streaming water. During the dry season, these microbasins trap particles of soil and organic matter brought by the desert wind. As soon as the April rains come, farmers fill these basins with a mixture of organic matter – manure, plant debris, compost, ashes, household refuse – which has been dried in the sun and turned into powder; this then attracts termites of the *Trinervitermes* genus, which dig tunnels at the bottom of the basins in which streaming water collects, resulting in deep pockets of moisture safe from rapid evaporation that allow families to sow in the basins.

Inspired by the *zaï* system, Niger farmers in Illéla and Badeguichiri have been reviving with excellent results another almost-abandoned traditional technique – the *tassa*. In West Africa, where millet yields are usually less than 350 kg per hectare, *zaï* holes can give as much as 1,000 to 2,000 kg. Yet the technique is operational only in Sahel–Sudanese regions with an average annual rainfall of 300 to 800 mm. The peasantry also knows that a combination of manure and light mineral fertilizer improves this traditional technique to the point where it can increase markedly the output of cereals and fodder, thereby alleviating food insecurity and pressure on cultivable land. Thus, so long as one takes the trouble to study ancestral methods, it is possible to draw precious lessons from them concerning the use of soil and water, which can only help to secure the human and livestock food supply. Armed with spades and mattocks, often carrying a child in their womb, women from the Keita district in Niger have been successfully pushing back the desert. Further inspiration has come from the building of low stone walls to protect fields from erosion (called *jessours* in southern Tunisia) – an old technique that has enabled these women to trap the little rainfall (300 mm per year) by reducing the speed of streaming, so that it seeps through the soil into the groundwater level. A further advantage of this is that it is no longer necessary to water trees and plants for months on end. In the space of fifteen years, more than 25,000 hectares have been recovered through these efforts: 16 million trees have been planted in supposedly barren land that had been abandoned for fifty years or more. *Le Soleil*, published in Dakar, writes lyrically of this regeneration:

> The sight is fantastic, almost unreal.... On the arid plateaux ... they are planting forage species ... for livestock. Further down, they are transplanting trees that can withstand the devastating force of the wind and give shade and nutrients to the soil. In the areas in between, they are growing millet and sorghum, but also wheat, onions and sunflowers. Nurseries and market gardens run by women are flourishing near the dams.... Who said that it is impossible to conquer the desert?

In Niger fishermen are commonly called *sorkos* (water masters), for not only do they have deep, almost carnal knowledge of the Niger river and Lake Chad, they can also tell you the period, cycle and area of reproduction for each kind of fish living there. Theoretically, Niger has at its disposal 31 billion cubic metres of water a year (29 billion of it from the Niger river) plus 4.5 billion cubic metres of underground water, but only 1 per cent of this potential is actually mobilized for the needs of the population, livestock, industry and irrigation. A lack of political will, financial pressures and a highly variable rainfall, combined with the local lifestyle and scattered settlement patterns, ensure that the water issue is constantly and cruelly posed.[10] One result is the prohibitive price for water: in Zinder, in southern Niger, 18 litres cost 1,000 FCFA francs (€1.50).

The spiritual identity of many communities around the world is closely bound up with earth and water, and their capacity to feed them. In 1988 the Indian government honoured the Bishnoi people for their heroic struggle to defend the fauna, flora and water of the Rajasthan desert. As their economy is based on livestock – agriculture would be too risky – the little water collected in their tanks serves first of all for the production of fodder, which provides people with milk and wool to live on.[11] In Africa, various peoples used hydraulic systems to improve their farming methods, and the new knowledge, exported to the USA via the slave trade, led to the growing of rice in the southern States and the making of many a fortune.[12] When André Gide visited Chad in 1925, he was all admiration for the irrigation methods on the Logone river: 'Nothing more primitive and more ingenious than this elementary machine of Virgilian elegance.'[13]

In Benin, however, the anarchic introduction of *acadjas* – systems involving the use of branches to trap fish – has caused catastrophic filling of the Ouémé delta in a number of places. Traditional techniques do not have only positive effects: it is necessary to separate the wheat from the chaff, and to avoid a potentially disastrous kind of naive optimism. Objective criteria must be used to measure the economic and social-cultural impact of various techniques, in relation to the nature of the soil, erosion factors, the availability of water, and so on. Unfortunately, moreover, the water that is indispensable for agriculture, creating wealth and offering the key to food sufficiency (and therefore independence), attracts the envious gaze of others. Struggles for power are never far away, and water is a significant variable in current strategic equations.

4

Geostrategy, power and struggles

Water is the Earth's gaze, its device for watching time.

Paul Claudel

In the course of history, water has often been an instrument in the hands of politicians and an instrument of geostrategy. A textbook case is the Aswan dam in Egypt: under pressure from Washington, which was opposed to the Nasser regime, the World Bank in July 1956 reneged on an agreement of principle that it had signed with Cairo to fund the building of the dam. The project was finally completed in 1970, thanks mainly to Soviet aid. More recently, former US Secretary of State Madeleine Albright made known the importance she attached to water issues in foreign policy when she proposed an 'alliance for global water security', at the Earth Day in April 2000: 'I have in mind not an alliance such as NATO that is limited to certain countries and comprised of governments alone, but rather a less formal alliance open to all who comprehend the urgency of working together to conserve transboundary water, manage it wisely and use it well.'[1] And, after the Iraq War in 2003, her successor, Colin Powell, deplored the fact that 'more than a billion people lack clean water', and that 'two billion lack adequate sanitation'; but he argued that President George W. Bush's 'Millennium Challenge Account' (MCA) was a powerful means to 'draw whole nations into an expanding circle of opportunity and enterprise'.[2]

Power games

Some Arab analysts think that the United States is seeking, through the Christian–Muslim conflict in Sudan, to control the waters of the Nile for Israel's benefit, their main ally in the region, and to gain a further hold over Egypt, the leader of the Arab world.[3] Karl Marx, for his part, described what we might call 'hydraulic societies', where the state directed and managed the collective performance of huge works.[4] Hydraulic centralism (despotism?) in the Egypt of the Pharaohs, in Mesopotamia, China and elsewhere. In the case of Egypt, historians have a go at explaining that 'unity is necessary to keep a watch for rises in water level, to organize and extend the beneficial flooding of the Nile'. They also try to find reasons for the divine power of the pharaoh, who, in the words of a vizier of the New Empire, 'is a god whose actions bring life'. In fact, it was thanks to his divine power that harvests were abundant, since he commanded the respect of the Nile god, the source of all prosperity.[5] History does, it is true, show that in Babylonia and Egypt regular order and discipline were vital for the proper use of river water and the rational exploitation of their natural fertility. But, Michalowski writes, there were a number of unexpected outgrowths:

> The centralization of power resulting from the country's unifica-
> tion was undoubtedly a far-reaching political act that led to the
> strengthening of the state. The administration of such a large
> area, the supervision of a complicated irrigation system and the
> construction of canals and dykes led to ... the development, or
> rather overdevelopment, of bureaucracy.[6]

Paradoxically, this situation is still more or less with us today: water remains an instrument of population control. During the Mexican presidential elections in 2000, for example, in the god-forsaken dormitory town of Chimalhuacán (pop. 1 million), the PRI candidate *La Loba* (the She-Wolf) – who was in charge of the local distribution of drinking water – 'did not shrink from cutting off the water supply to ensure that she got people's votes'. The municipal water lorries then remembered the existence of the slum inhabitants and finally began to supply them with water, which led one observer to comment: 'If a business can be made of poverty, where is the democracy?' Similarly, when the government of Africa's richest country, Botswana, decided to force the Bush-men people to live in settlement areas and enjoy 'the benefits of civilization', President Festus Mogae curtly explained that 'people can no longer live from hunting and gathering' – but the real reason, according to one newspaper,[7] was that 'the state wanted to get its hands on their land'; so, it stopped supplying communities living on the reservation with water, on the grounds that transportation costs were too high (even though the European Union had declared its willingness to put up the cash). Unfortunately the tactic worked only too well and virtually emptied the region of its inhabitants, many of whom said that they had no alternative if they were not to die of thirst. A representative of the NGO Survival International stated: 'They take away their water to force them into government camps, where they are stripped of their tribal way of life and reduced to the listless state of drunkards and beggars.'

Further north, in Sicily, water has become an issue of power for the Mafia and crooked politicians. In May 2002, to tackle the water shortages that had led to religious processions and sometimes rioting in Sicilian villages,[8] the government set up a special organization to run the island's dams, to equip ships with emergency desalination equipment, to develop or repair the water mains system, and to make compensatory awards to drought-stricken farmers. This effective assumption of powers devolving to the Sicilian regional council, which had been paralysed for months by political quarrels, provided a context highly favourable to Cosa Nostra. In fact, the Roman paper *L'Espresso* reports that much of the water shortage seems to have been organized:

> There is water everywhere in Sicily. There are even dams that could supply whole provinces with running water twenty-four hours a day. But they are not working – for example, the Gibbesi dam, a quarter of an hour from Ravanusa [where 'water-carriers' operate, as in the good old days]. Who profits from this situation? Everyone, except the users and consumers of water. First of all, it profits the politicians and their clientele: in Sicily there are 451 organizations, institutions, consortia and public enterprises that look after the harnessing of water. Multiply that by the number of chairmen, directors, council members, workmen and guards, and you will have an idea of what a subsistence economy based on chronic dysfunctionality actually means. Then there are the private enterprises. For a long time the Mafia controlled water distribution, explains Domenico Sabatino, from the Committee for the Global Contract for Local Water. 'In the 1950s a large number of water merchants were in the pay of the Mafia, and in the 1970s many wells belonging to clans ... were confiscated. Then a series of laws made Cosa Nostra's business more difficult.'

And the *Espresso* article concludes: 'No one will ever tell you which of all these people who make money from water actually pay their tithes to the Mafia.'

In Tunisia, donations fund the installation of running water in some parts of the country, and it is duly inscribed in marble as an 'achievement of the President', for people to read as they enter the area. Only rarely, however, is the supply of drinking water matched with adequate drainage works – even though 80 per cent of it ends up as wastewater.

The water weapon

The marshlands of the Nile delta enabled Christian Bashmur communities to escape the Islamization of Egypt. Many other non-Muslims were ruined by the taxes that Islamic law demanded from them as *dhimmis*, but during the uprising of 831–32 the marshy labyrinth, with its mangroves, bulrushes and crocodiles, was a natural fortress that held at bay Arab fighters unfamiliar with the area. However, dominated groups also know how to use water as a weapon. In 1881, to resist the French occupation, Tunisians sabotaged the aqueduct supplying Tunis. 'Disused tanks had to be brought into service and water was rationed', lamented one diplomat. 'The existence of a city with more than 100,000 inhabitants was threatened.'

The historian Gamal Ghittany maintains that, in the fourteenth century, the Mameluk rulers of Cairo used water to control its more turbulent districts – just as the Israeli authorities routinely use water as one of their brutal measures against the Palestinian intifada. On 12 March 2002, for example, the Israelis cut the water supply to the whole of Ramallah, as a collective punishment for resistance; and, whenever the IDF lays siege to Palestinian areas or villages, its tanks begin by methodically destroying the mains water system (as in Jenin, in March 2002).

Under the Ottomans, and right down to the 1920s, the Tigris ensured the social division of Baghdad between rich and (regularly flooded) poor areas. Similarly, the Shatt al-Arab – the fertile ecosystem at the confluence of the Tigris, Euphrates and Karun rivers, containing the largest palm groves in the world – has long been home to a culture and civilization particularly opposed to Baghdad. One fourteenth-century visitor to the region, Ibn Battuta, wrote of its spell: 'It has inherited wealth and opulence, being at the confluence of two seas, one brackish and one fresh.' Saddam Hussein dared to drain in part this unique ecosystem, for his own base needs of police control. But, in prosperous times, Saudi Arabia has carried out expensive drilling operations to draw water from fossil aquifers in areas bordering Iraq, in the hope of winning over Shiite tribes in revolt against the Wahabi regime in Riyadh and stopping their ears to the siren songs of Iraqi Baathists or Iranian ayatollahs. The non-renewable water in question served to irrigate wheat fields – a crop that the kingdom bought at above the world price or exported with the boast that it had succeeded in greening the Rub' al Khali desert. And indeed, for reasons of prestige, the Saud family did export the country's fossil water, in the form of wheat!

In a Libyan parallel, the Great Artificial River created to supply the coastal towns draws water from fossil aquifers beneath the Sahara some 35,000 years old, and official propaganda exploits the achievement to sing the praises of the long-ruling Colonel Gaddafi.

At Mar del Plata in 1977, Dublin in 1992, Paris in March 1998 and the UN in June 1998, the international community has repeatedly stressed its concern over the water issue and posed the problem of global governance for this vital substance. The 1981–90 period was declared the International Decade for Clean Drinking Water, and, more recently, 2003 was the International Year of Freshwater. A quarter of a century ago the United Nations organized a conference on the environment, in Vancouver, where the main theme was the visible water crisis in the South, usually resulting from the weakness of the state. Today it is globalization and the associated privatizations which are causing often dramatic crises in the United States, Canada, Britain and elsewhere and acutely posing the problem of water at a global level. Among the pernicious effects, we might mention here the abandonment of Japanese rice fields, resulting in floods and contamination with accumulated pesticides and fertilizer, which has followed the imports of cheaper rice from Thailand.

On the other hand, public opinion now pays greater attention to the issue of water, demanding greater justice and a more ethical approach to its management and consumption. The *Guardian* (26 May 1998) reported that, as soon as the new Indonesian regime had ousted Suharto, it cancelled the far from transparent contracts linking the city of Jakarta to two water corporations (the French Lyonnaise des Eaux and the British Thames Water). The newly renegotiated contracts have also been sharply criticized, however, both because of the lack of openness and because Suharto's son continues to have a large shareholding in the company that runs the capital's water supply. Water is such an acute problem in Jakarta that, according to the World Bank, avoidable health costs due to mismanagement represent a burden of $40–700 million on the national economy. The Bank itself, which has lent Indonesia $300 million to improve this sorry state of affairs, states that water-related problems are likely to hamper severely the country's economic development and jeopardize its food security, as well as degrading public health and inflicting irreversible damage on the aquatic environment.[9]

The widely quoted slogan of the ecologist René Dubos, 'Think globally, act locally', is not very relevant to water, since it passes over the intermediate, regional level where issues of development and resource allocation are decided. The world is crying out for an ethical water policy, one that can provide the guidelines for a more just global distribution and end the disgraceful games that rulers and pressure groups are playing with the resource. Only that will be able to reduce, perhaps even eliminate, the water-related conflicts that rage with greater or lesser severity around the world.

5

Water and conflicts

Whiskey is for drinking.
Water is for fighting over.

Mark Twain

It is significant that the words for river and rivalry have the same
Latin root. A Swedish academic book published in 1995, *Hydro-
politics*, quoted a (perhaps self-interested) prediction made by Ismail
Serageldin, former vice-president of the World Bank and chairman
of the World Water Commission: 'The wars of the next century
will be fought over water.' The same prediction was made by Wally
N'dow, director of the UN's Centre for Human Establishments,
who said in March 1996:

> I believe that if by 2010 great improvements are not undertaken
> to provide and save water, we'll have to face a monumental
> crisis....Whereas the grounds for the last century's wars were oil,
> I am firmly convinced that many political and social conflicts of
> the twenty-first century will focus on water.

Hydropolitics

In fact, conflicts are taking place on all five continents. There are frequent disputes between Mexico and the United States over the waters of the Colorado, which are so heavily depleted on the American side that they only sporadically reach the Gulf of California. In the view of certain analysts, the flows of the Rio Grande and the Upper Colorado are in danger of falling by 75 per cent and 40 per cent, respectively, in the course of the next century. In early February 2001, the Mexican foreign ministry lodged a protest against US plans to exploit the Colorado basin, which threaten the water supply to many communities in the Mexican province of Baja California.[1] It should be borne in mind, however, that, because of water pollution by the *maquiladoras* (foreign-owned firms producing jeans, electronic goods, toys, pesticides, and so forth, attracted to Mexico by its cheap wages and lack of environmental controls), mothers often give their children Pepsi or Coca-Cola to drink. Obesity, diabetes and overexcitement are some of the consequences. Not by chance was Mexico the destination for Bush's first trip abroad after his election in 2000.

Conflicts over water have been a theme for novelists, such as Tom Clancy: 'Rodgers looked at the screen. There was only one explanation.... I think it's a mass of water.... Colonel, I think someone's just made a breach in the Ataturk dam.' Middle Eastern water wars thus appear in his techno-thriller,[2] where he imagines Kurdish separatists blowing up the Great Anatolia Project dam in Turkey (actually twenty-two dams and seventeen power stations). But, on the ground in the Middle East, fiction is lagging behind reality. Already on 17 April 1967 four Israeli Mirage jets bombed and destroyed the Syrian–Jordanian Khaled Ibn Al Waid dam on the Yarmuk river. An international convention signed in Geneva in 1947 prohibits the bombing of dams. Nevertheless, John McNaughton, in the name of the Pentagon, put forward the following odious proposal during the Vietnam War:

Strikes at population targets (per se) are likely not only to create a counterproductive wave of revulsion abroad and at home, but greatly to increase the risk of enlarging the war.... Destruction of locks and dams, however – if handled right – might ... offer promise. Such destruction does not kill or drown people. By shallow-flooding the rice, it leads after time to widespread starvation (more than a million?) unless food is provided – which we could offer to do at the conference table.[3]

In fact, a number of conflicts come to mind in relation to water: both between countries (Turkey–Syria,[4] Jordan–Israel, Israel–Palestine, India–Bangladesh, Iran–Iraq, Namibia–Lesotho, Senegal–Mauritania, Hungary–Slovenia, Uzbekistan–Kazakhstan– Kyrghyzstan–Tajikistan over the Amu Darya, Syr Darya and Aral Sea) and between states of a federation (as in India, Malaysia or the USA). The dispute that has been raging for six years between Virginia and Maryland over the waters of the Potomac is due to come before the Supreme Court: Maryland, invoking a royal charter going back to 1632, prevents Virginia from pumping water for the needs of its expanding cities.[5]

In 1970, an armed conflict was only just avoided between Syria and Iraq over the waters of the Euphrates. And, in the view of many observers, control of the Mesopotamian delta of Shatt al-Arab was one of the causes of the Iran–Iraq war in 1980.

Water conflicts may also break out inside a country. For example, the diversion of water from north-western Tunisia (which has plentiful water and a good hydrographic system) to the Sahel and Cape Bon is considered by many to be the 'hold-up of the century', carried out at the expense of politically weak communities that Bourguiba's regional policy kept marginalized in favour of his native Sahel. More recently, the planned diversion of water from the Rhône to Catalonia is encountering opposition on both sides of the Pyrenees, and, in line with EU directives for any such project, Pedro Arrojo of Saragossa University is demanding a proper study of its ecological impact. He has even gone so far as to say:

The bill for the work would no doubt be largely paid by the European Community and the public authorities. And why? Not because ordinary citizens need the water – there is no shortage in the area – but perhaps in order to supply more hotel toilets on the Costa Brava and golf courses. In other words, it is a question not of European solidarity but of public money in the service of private speculators.[6]

On the French side, competition is the main fear, since the water could give a boost to Spanish agriculture and increase its output. On 11 March 2001, a huge protest demonstration took place against the planned diversion, as well as the sharing of the Ebro's waters with the Spanish South in the framework of the Áznar government's ambitious National Hydrological Plan and its related political manoeuvring. In fact, water standards and funding are a matter for the European Union. In Andalusia, there is no water but there are many tourists – and greenhouses. The diversion of water from the Ebro would make it possible to meet the needs of the tourist industry, and to continue growing highly water-intensive crops under glass (or plastic). Such crops bring the manna of export subsidies from Brussels, which has thus turned local farmers into bounty-hunters. In France, clashes have occurred between Breton livestock farmers – Finistère alone produces 5.3 million pigs a year – and ecologists who accuse them of polluting the region's water. It is well known that only 70 per cent of farmers in the Aber Benoît, near Brest, comply with official standards for the storage of liquid manure, and unless measures are taken to control its use the opposition is expected to grow to a roar.[7]

Internal wars

Whereas, in the 1980s, India's national water policy established that the poor have priority in the development of river basins, the states of the union with the most resources jealously guard them against the others. Thus Karnataka did not wish to give up water from the Cauvery river for the benefit of Tamil Nadu, but after the violent incidents of 1991, which left 125 dead, the Supreme Court finally took action in late 2002 to force such transfers.[8] Within the Malaysian Federation, the state of Johor Baru prefers to sell its abundant water dear to cash-rich Singapore, rather than give it up to its Malaysian neighbours. Similarly, in the federation of Pakistan, which possesses one of the world's largest systems of continuous irrigation, drought has been fuelling tensions between its various provinces. Early in 2001, violent disturbances broke out in Karachi over the issue of water shortages, and strikes have taken place in Hyderabad (where the temperature can rise above 45°c). Yet, according to Dr Shashana Urooj Kazmi, a microbiologist at the University of Karachi, the city's water is a veritable culture fluid for a variety of 'skin conditions and gastro-intestinal disorders'.[9] Pakistan has its own nuclear weapons, like neighbouring India, but throws in the towel when it faces the basic public health task of providing its children with clean drinking water. In the Sind, the local population does not hesitate to challenge the military authorities, who, like the state bureaucracy, are largely made up of Punjabis. For the Sind, the last province downstream from the Indus basin, is convinced that it is the victim of hegemonic ambitions on the part of powerful Punjabis, and it accuses them of keeping water supplies for themselves. One Pakistani agricultural official stated: 'It's a tragedy, and in the end the country will fall apart, because everyone in the Sind is affected and everyone knows that the Sind is not getting its share of water.' A former senator added that 'this crisis has been the last straw in the long-simmering dispute between the three provinces (Sind, Baluchistan, North-west Frontier) and the Punjab', and that 'it may have grave consequences unless it is rationally explained to the population'.[10]

Water problems are thus valuable social-economic and political indicators. When people can no longer drink the water, this does not increase their confidence in the capacities of the state or the cohesiveness of society.

Water and the Israeli–Arab conflict

We should be wary, however, of linear thinking and generalization: it is difficult to prove that water is the cause of a conflict, because often there are several causes. Sometimes, as in the Middle East, it is mainly an issue of sovereignty for states that are very touchy about it, although Jordan mainly depends on the (Israeli-controlled) river of the same name for its water supply. Under the terms of the Madrid accords, Israel guaranteed it 'the minimum survival requirement for domestic purposes'.[11] It should be borne in mind that two-thirds of Jordan's water comes from territories forcibly acquired by Israel: the Golan Heights and the West Bank of the Jordan, and that a quarter comes from aquifers in the occupied territories. In other words, there is a 'water war' around the Jordan basin, 75 per cent of whose resources are exploited by a single country (Israel) covering less than 25 per cent of the surface of the basin. In Palestine, more than 55 per cent of the population do not have access to sufficient drinking water, while in Israel per capita water consumption is 500 cubic metres a year, rising to 700–800 cubic metres for West Bank settlers. In Israel water is the responsibility of the ministry of agriculture, but the Palestinian water supply is placed under the iron rule of the Israeli defence ministry. Military Ordinance No. 158, dated 30 October 1967, contained a particularly explosive provision: 'It is forbidden for anyone to utilize or possess hydraulic installations without prior authorization from the military authorities.' Prime minister Ariel Sharon, for his part, could hardly have been clearer: 'It is no accident that the settlements are where they are. It is necessary to keep the West security zone on the West Bank of the Jordan, the East security zone, the roads linking Jerusalem and, of course, the aquifer ... from which a third of our water comes.'[12]

On 18 August 1990, on a full page of the international edition of the *Jerusalem Post*, the Israeli agriculture ministry admitted that relinquishing control of the West Bank would have 'an immediate and significantly detrimental effect on the Israeli water supply', and that giving up Palestinian water would endanger the existence of the State of Israel. Referring to the Jewish settlements in the occupied territories, an article in the Palestinian paper *Al Quds* said that the first construction to spring up after the uprooting of Palestinian fruit trees was 'a huge water tower surrounded by barbed wire' – which underlined the importance of water for the future settlement and the fears it would have in its parched environment.[13] The Egyptian analyst Sid Ahmed has noted that on 28 September 2001, after the beginning of the second intifada, the Israeli armed forces dealt a series of harsh blows to the Palestinian water supply, destroying artesian wells, reservoirs and pipes for drinking water.[14] (We should remember that, during the first intifada, Yitzhak Rabin ruled that any Arab village whose children threw stones at Zionist troops should be deprived of water as a punishment.) Sid Ahmed also claims that Avidor Libermann, a man close to Sharon, threatened Egypt with a bombing raid against the Aswan dam if it ever actively supported the intifada. For a long time, of course, Israel occupied a strip of territory in southern Lebanon, including access to the country's only major river, the Litani – which means that in Lebanon, as elsewhere in the region, any evaluation of national water resources is now seen as a strategic matter. Further evidence of the importance of water in the region came in June 2001, when Lebanese president Émile Lahoud told visiting Arab ministers responsible for water issues that 'water is the new oil of the Arab countries'.[15]

Ariel Sharon also claimed that 'from 1948 to 1987' Syria 'carried on a war of attrition against Israeli civilians by attempting to divert vital water resources from Israel',[16] his aim probably being to justify the Israeli bombing of the Unity dam that Syria and Jordan had begun to build at that time. But the same Sharon has done much worse things in the register of horror and inhumanity. In May 2002, following a visit to Israel in March, Christian Salmon published an eyewitness account of the destruction of 'Jericho's irrigation systems'.[17] In fact, Israel tramples on Protocol 2 supplementing the Geneva conventions of 12 August 1949, which states that it is 'prohibited to attack, destroy, remove or render useless ... objects indispensable to the survival of the civilian population, such as foodstuffs, agricultural areas for the production of foodstuffs, crops, livestock, drinking water installations and supplies and irrigation works'. According to Dominique Vidal, at the peace talks with Syria in 1999, Ehud Barak 'failed to impose on the Syrian president, Hafez al-Assad, an agreement leaving Israel complete sovereignty over Lake Tiberias'[18] – which indicates that water was the object of bitter wrangling between the belligerents.

Historically, water has often been the catalyst of economic, ethnic or religious rivalries. It is true that there is considerable potential for conflicts over water, since no fewer than two hundred river basins are shared between more than one country: the Congo and the Nile flow through nine countries each, the Zambezi eight, the Amazon seven, the Mekong six, and the Tigris–Euphrates four. Egypt – the last country on the course of the Nile – is a special case, because, unlike the other eight, it adds no water to the river and is almost totally dependent on it. (Egypt and Hungary are more than 95 per cent dependent on water coming from beyond their frontiers: comparable figures are 82 per cent for Romania, 89 per cent for the Netherlands, 51 per cent for Germany and 33 per cent for Belgium.) As long ago as 1898, Britain threatened to go to war with France over its attempts to control the sources of the Nile. Further south, Botswana has recently purchased new tanks, as the peace between Angola and Namibia threatens to create increased pressure on the Okavango: Namibia plans to build a pipeline to divert water from this common river to its eastern regions.

In the recent past, most settlements of water disputes concerned navigable routes in the former Ottoman Empire. Theory evolved from an emphasis on the rights of upstream states (the Harmon doctrine of 1909, covering Canada and the United States) to a concept of just division, but there was no mechanism to enforce decisions. The Red Cross states that, despite the international conventions, a number of armed conflicts (such as those in the Balkans) have targeted water conveyance as a way of quickly bringing the enemy to its knees. And it adds: 'Water and sanitation are the backbone of emergency aid.' The war against Iraq, in March 2003, and the war against the Palestinians are further convincing proof of these points.

An international body with the power to settle water disputes has become a necessity for the preservation of peace and the equitable distribution of the resource. It would also be a valuable step in the direction of global governance for water.

6

A painful issue in Algeria

O billows, how many sad stories you know!

Victor Hugo

Astronauts see a blue planet, yet freshwater accounts for only 2 per cent of all the water on Earth, compared with 98 per cent for saltwater. Moreover, river water takes 16 days to be entirely replaced, swamp water 5 years, lake water 17 years, and aquifer water 1,400 years. We need to think about these figures, to understand the gravity of our actions and to keep in mind the timescale involved.

Over the last fifty years the world's population has trebled, while irrigated areas have increased sixfold and the demand for water sevenfold. Over the last ten years the global consumption of water has quadrupled.

Resource pressure

In fact, demand has been increasing at twice the rate of population growth, and at the same time pollution has been reducing by a third the reserves at our disposal. For example, the level of the Ogallala – the fossil aquifer beneath the Great Plains in the United States, which alone provides a fifth of the country's irrigation water – has fallen by 50 per cent, and some parts of it are now irredeemably polluted by agrichemical and industrial products; if depletion continues at the present rate, the aquifer will lose all of its 4 trillion tonnes of water over the next 140 years. As for the fossil aquifer of central Arabia, solvents used by Western tanks and aircraft during the Gulf war have now seriously polluted it.[1] Contamination of these ancient fixed aquifers is much more disturbing than what happens to watercourses capable of eventually shedding much of their foreign matter. Much has been written about the fate of the Aral Sea, which intensive growing of rice and cotton under the sacrosanct Soviet plan turned into a toxic broth, and which irrigation has reduced to a third of its previous area. Less well known perhaps is the case of Lake Owens, which eighty-five years of water diversion to Los Angeles has shrunk from 300 square kilometres to little more than a desolate dustbowl. Eighteen years ago, the city shirked its responsibility to take expensive remedial measures for the sake of the environment and those living on the shores of the lake.[2] In the 1998 election for governor, the issue of California's water needs was described as 'explosive':[3] not only did the Democratic candidate argue for water economies, including the recycling of farm waste, rather than the building of new dams; he also proposed lower taxes for farmers who agreed to irrigate their land more sparingly, and demanded harsher penalties for industrialists who rode roughshod over the environment.

The water issue has aroused the American public to such an extent that on 30 July 1998, at the height of his problems with the courts and the Monica Lewinsky affair, President Clinton found time to launch the 'Save the Rivers' environmental project in North Carolina and to declare its New River part of the protected 'American Heritage'. On 30 March 2002, the *Los Angeles*

Times published an editorial on the water shortage in New York, and, after recalling the chronic problems in southern California, stressed that 'ordinary water will remain an exceptional problem at national level'.

While Lake Owens was plundered to supply millions of California's inhabitants, the pretty mountain lake of Dayat Aoua in Morocco, a resort with a charming hotel, 30 kilometres from Fez, has rapidly seen its water vanish by order of King Hassan II, who wanted its feeder spring to serve the needs of his castle at Ifrane, where he spends a couple of weeks every now and then.

The ambiguity of water

Without water, poverty becomes more widespread and extreme. In India 69 per cent of people living in areas without agricultural irrigation are poor, compared with 26 per cent in irrigated areas. In connection with the famine still affecting southern Ethiopia in 2003, it is thought that only investment in the organization of water and agriculture could break the cycle of drought and exhaustion of family goods such as seeds.

Yet water is not always a blessing. According to a UN report dated March 2003, the period between 1991 and 2000 witnessed 2,557 natural disasters, causing 665,000 deaths. Of these, 90 per cent were due to typhoons, cyclones, landslips and other phenomena related to water; 50 per cent involved flooding, 28 per cent water-borne and carrier-borne illnesses (malaria, schistosomiasis, helminthiasis, etc.), and 11 per cent drought. Flooding was the cause of 15 per cent of deaths due to natural disasters, and drought of 42 per cent. But the tragedies associated with drought are often silent and less spectacular than landslips or typhoons: it is often too late to do anything by the time the damage is visible in the shape of dead animals and trees, dried-up wells or food shortages.

Paradoxically, in some countries such as Malaysia, flooding causes more casualties because the peasantry is somewhat better off. In the past, people used to leave their home as soon as water levels began to rise, whereas now they often own a television or refrigerator and wait until the last minute to make tracks, and by then, alas, the current may be strong enough to carry them and their few goods away. In 1999, the losses owing to natural disasters were estimated at $70 billion, but allowance must also be made for hidden social costs, loss of livelihood, farming equipment, and so on. During the terrible drought that hit Brazil in April 1998, causing widespread hunger among millions of small farmers, neighbouring Argentina reported seventeen deaths in Chaco as a result of flooding that forced half a million people to abandon their homes. Since then, at the other end of the world, a terrible tragedy has again thrown the Algiers district of Bab El Oued into mourning;[4] the floods of December 2001 tore at the fabric of the city and caused more than a thousand casualties. But did humans not have some responsibility for what happened? We should remember that the Islamic Salvation Front (FIS) was founded in Algiers, in October 1988, following riots due to water shortages in the capital.[5] In the course of July 2003, water riots also shook the east and south of Algeria, while the west was suffering cases of cholera, meningitis and even plague (according to Agence France-Presse, quoted by the Tunisian press on 14 July 2003).

An emblematic case

It is often forgotten that, due to negligence, poor maintenance, theft, leaks (totalling nearly 40 per cent, according to *Le Monde*[6]) and failure to keep up with demographic growth, the inhabitants of towns like Algiers or Oran have for thirty years been living through a veritable ordeal, in which water has been available for only a few hours a day. The major demonstrations of June 2001, in Kabylie as well as Algiers, shed great light on this central popular grievance. *Le Monde* reported in September: 'A delegation told the prefect of Annaba, who had been promising to take the necessary measures: "We're at the end of our tether. We're not going to spend the whole summer filling jerrycans. Do something – otherwise it'll be war".' But the paper did not hold out much hope for the future: 'The people in charge of the Algiers water distribution company [Epeal] are unwilling to add to the restrictions currently in force, but they plan "time slot improvements" – in other words, a reduction in the length of time during which water will flow from the taps.' One perverse effect of rationing is that 'Algerians use the hours when water is available to build up stocks and waste the precious liquid', but the press is also full of reports of 'breaks in the supply lasting as much as ten days in outlying areas'. After noting that 'drought is not the only factor', since the state has invested much less than Morocco in dam construction, *Le Monde* concludes:

> For many Algerians things are not getting any better. Young
> kids on water duty, roaming the streets with a jerrycan, are still
> a common sight. Several years ago, an Algerian prime minister
> maintained that the water shortage threatened to become a real
> public order problem. News reports in the last few months have
> largely borne out those fears.[7]

The writer François Maspéro, who spent a month with an Algerian family in the summer of 2001, reported:

> During my stay there was one big event: the water pipe was
> connected to the future kitchen. But I never saw water running
> there before I left. It comes on every two or three days, usually
> in the early hours of the morning. Until now it was from the tap
> in the yard. And, as the flow is weak, several hours are needed to
> fill pail by pail the blue plastic tuns. Often it comes on late, after
> the reserves have been exhausted. The richest have installed

storage systems, but generally the life of Algerians is punctuated day and night by the wearying handling of pails.[8]

Rostomi Hadj Nacer, former governor of the Bank of Algeria, has revealed what is behind the suffering, what are the roots of the evil:

> People in Algiers risk dying of thirst, yet the Taksebt dam, 130 km away in Kabylie, is filled with water. The problem is that there are no canals to bring the water for people to use. Why? Because, after four years, no decision has been made about the method of allocating markets. The lack of economic administration, the shortage of experts, the incompetence and the short-term management of government stock: all these things together mean that an asset-destruction system is reproducing itself ad infinitum in Algeria. We needed the state to become stronger as we moved down the road to liberalism, but the opposite is what happened.[9]

Early in 2002 the situation was quite disturbing for the town of Sétif – the ancient Sitifis, which the Romans thought of as their granary – even though it has a dam, a number of boreholes and the waters of the Oued Bared. The authorities announced that water would be available for only one day in three, without mentioning what a friend called 'the taste and smell of the supply'. Despite Hadj Nacer's list of local shortcomings, the Algerian government is desperately looking for international finance and cooperation agreements. Early in February 2002 the water minister travelled to Tunisia; he also received the chairman and a delegation from the African Development Bank (ABD), asked them to finance repairs to the drinking water systems in Constantine, Annaba and Jijel, and proposed major renovation work on nine water recycling plants as well as dam projects and agricultural hydraulic schemes.[10] This raises the whole problem of water governance, and confirms the rule that water issues are an excellent indicator of the social, economic and political dynamics in any given country.

The painful issue of water resurfaced during the legislative elections of 30 May 2002. Writing of President Bouteflika's inspection of work on a water treatment plant and a desalination plant, the 'frontline leader in the battle for water', Florence Beaugé, wrote: 'The water shortage in the capital means that there is no alternative to drastic rationing. Tap water runs only one day in three, or one in six in some parts of Algiers.'[11] She also reported a comment by the Algerian head of state: 'The battle for water is not lost in advance for Algeria, but it is clear that if we nod off we'll have a rude awakening in 2010, and 2010 is already tomorrow.' Meanwhile, advertisements for mineral water are appearing on all sides, like the one promoting Mont Djurdjura 'natural mineral water' in the Algerian daily *Le Matin* on 31 December 2002. 'Treat yourself to health', it shouted, 'at an unbeatable price and quality' – without offering further details. It is unlikely that most Algerians will be able to afford that kind of water.

Florence Beaugé took up the question again in an article entitled 'The water supply has become a nightmare for the inhabitants of Algiers'.[12] 'The water shortage', she wrote, 'is such a nightmare in Algiers that it overshadows other problems such as housing, jobs or safety. It is driving us crazy. Lack of water could turn us into terrorists! people at the end of their tether admit when the thermometer inches above 30°c.' Others confided in her: 'You feel dirty, you feel ashamed of yourself. Just think that this is how things are, in the age of the Internet!' Because of neglect and official lack of foresight, in addition to the drought conditions (which are not so uncommon in the Mediterranean), 'the capital is currently receiving only a half of its water needs'. One expert emphasized:

> There have been huge efforts on this issue since independence, but serious thought has been dramatically lacking. Aberrations, lack of basic common sense have been uncovered. A dam is a combination of three elements that have to be made to function

at the same time: immobilization, transportation and distribution of the water. Two times out of three, however, they thought about the first part, but not about the second or the third! It's that kind of farcical negligence which we now have to get on top of.

In emergencies, water tankers serve some districts and, in doing so, threaten to create hygiene problems.[13] Desalination units are on the drawing board, but rationing will remain in force, with perhaps some minor improvements. This means that the nightmare is far from over for people living on upper storeys. Repairs must also be carried out on the system, which is more than fifty years old and sprang 25,000 recorded leaks in 2001. *Le Matin* of 8 January 2003 not only mentioned the first leaks of the year, but pointed to several paradoxes:

> The communes of greater Blida ... are reporting numerous leaks of water, especially during the winter season when there is an increased supply of drinking water. The Blida water board has tracked down a number of these leaks.... Illegal building over the reverse flow and distribution pipe seems to be the cause of these leaks, and all means are being employed to seal the holes.[14]

Evidently all this affects people's health and daily life in Algiers and the rest of the country. One woman, Djemel, explained why she would not be voting in the legislative elections in May 2002:

> The water will be off, like every Thursday. Up from six in the morning to go looking for the precious liquid. There is a well at the hammam and two queues: one for children with plastic bottles, one for adults with jerrycans. After five trips back and forth between the hammam and my fourth-floor flat, I'll be tired: I'll lie down to rest and fall asleep. So, I won't be thinking of the election. It's as simple as that![15]

In the view of the magazine *Jeune Afrique l'Intelligent*, 'it is not water that is lacking' but political will:

Silted-up dams, almost dry reservoirs, towns with water rationing.... The scenario in Algeria has a déjà-vu quality to it. For
people here know about all that. It's been going on for twenty-
five years, the general secretary at the Algerian ministry of
agriculture recalls. Suddenly, he says, politicians have had to
build the rainfall deficit into the picture as an everlasting fact,
a structural problem. So, nothing really new – except that, for
the past two years, the situation has been growing worse, and
the recent rain doesn't alter the terms of the problem. In fact, it
looks as if it will be a scorching summer, and this year could be
the worst we've had for five years, with an average deficit around
35 per cent.... In the end no part of the country is spared, they
admit at the ministry of agriculture. Algiers is no exception, and
its inhabitants have to resign themselves to their fate. The Orsec
Plan, adopted here as in most large urban areas, gives them a
right to drinking water only one day in three. At least in theory
– one journalist tones it down. For in some outlying areas it's one
day in five, and even less if you live in a block where the pressure is too weak for water to reach the upper floors. The only
solution then is to fill a can at the closest fountain, or to instal a
high-pressure device to conquer the height of the building.[16]

Today, with 10 billion dinars (€142 million) in emergency funding allocated to it, water has become the number-one priority, as
the exasperation of ordinary Algerians at the incompetence of
their rulers threatens to turn into the kind of public order problem
already glimpsed in Kabylie. Official encouragement is also being
given for the use of water-saving devices, and for a shift away
from rain-dependent grains to vines and almond trees. But it is
management issues that are the core of the debate – even if the
ministry uses wooden language and speaks of 'rationalization', in
a country where 85 per cent of annual precipitation evaporates
and the traditional North African domestic catchment tanks disappeared half a century ago.[17]

Despite its 112 dams, Algeria seems incapable of managing more
than 10 per cent of its water resources. Kaci Djerbib from the APS

press agency claims: 'We have the infrastructure, but it is often run-down and inadequate. Just in Algiers 30 to 40 per cent is being lost.' One idea is to use desalination (50,000 cubic metres a day) to supply Algiers, Tipaza, Boumerdès, Skikda and Tlemcen, but the water will cost 200 dinars per cubic metres instead of the present 25 dinars; it is a technological fix that addresses neither the problem of leaks nor social priorities nor the bureaucratic dysfunctions. For the moment, the Algerian government is using all the means at its disposal and has even created a water resources ministry, supposedly to cut through bureaucracy. But the ministry allows itself to be courted by French multinationals in the country, and has created l'Algérienne des Eaux under the influence of economists who have eyes only for imported models. This corporation began with an irresponsible round of price increases, in a situation where unemployment has reached record levels, but mass demonstrations eventually forced it into a shameful withdrawal.

Although the Algerian case is emblematic, it is true that Algiers is far from being the only capital city with shortages where the water taps run only once in three days, often at night. Remaining in the Arab world, we might also mention Damascus – which has water only six hours a day – or Amman, where a minister was recently sacked following water shortages and the contamination of drinking water. Nor is it enough to provide water; there must also be drains to carry away the waste.

Algeria's many serious problems relating to water play a key role in the cycle of violence that it has endured for the past decade, and in the *mal de vivre* felt by the population. On the issue of waste water, here is a report from Douzi III housing estate in Bab Ezzouar, which was built 'just a few years ago':

> The most crucial problem is indisputably the diversion of
> waste water into septic tanks, given the lack of proper drains.
> Of course, this exposes the life of citizens to a danger that may
> result in water-borne diseases … if the groundwater becomes

contaminated. This ordeal of the inhabitants of Douzi III ... is not limited to the septic tanks, as drinking water is not always on tap. The sight of children holding jerrycans is ubiquitous, and this forces residents to buy tanks for large sums of money, without being sure that the water is always drinkable.[18]

The terrible earthquake that struck in May 2003, causing 2,500 deaths and devastating the Boumerdès region, highlighted the reserves of solidarity and generosity among the Algerian people, which admirably compensated for the shortcomings of politicians and soldiers. Young *hittistes*,[19] in particular, spontaneously came to the aid of victims, digging them out with bare hands, taking them to hospital, erecting tents and providing water.[20]

Once again, the situation is far from unique to Algeria; wastewater regularly causes tragedies in Egypt too.

Algeria is not the only case

Although the situation is by no means as serious in Tunisia, it has led some people to write to the press to demand drinking water.[21] As if in response, on 30 October 2001 a minister visited the governorate of Siliana to launch a water supply project for a thousand households;[22] but it is not unusual to see in the suburbs of Tunis – for example, at Nahli, on the way from the Ariana – women carrying water in a cart. However, things are evolving. On 27 September 2001, the agriculture ministry organized a 'national seminar on the more economical use of water', in line with a 'profound change from the mobilization of hydraulic resources to the rationalization of consumption', from a liberal supply policy to one involving greater care and attention. Thus, a decision has been made to 'diagnose' the water consumption patterns of four thousand large users in industry, agriculture and tourism. But the gravity of the situation is evident in the talk of 'unconventional resources such as desalination', although the country is not exactly rich in the energy to power it. In an editorial on the issue, *La Presse* mentioned 'a decree to extend benefits under the investment code to audit and consultancy activities in the more economical use of water'. 'This measure,' it commented, 'which is meant to encourage the private sector ... to engage in this vital activity for the future, gives concrete expression to presidential decisions ... designed to strengthen the national water mobilization strategy, to create better conditions for its implementation, and to establish more economical patterns of water use.'[23]

At the other end of North Africa, in the Moroccan High Atlas, local people who staged a sit-in in March 2003 to demand 'basic infrastructure', especially water, ended up spending forty-five days in prison. Berber tribal chiefs also bitterly criticize the regime for neglecting irrigation and the battle against drought.[24]

Similar problems are familiar in Egypt, where a former economics minister speaks of the Nile as an 'open sewer'. In May 2003 a serious crisis shook the governorate of Gharbiya, where the authorities responded to pollution of the Nile by cutting the flow of water to irrigation canals,[25] and the resulting losses led farmers to accuse the regime of breaking its promises. In the same month, following constant complaints about poor water quality and worsening pollution, the Egyptian water resources ministry finally decided to impose controls on pesticide and nitrogen fertilizer contamination.[26]

So far as Iran is concerned, no one can fail to be struck by the open drains that cross the imposing Vilayati Street in the heart of the capital, or the sight of people sometimes washing their hands in them.

In some countries in the South, women (or more often girls) expend 85 per cent of their daily calorie intake providing the family with water – usually without even finding the 50 litres necessary per head. According to the WHO representative at the

World Water Forum in Kyoto (March 2003), a mains supply of
domestic drinking water would probably bring about the greatest
single improvement to people's lives. Such a supply at home, or
within a kilometre of it, would make it possible to educate many
more girls at school by releasing them from water chores – a
real advance, both for the families and for the community as a
whole.

The quality of water is scarcely adequate in the former USSR
either. I remember one hotel in Barnaul (Siberia) in the days of
the Soviet Union, where the water ran brown, and in 2002, at the
best hotel in Kiev, guests were advised not to drink water from
the tap.

As we can see, in Algeria and elsewhere, water distribution
is inseparable from problems of social and spatial inequality
(rich–poor, male–female, shanty town–smart area). The geographer Swyngedow has shown this in the case of Guayaquil in
Ecuador, while in North Africa the weakness and deficiencies of
the state are also highly significant. As to Spain, he explains how
modernization of the state has gone hand in hand with fundamental changes in the use of water. Water policies, water culture and
hydraulic engineering have all been of major importance: 'Almost
nothing in the social, economic and ecological landscape of contemporary Spain can be understood without explicit reference to
the changes in water use in Spanish society taking place in front
of our eyes.'[27]

Nevertheless, it is regularly argued in some quarters that the
world is on the brink of a 'water crisis'. We need to consider
now whether this is a self-serving prediction or an inescapable
reality.

7

A water crisis?

Humans are not alone in yearning for liberty. The whole
ecosystem cries out for it. The revolution is also for the lakes,
rivers, trees and animals.

Father Ernesto Cardenal, culture minister in Sandinista Nicaragua

Many believe that a crisis is looming. The United Nations predicts
that in 2025 two-thirds of the world's population will live in regions
suffering from water shortage. But, of course, this makes sense
only if we assume that management, consumption and resource
levels remain unchanged between now and then.

In May 1996, a report on water management in North Africa
and the Middle East by Canada's International Development
Research Centre (IDRC) made the following predictions:

By the year 2025, the amount of water available per person in
North Africa is expected to drop by 80 per cent in a single
lifetime, from 3,430 to 667 cubic metres.... Within ten years
Kenya's water supply will dwindle by 50 per cent and Nigeria's
by 40 per cent.

In fact, by 1997 a total of twenty-six countries around the world
were in a state of 'hydric stress' – that is, had less than 2,000 cubic

metres of water a year per head at their disposal. Malin Falken-
mark, who defines the terms 'hydric stress' and 'water shortage'
by an index of freshwater needs per head of population, estimates
minimum water needs at 100 litres per person per day, for both
vital and domestic needs (drinking, cooking, body hygiene and
waste clearance). Agriculture and industry need between five and
a hundred times more, depending on the economic development
of the country in question.

A number of international organizations have used these concepts to make simulations and projections concerning per capita
water availability and water shortages for the years 2025 and 2050,
it being understood that the calculations are based on renewable
freshwater resources and do not include any drawing of fossil
water (which, in our timescale, is obviously non-renewable). On
this basis, it may be said that a country is in hydric stress if its
annual supply of water falls below 1,700 cubic metres per person.
If the figure is between 1,700 and 1,000 cubic metres, the country
will probably experience periodic or limited shortages; if it falls
below 1,000 cubic metres, the country will be very likely to face a
chronic shortage that threatens food production, inhibits economic
development and does lasting damage to ecosystems.

Scarcity or mismanagement?

In a study published in September 1998, the Johns Hopkins School
of Public Health in Baltimore estimated that 458 million people
lived in the thirty-one countries which, in 1995, faced either hydric
stress or water shortage. However, at the World Water Forum in
The Hague, in March 2000, the Delhi-based Centre for Science
and Environment argued that 'there was no scarcity of water', and
that the solution to the crisis was to end 'mismanagement of the
resource'. For its part, the Israeli newspaper *Ha'aretz* published

an article by Nehemya Strassler criticizing politicians for Israel's water shortage and its imports of water from Turkey. Strassler concluded:

> The water shortage hitting Israel is purely artificial: it is the result of political choices by our establishment. This is why the imports of Turkish water are a heresy. The maintenance of a skewed system of subsidies and quotas favouring unprofitable and expensive sectors is the work of our politicians. If no reform project has yet succeeded, this is because many of our politicians have a direct interest in these subsidized sectors of agro-industry.[1]

The crisis may be a construct of the industrial lobbies, like the one in Santa Barbara County, California, in the 1980s, when stage-managed perceptions of drought led people to vote in a referendum for the State Water Project to be extended to their area. If the aim of those behind this was to boost development and economic growth, they certainly never expressed it in those terms; what they actually argued was that the project offered people some future protection against drought.

> The water lobby used three ploys to steer debate in the direction it wanted: (i) it organized the Committee in a way that avoided any involvement of the population in decision-making; (ii) it avoided the use of water-saving technologies from the start of the drought; and (iii) it defined the drought in public discussions as a 'crisis'.[2]

If we now look at things from the point of view of the Third World, we are immediately struck by the fact that poverty is at the root of water shortages and lack of sanitation. Where water is scarce, poverty and destitution are the common lot. This must be built into the picture when there is talk of a 'water crisis'.

While the 'global village' grows, agricultural land is being turned into desert as ill-conceived or ill-conducted irrigation schemes bring about salination and hydromorphism. The UN estimates that 850 million people around the world are affected by desertification, 135 million of them severely; it is easy to imagine the hardship and tragedies that they endure as a result. The large-scale droughts of the 1970s ended in a veritable ecological and human catastrophe in the Senegal river basin, and in April 1998 3 million people in Niger suffered hunger under the combined impact of drought and desertification.[3] Many in these conditions set their sights on work abroad, so that they can then send money back to their nearest and dearest, or help their home village to prosper (as the Immigration Développement Sahel (IDS) association has been doing in France). According to the IDS, the struggle to keep the desert from advancing further mainly requires

> access to water, both for human life and health and to water the livestock ... that are the key source of income. As the area succumbs to desertification, it depends on the vagaries of very low rainfall.... The state of the ground, as well as the violence of the rains during the few months that they fall, explains the premature drying-up of ponds, rivers and wells, which often puts at risk the harvest and the supply of drinking water.

With these points in mind, the IDS decided to promote work on a water system to supply 195,000 people in the Kayes region of Mali, showing a great sense of solidarity and cutting the ground from under the feet of those whose aim is the commodification of water.

The costs of desertification – which mainly befalls Asia and Africa – amount to some $42 billion. Some reproach the Global Environmental Facility for its lack of concern, which they attribute to the fact that the phenomenon scarcely affects the rich countries. But drought is no longer limited to the countries of the South. In March 2002 it hit the United States, and a *New York Times* editorial called for 'conservation' of water and stated that the Northeast was preparing to introduce emergency restrictions.[4] On 4 March, the director of the Pacific Institute for Studies in Development, Environment and Security, Peter H. Gleick, maintained that the drought ravaging East Coast areas was the worst for a hundred years, and lambasted the authorities for their passivity and lack of preparation, as well as their subsidization of water-guzzling crops. Voluntary restrictions, he argued, were necessary but insufficient to tackle the situation. 'For the planet as a whole, January 2002 was warmer than any January in 123 years' – and so there also had to be cuts in greenhouse gas emissions. 'The evidence is growing that this year's drought could be merely a taste of the future.' And, to underline the light-mindedness of officials, he quoted from John Steinbeck's *East of Eden*: 'And it never failed that during the dry years the people forgot about the rich years, and during the wet years they lost all memory of the dry years. It was always that way.'[5]

Two months later, the *New York Times* drew a bleak picture of drought in thirty States of the USA, with less than one inch of rain recorded since June 2001 in Montana, Colorado and Wyoming.[6] In October 2002, when Nevada was declared a disaster area because of drought, people were somewhat reminded of the 'dustbowl' 1930s, which, together with the Depression, threw millions of ruined farmers on to the roads; then in 2003 Montana farmers were forced to reduce their livestock. Intensive agriculture, subsidies and the effects of globalization – too much wheat in the world – have further worsened the social effects of drought in the United States. Virginia has asked people to save water to offset three years of drought, while Nebraska has requisitioned tankers from the dairies. In Kansas, where farmers are finally eager to spare the Ogallala aquifer, cotton is tending to replace the more water-intensive corn.

For its part, the Bush administration decided in May 2003 to launch a major drought-prevention initiative in the arid Southwest, through the creation of water banks to transfer resources between the farms and cities. One aspect is to modernize irrigation and to hunt down leaks. Above all, however, Washington is stressing the importance of conservation and resource-sharing, rather than the dam construction that it used to favour.

In France, the drought of August 2003 forced fifty-six *départements* to introduce water restrictions. The ecology minister warned in *Le Monde*: 'There is no major disaster for drinking water, but those in charge of supply systems must be extremely vigilant and, if necessary, strengthen the existing restrictions.' But the situation remained less critical than during the great drought of 1976.

A man-made crisis?

Contrary to a shallow belief, technology alone cannot provide a lasting solution to the problems, especially as its success largely depends on public attitudes and the way in which it is fitted into other projects. Thus, the seeding of clouds with silver iodide to trigger rainfall gives mixed results, and of course no one can bring about rain in the absence of atmospheric moisture. Some hopes have been pinned on desalination and the purification of wastewater, but caution must remain the guiding principle in relation to all such techniques.

Moreover, it is especially important in the South to coordinate the various techniques. Otherwise, one ends up with the kind of situation we see in Kenya, where backers have installed sixteen different models of pump, with all the related problems of maintenance.

The Moroccan geographer Mohamed Naceri has appealed for us to draw more on the treasure of traditional knowledge, while the Delhi Centre for Science and Environment (CSE) has published a magnificent summa of such knowledge in the Indian subcontinent. 'The nationalization of water in India has only worsened the situation', its authors argue. 'Let us allow the local populations to look after it – those who use water, and for whom it is synonymous with all goodness and all wealth.'[7]

Indeed, some are prepared to pay the supreme price so that their community may have enough water. Retired civil servant Devidas Lahane cycled day after day to demand that officials supply drinking water to his village of Sundarkhed, 386 km north of Bombay. He wrote letters, drew up petitions, declared hunger strikes and threatened to commit suicide. But it was all to no avail. There was no response from officialdom, in a country capable of producing nuclear weapons that cannot even quench the thirst of all its children – half of India's do not have adequate drinking water.[8] Then, in the depths of despair one sad October day in 1998, he finally poured kerosene over himself and struck a match; he died the same evening, at the age of 65.[9] Water kills a million and a half people a year in India, as a consequence of diarrhoea and related disorders. During the period from 1970 to 1997, 19 per cent of the population were without access to safe drinking water, and 71 per cent without sanitation. But the government has different priorities. The capital, with a population of 12 million, has just treated itself to an ultramodern underground system, but the brown, fetid waters of the Yamuna continue to cross the city. In the eyes of some politicians, achievements in relation to water are much less glorious and worthy of publicity than a new metro or dam.

Water also kills in Latin America and elsewhere in the South. 'In Honduras, on 10 November, a guard shot and killed at point-blank range 9-year-old Jenny Vanezza Gómez, who was stealing a bucket of drinking water in the town of Comayaguela after its devastation by Hurricane Mitch.'[10] On 13 May 2000, Eusebio de Haro Espinosa, a 23-year-old illegal Mexican immigrant, was killed by a Texan farmer, Samuel H. Blackwood Jr, whose property he had approached to ask for a little water.[11] And at Nablus in occupied Palestine – a town reeling under a 120-day curfew, which, like Jenin, is coveted by Israel for its water[12] – 29-year-old Amjad Catani was killed on 9 April 2002 when he 'went to look for water at a fountain because he no longer had any at home'.[13]

The same tragedy was repeated on a different continent, in Tunisia. In 2002 a magazine reported a drought drama under the title 'Agriculteurs voleurs d'eau'.[14]

> People in a village in the northwest adopted a traditional method for sharing the water from a providential mountain spring. Despite the shortages, everything went well and the water was distributed fairly and without incident, under the watchful eye of a man known for his integrity and rectitude. Then, one day, a villager who had risen earlier than usual to take his animals to market saw something strange going on near the main fountain. In the half-dark he noticed one of his neighbours interfering with the channels to divert water to his own field. He tried to dissuade him from continuing with an action that threatened to end the fragile order in the village – without success. The cheating neighbour was determined to pump all the water he needed to irrigate his orchard. After some argument, the first man said that he intended to make a complaint, and then the water thief and his son struck him down with a spade that brought his days to an end.

'Is that how people live?' the poet Aragon once asked in amazement.

Several years of continuous drought pose a major threat to many countries, which should be taken all the more seriously as climate changes loom on the horizon. For the moment, the scale of such changes is difficult to measure; the whole picture looks quite uncertain. But most experts agree that the climate will become more uneven: for example, in the course of the twenty-first century, growing aridity in the southern Mediterranean will both reduce water resources and increase people's needs, as drought and rainfall evaporation become more severe; in northern Europe, by contrast, higher levels of winter rainfall will go together with dry and erratic summers, producing serious consequences for water planning, especially during the summer season. It is therefore to be feared that, as recent flooding in Europe tends to confirm, the scale of public works suited to past patterns of rainfall will no longer be adequate in the future.

When asked whether we will run short of water, one expert replied: 'That would mean that big agricultural countries like China or the United States prioritized certain uses of water over the need to supply their own population. Is that credible?'[15]

Clearly, choices will have to be made if we are to solve the water challenge, for we should never forget that the supply of water on Earth is limited. The challenge is much greater for the poor than for the rich, as some do not have water to drink while others complain of not having enough to sprinkle their flowerbeds, clean their car or fill their swimming pool.

We have to move towards 'a society that is economical in its use of water' – both in our own interest and for the sake of future generations and the whole realm of living beings. Water therefore poses a real question for society. It shows that there will be no salvation without sustainable development (or, rather, eco-development), especially as our health and well-being depend so much on this precious resource.

8

A common good
coveted by the market

Some advocate population control as a way of reducing demand. Obviously this is a delicate issue that affects the rights of individuals, and in any event it could not have an immediate impact. Besides, the nature of the demand for water (luxury goods, swimming pools, golf courses, industrial production) is an aspect at least as important as raw population statistics. We must always bear in mind the great differences in consumption: a German consumes ten times more water per day than an Indian, and an Israeli settler six times more than a Palestinian. Demographic trends are therefore not as significant as they might appear, for, as a UN report put it in March 2003, 'industrial production, which is evidently dependent on water, has risen faster than the world population, and nothing indicates that the trend will be reversed'. Malthusian positions have a regrettably long life, even though the past has refuted them and they no longer seem relevant to the future. 'When it comes to water consumption, hardline Malthusians should first of all attack the privileged. René Dumont once said: "At the level of the planet, it is the rich who waste and pollute the most; and the great majority of them reject a minimum degree of austerity".' Anil Agarwal was addressing the experience of water management in Himalayan villages when he wrote: 'Increased demographic pressure does not necessarily mean an irreversible tendency to environmental degradation. It simply means better management of the environment, which is usually not possible without involving people and keeping to a minimum the role of the authorities.'

For others, the primacy of physics in water matters needs to be replaced with the primacy of the market (the 'natural condition of society', according to Alain Minc). But Sandra Postel, of the Worldwatch Institute in Washington, is quick to underline the limits of the market: water is fifty to a hundred times more expensive when used in cities than it is in irrigation;[1] the European Parliament's Development and Cooperation Commission requires access to water to be financed out of consumption, but this principle is not consistently applied to industry, agriculture or the production of energy. Water is not a product like any other. In 1997, when Mexico was hit by a terrible drought, it asked its mighty neighbour to the north to grant it a loan in dollars and, for a brief period, to adjust in its favour the 1944 treaty regulating the division of the Rio Grande waters between the two countries. The US Congress immediately came up with the greenback loan, but ruthlessly turned down any extra allocation of 'blue gold' from the frontier river. Since the drought has continued, this means that in five years Mexico has accumulated a debt of half a trillion gallons of water from the Rio Grande, causing US harvest losses that Texan farmers put at a billion dollars.[2]

Water privatization in Britain

The World Bank, for its part, advocates price increases as the way to reduce water consumption. Such a policy would have an impact only on the poorest sections of society, who would no longer have access to water, while those with the money would continue to waste the resource despite the higher charges. Yet the World Bank loudly proclaims the virtues of 'market efficiency', and maintains that 'the development of markets, together with market-based pricing, allows the peaceful transfer of most resources between nations'.

The market – in the case of water, at least – is not a panacea, as we can see from the shortages, accidents, price rises and assorted scandals that followed complete privatization of the sector in Britain. Since the collapse of communism, capitalism has been face to face with itself alone. Public Services International (PSI) reports in its publication that, between 1989 (the year of water privatization) and 1995, British consumers saw the price of water rise by 106 per cent, while operators' profits soared by 692 per cent and the highest-paid director of North-West Water received 708 per cent more in emoluments.[3] The result: the number of consumers whose supply has been disconnected is up 50 per cent, and the British Medical Association has vigorously denounced the damage being done to people's health.

The harm inflicted on the countries of the South is considerably more deadly. But this does not prevent some experts from offering free publicity for the water merchants – for example, by suggesting privatization because of 'the infrastructural costs and huge demand for funding that the countries of the South cannot easily meet'.[4] Patrick Point insists, without giving a single example, that 'the appeal to the private sector has often been a source of improvement'. And then he continues:

> It should be noted, however, that the delegation of public services may also generate inefficiencies. The causes ... lie in asymmetry of information between the delegating public body and the company that has to be regulated, an especially significant phenomenon in a highly oligopolistic field organized around a few global groups. Monitoring should therefore focus on the quality of the service, judged by the contractual objectives and the level of prices. Such monitoring may prove very difficult to carry out....

> It cannot be disregarded, however, that private groups rarely
> have an interest in supplying rural areas of developing countries
> with drinking water.[5]

Some market-obsessed experts forget that most people in the
Third World live in the countryside, and that the state is not
strong enough to resist the demands of the water giants. In Chad,
Burkina Faso, Mali or Gabon, for instance, management contracts
often cover nothing more than mere distribution and the recovery
of costs, leaving the government to foot the bill, or incur the debt,
for repairs and new infrastructure. On the other hand, there are
cases where the local population does not knuckle under to the
'global corporations' but responds by getting directly involved
and keeping a watch on their activities. In Argentina, a popular
referendum in Santa Fe led to the renegotiation of a contract
dating back to 1995 with a branch of the Lyonnaise group, and
in Tucumán a payments strike forced Vivendi to decamp alto-
gether. Water privatization has been a complete failure in Manila:
undertakings given by the Suez corporation have not been kept,
the price of water has risen fivefold since 1997 in the half of town
assigned to it, and sevenfold in the half run by Bechtel. In fact,
Suez is now pulling out of the Philippines capital, on the grounds
that the regulator only partially approved its plan for more rapid
price rises; it is claiming financial compensation and appealing
to the International Chamber of Commerce in Paris. In the view
of the Water Vigilance Network in the Philippines, this case has
major implications for sovereignty, as 'Suez is trying to subvert the
power of the local regulator in Manila' and 'the French embassy
is continually lobbying hard in support of Suez'.

In mid-June 2003, Suez announced that it was also withdrawing
from Ho Chi Minh City in Vietnam, for 'group strategy reasons'.
One can appreciate the logic of these multinationals, which do not
hesitate to sue the public authorities for any breach of contract,
or even when they simply deem their profits to be lower than

expected. This did not prevent Vivendi, in September 2002, from carrying off a thirty-year purification contract worth €1.5 billion in the Netherlands. As for Ondéo, a subsidiary of Suez, it has signed the largest maintenance contract ever concluded with Puerto Rico, which will bring it in $4 billion over a ten-year term. The same company has also netted two projects in China worth a total of €460 million.

Water privatization has worsened the situation in the South

Privatization has also brought to South Africa the worst cholera epidemic in its history, according to the San Francisco magazine *Mother Jones*.[6] Under the apartheid regime, the poor had to use water supply pipes that were often a kilometre or more from their home. In 1996, when the new government, under World Bank and IMF pressure, adopted the 'cost recovery' requirement that public services should be self-financing (which usually meant sharp price rises), many municipalities turned to Vivendi or Suez for the distribution of water. 'The ANC then virtually disowned its Marxist origins', as *Mother Jones* put it. The water bill became unbearable for underprivileged layers of the population, who turned instead to polluted river water – especially as supply interruptions became more common and public standpipes disappeared. One woman villager complained: 'There are no jobs. We're forced to choose between food and water. So, we buy something to eat and pray that the water won't make us ill.' Free of apartheid, South Africans now say: 'If we could have water we'd be really free.' The situation has elements of a sick farce: doctors claim that the government could have averted a cholera epidemic if it had reviewed its cost-recovery policy, and in the end the treatment of cholera due to water supply failure has cost it more than it would otherwise have had to pay. This error of judgement cost the lives of 260 people. Meanwhile, as in South Africa, water privatization in Abidjan has forced the poorest layers to dig wells, some of which communicate with septic tanks, leading to numerous cases of cholera. In both cases, although the government tried to extend the supply of drinking water, it unfortunately did nothing to improve the sewerage system that was the source of the epidemic.

In the World Water Council document produced on the occasion of the Paris Conference in March 1998 – whose main aim was to popularize the idea that water is an economic good and that the market has to determine its commercial value – we read the following: 'Water distribution monopolies must be controlled or regulated in such a way as to ensure that the appointed distribution company does not abuse its position.... The British system has created a regulatory body whose independence reinforces its powers.' And yet, in December 1997, Britain's National Audit Office criticized the regulator on the grounds that he was not using his independence to create his own norms for the industry, and that his conclusions derived from a simple 'comparison among the twenty-nine water distribution companies currently enjoying a near-total monopoly'.

In the United States, there have been cases where private distributors have pressured Congress to loosen drinking water standards. As a result, in 1993 and 1994 a total of 53 million Americans drank water contaminated by lead, pesticides or volatile organic compounds, and 11 million water contaminated by faecal coliforms; while 43 million were exposed to *Cryptosporidium* in the water – a microorganism that struck at a hundred victims in Milwaukee in 1993. In Ontario, in May 2000, the small agricultural town of Walkerton suffered a number of deaths due to the contamination of drinking water by the *E. coli* bacterium. Graham Fraser gives us some clues to why this happened, following the election of an ultraliberal prime minister:

Many factors are involved: environmental deregulation, massive industrialization of agriculture, a downward shifting of responsibility in a climate of irresponsibility and incompetence. Since its election in 1995, the government of Mike Harris has done everything to undermine the regulatory power of the Ontario environment minister, who is perceived as an obstacle to market growth. Laboratories have been closed down, inspection jobs eliminated, responsibilities shifted to local councils, and rules and regulations altered. At the same time, there has been rapid growth of what is known as intensive agriculture.... The 3.8 million pigs in Ontario produce as much excrement as the province's 10 million human inhabitants. The purification of slurry is only minimally regulated.... The privatization of provincial government laboratories has further reduced the process of communication with citizens.[7]

In May 2001, three more deaths probably due to *Cryptosporidium* in the water were reported at North Battleford, in Saskatchewan province. The preliminary inquest revealed that, at the local water treatment plant, the wells were inadequately protected and traces of mice had been discovered in the equipment.

In May 2000, at the request of industrial chloride producers, the American courts forbade the Environmental Protection Agency (EPA) imposing a zero-tolerance regime for chloroform in drinking water, although it has been known for a long time that this substance is harmful to the liver; the reason for the judgment was that, in the view of experts, chloroform is only 'probably carcinogenic' (that is, it does not act directly on cellular DNA to cause cancer, but uses other mechanisms to induce a tumour). If this judgement is upheld, Americans will in future drink water from which chloroform is not absent, and it will be the first time that the EPA accepts a standard other than zero tolerance for a carcinogen in drinking water[8] – a real regression, then, in a country with the technical means to achieve this health-protection objective. At the same time, Congress finally approved in 2000 the ending of a programme to stop watercourse pollution by discharge from farms and industry. The EPA estimates that 40 per cent of the country's rivers – more than 20,000 watercourses and lakes – do not meet water quality standards. For EPA spokesperson Dave Cohen, 'this is a new anti-environmental assault by the Congress leadership on the Administration's efforts to place cleaner and safer water at the disposal of all Americans'. In 1994, the Physicians for Social Responsibility association stated that 14 million Americans were regularly drinking water contaminated by such herbicides as alachlor, atrazin, cyanazin, metolachlor and simazin, 'particularly dangerous ageless toxins developed in the 1950s, which today would not be approved because of their toxicity and their mobility in water'. David Rall, an official in the association, added that 'their risks are additive (cumulative), and that there are strong reasons to be worried for babies and young children, for whom there is no animal model'.[9]

When politics gets mixed up in it

Official bodies in the United States have carried out 20,000 tests of tap water to check for the presence of these contaminants. Each spring, farmers spray no fewer than 150 million pounds of pesticide, and this is why 3.5 million people in 120 cities face cancer risks ten to a hundred times higher than the federally approved maximum of one extra lifetime cancer per million persons. In June 2000 the Clinton administration, acting through the EPA, proposed to lower from 50 parts per billion (ppb), the level set in 1942, to 5 ppb, the maximum permitted concentration of arsenic in drinking water.[10] The Association of Drinking Water Administrators (ASDWA) stood out against this and called for the new norm to be set at 20 ppb, until fresh studies had been concluded. Since then, President George W. Bush has championed the cause of industry and opposed setting the maximum concentration for this poison (responsible for skin, bladder and lung cancers) at the level required by the WHO and applied by the EU and Japan. In fact, Bush is unable to refuse anything to the timber industrialists (large users of arsenic), or to the mining and electricity sectors – coal contains arsenic – that so generously contributed to his election. Democratic Party senators bitterly pointed out: 'This is another case of payback or return favours to an industry that gave millions of dollars for Bush's election campaign.' We should recall that in 1999, because of the cancer risks, the American Academy of Sciences had asked for the maximum arsenic level to be lowered 'as soon as possible' to 10 ppb;[11] and that water distributors would have had to pay between $400 and $500 million to comply with the proposals of the Clinton administration. Arthur Miller commented: 'The Bush administration has ruined … the social security system, water reserves, the environment…. We are going from calamity to calamity. All we know, one year after Mr Bush's election, is that if you're a polluter you stand a good chance of joining the government! This is an administration we should really feel ashamed of.'[12]

The decision of the Bush administration put an end to the decade-long struggle of ecologists, scientists and town councillors to reduce arsenic levels to 10 ppb over a period of five years, in the drinking water of 13 million Americans spread among 3,000 communities in the Southwest (mostly small towns and rural areas, but also the city of Albuquerque).

Do industry and politics always work hand in hand at the expense of the environment? Take another case: that of Jeb Bush, governor of Florida, whom some accuse of being a 'puppet of the sugar planters'. Through the Everglades Forever Act of 1994, Washington and the State of Florida undertook to restore the unique ecosystem of the Everglades swamps, which had been degraded by years of fertilizer and pesticide contamination from the sugar plantations, while industry, for its part, agreed to limit the release of phosphorus to 10 ppb by the year 2006. However, in April 2003 it asked for a twenty-year moratorium, and ecologists and affected Indian tribes organized a press campaign to persuade the governor not to allow the Florida Senate to grant the application.[13]

The water issue certainly worries a lot of Americans. The film *Erin Brokovich*, starring Julia Roberts, portrays legal experts defending a community whose present and future generations are at the mercy of invisible chromium pollution of its drinking water; the industrialists responsible for it, when faced with untreatable cancers and indescribable sores and deformations inflicted on the children of low-income families, can think of nothing other than their profits.[14] In May 2003, the firm Honeywell was actually sentenced to clean up a New Jersey contaminated by chromium, the dangers of which it had been aware since the 1980s.

Robert F. Kennedy Jr has explained 'why the New York water supply is not yet safe', and accuses the government of being too soft on property developers and agricultural polluters, whose pressure on the city's water catchment area could eventually make it necessary for taxpayers to foot a $5 billion bill for a treatment plant.[15]

In February 2003, the city of Stockton, California, awarded a twenty-year water management contract worth $600 million to OMI–Thames Water (an Anglo-American joint venture linked to the German RWE conglomerate), the largest contract ever signed in the state. This is a test case for the water merchants, who see a rosy future for the private sector, which at present accounts for only 10 per cent of the water business in the United States.[16] But consumer associations are turning to the law to fight the deal, causing great discomfiture among the private electricity groups in California. They are especially afraid of the evils that usually accompany privatization: excessive price rises, poor service, court litigation and inadequate staffing levels, as documented in October

2001 by Ralph Nader's NGO Public Citizen, with special reference to San Francisco, New Orleans and Charleston.[17] Stockton municipality claims that its contract with OMI–Thames Water will save it not only capital and operational costs but also any environmental fines (which will now be charged to the contracting companies). However, although consultants estimate that the city might save between $154 million and $175 million in this way over twenty years, an Oakland research institute calculates that the contract with a private firm might end up costing the city $1.7 million a year more. It is worth noting that the largest water management contract ever signed in the United States – it covered Atlanta and was due to run until 2019 – was broken in January 2003 following complaints about the quality of service and interruptions to the water supply. The city has now sent United Water (a Suez subsidiary) packing and taken back control of its water services.

A recent book analyses problems with the water service in Australia, such as the flooding caused by Big Pong reservoir in Adelaide in autumn 1997 or the contamination in autumn 1998 that meant people in Sydney had to boil water for several days.[18] The book amounts to a devastating criticism of the 'economic rationality' of handing water services over to a private French company, and of the state's abdication of responsibility for an industry worth some Aus.$90 billion – or more than the electricity industry. In the author's view, 'economic rationalism' is a 'very bad guardian of public health, and private profit and public responsibility are not compatible with each other in the field of essential public services'. His conclusion is that 'water privatization not only increases the number of supply failures but releases "animal spirits".... Water is a special substance in society, and it should have a special place in national politics.'

The Belgian geographer Pierre Cornut notes that in Belgium the laws of 1907 and 26 August 1913, as well as the ministerial circular of 1909, place the whole drinking water sector out of the reach of private capital and private profit, on the grounds that these are 'incompatible with the smooth functioning of a vital service that has to be accessible to the greatest number of people'. No similar measures were taken with regard to gas or electricity; it is water that the Belgian legislature regards as a vital and indispensable need. In Cornut's view, what is mainly involved in today's privatization is 'the making of a profit by selling a good necessary to life and public health – profit that reverts not to the community that consumes the water but to a few privileged legal or physical entities making their money work for them'. If these practices are allowed to develop, they 'threaten to endanger universal access to water ... and to deepen social inequalities'.[19]

A number of authors, such as Caspar Henderson,[20] have shown that water privatization is clearly not cost-effective, as we can see from a simple price comparison between Swedish and British towns of the same size: Swedish municipalities supply water at a third of the price and at half the operating costs, and deliver a return on capital three times higher, than the levels achieved by Britain's privatized companies. In Puerto Rico, Trinidad and Budapest, the government authorities have recently uncovered serious deficiencies on the part of Vivendi, Severn Trent and Suez–Lyonnaise respectively, in maintenance, repair, administration, operation and finances (especially a growing deficit). Puerto Rico further blames Vivendi for a major catastrophe in 1998, when a reservoir overflowed and was then ravaged by a typhoon. However, this did not prevent the corporation from landing, in March 2001, a 25-year concession worth $350 million for the supply of water and energy in the Moroccan towns of Tetouan and Tangier,[21] at a time when Morocco is the object of keen interest in water industry think-tanks and the various institutes dealing with 'Mediterranean water'. Did not the first World Water Forum take place in Marrakesh, in 1997, under the auspices of the Marseilles-based World Water Council?

It is said that privatization can bring the economic benefits associated with competition, but the fact is that a handful of companies dominate the global water market and that they often subcontract the actual work to their subsidiaries. The private market is 70 per cent controlled by the French firms Vivendi, Suez–Lyonnaise and SAUR/Bouygues; the German RWE and its subsidiary, Thames Water, are featherweights in comparison. But the American Bechtel might prove a formidable rival, given the manna falling from Iraq by courtesy of the US State Department, and it has a stake in more than two hundred water and sanitation networks through its various subsidiaries and crossholdings (Edison Italia, United Utilities in the UK, and so on). This does not mean that it is a perfect market, however. In 2002, when Vivendi shares plunged 54 per cent and those of Suez fell 75 per cent in a couple of weeks, the public body EDF mounted an operation, with support from the Élysée palace, to rescue the over-indebted Vivendi.[22] For some capitalists, water is looking like the 'new frontier' that will allow them to make a lot of money fast; and money is, of course, the number one consideration in the varied activities of the water multinationals, especially in the purchase of television channels, for, as the saying goes, he who has the television has the politicians. Yet, in 2003, Suez sold its British subsidiary to improve its debt position, partly because price controls and investment obligations had made the UK market lose some of its attractions.

Long-term monopolies (twenty to thirty years in France) distort the vision of these corporations and deliver to them a captive municipal clientele. We should stress here the huge asymmetry of power and finance between local councils and these mammoth companies, which may easily weigh in at €90 billion or more, although we should also bear in mind that water is the fifth largest industry in the G7 countries.

Comparing the performance of public and private services, Pierre Cornut gives the following edifying example:

In summer 1995 Yorkshire experienced an unprecedented
drought, and drastic restrictions were imposed on consumers.…
The apparent reasons for the crisis, as given by Yorkshire Water
Services, were unfavourable weather and higher-than-forecast
consumption of water. But this concealed deeper causes linked to
the operations of this private company.… For instance, it deliberately underestimated the likely consumption in order to obtain
higher price rises from the national authorities (the spreading
of costs over a lower number of cubic metres meant a higher
cost price and therefore a higher sale price per cubic metre).
The company also introduced changes in management which,
though improving its commercial efficiency, also brought a clear
loss of technical and social efficiency. The geographical division
of labour, involving deep knowledge of the system in each area,
was replaced by a functional division that made it possible to
contract out certain non-critical activities at a lower cost – and
this in turn hindered the capacity to combine information about
each activity and therefore to manage each distribution area
more adequately.[23] … Finally, we should note that, whereas the
crisis and water rationing have hit local communities hard, the
economic health of the private company has not been affected
in any way…; its staffing level has been cut by 50 per cent. By
comparison, the population of Brussels – whose drinking water
has come from a wholly public corporation for the last hundred
years – has never experienced such a supply crisis, even during
the major drought of 1976.[24]

Caspar Henderson and *The Economist* report that a dozen multinationals from Switzerland, France, Italy, Germany, Canada and
Sweden are currently being sued for irregularities in respect of
mega-contracts for the Lesotho Highlands Project.[25] In fact, in
every domain, corruption accompanies privatization as a cloud
carries rain. A World Bank publication explains that a firm may
pay to be included in the list of prequalified bidders or to restrict
their number. It may pay to obtain a low assessment of the public
property to be leased or sold off, or to be favoured in the selection
process. Moreover, firms that make pay-offs may expect not only

to win the contract or the privatization auction, but also to obtain inefficient subsidies, monopoly benefits, and regulatory laxness in the future.[26]

Privatization imposed on the South

For many countries in the South, the International Monetary Fund has imposed water privatization as a condition for debt relief and the granting of loans. In 2000 it again demanded it from forty countries, mostly African, which were candidates for the new poverty reduction and growth facility. However, if the poor do not have the means to pay for water, they are not going to get it from privatization. Some have the effrontery to advise Argentina, for example, to liquidate its debt by selling off part of Patagonia, as in the good old days of colonial rule, and indeed that region does have abundant water from the Andean glaciers and some of the largest freshwater deposits in the world.[27] In 1999, Mozambique obtained a loan of $117 million from the World Bank to improve its water services and to reschedule its debt, but only on the express condition that it carry out water privatization: SAUR/Bouygues expects to make as much as $9 million a year as a result. When people want it, however, they know how to roll back the water merchants. We have already mentioned the example of Argentina. And in 2000 the Bolivian town of Cochabamba – which means Mother Earth – reached boiling point when the new private operator, International Waters Ltd (a subsidiary of Bechtel), took possession of the public network and raised prices by 35 per cent. The police killed 6 demonstrators and wounded another 175, but the government was forced to annul the law of October 1999 that had ended water subsidies and given the go-ahead for privatization: the private company, for its part, had no option but to decamp, and the people of Cochabamba retook control of their water supply

– plus the debts left behind by International Waters. Bolivian intellectuals explained:

> For a number of years, successive governments have done not very transparent business with national and foreign corporations.... Since 1985 they have been privatizing public services. But people are dissatisfied because poverty has been growing all the time.... The peasants have joined the movement ... to ensure respect for traditional customs in the use of water in the countryside. The Cochabamba demonstrators demanded that water should not be controlled by 'the market', and that the state should keep its responsibilities to protect deprived sections of the population.[28]

Earlier, the privatization of Bolivia's national airline in 1985, and then of the railways, had not triggered such a huge wave of protest. Traditional Indian culture certainly had something to do with the different response, since water is a gift from the heavens and has been collectively managed since time immemorial; its privatization therefore shook one of the most solid and familiar landmarks, especially as the government in La Paz granted to farmers only a revocable two-year irrigation permit, which posed a threat to the livelihood of millions. Clearly, a city's water supply cannot be reduced to a feat of technology; its appropriation of nature often involves social and political prowess that needs to be placed in the wider context of a polarizing urban model of space and society, with all the consequences that entails. Moreover, La Paz was preparing to sell water to Chile, without carrying out the least study of its impact on Bolivian agriculture and the environment.

Privatized water is more expensive

In France, the law of 3 January 1992 opens with the statement that water is 'part of the common national heritage'. This implies that its development should take place in the general interest, even though some would like the catchment, treatment and distribution of water to be seen as a 'market commodity'. In 1983, when Jacques Chirac was mayor of Paris and had Alain Juppé as his assistant, the capital's water supply was privatized and divided up between Générale on the Right Bank and Lyonnaise on the Left Bank. More generally, 77 per cent of the water supply in France has now been 'privatized', although a number of large towns – Nantes, Reims, Tours, Strasbourg – have escaped the trend. Small municipalities were, in fact, the first to give the water merchants the slip. In 1997 the Durance-Lubéron regional syndicate in the Vaucluse put an end to forty-two years of cooperation with a Lyonnaise subsidiary, allowing it to reduce the unit price by 25–30 per cent and the purification charge by 25–50 per cent. Similarly, Cernay-la-Ville (in Yvelines), a commune with a population of 1,800, broke with Lyonnaise and was able to end years of budget deficits; today it can even boast a surplus of €21,000. To escape legal wrangling with the water merchants – it took Lyonnaise five years to let go after the courts ruled against the former mayor of Grenoble in 1996 – an ever greater number of communes are appealing for expert assistance.[29] Thus, at Athis-Mons, the purification contract with Vivendi was not renewed after a comparative study was made, and seven other municipalities have done the same in the Marne Valley and been able to reduce the cost by 24 cents per cubic metre.[30] Early in September 2000, the Competition, Consumption and Fraud Prevention Board referred to minister Marylise Lebranchu regional statistics which showed that the water bill for a family of four consuming 120 cubic metres a year was 14 per cent higher (€316 compared with €276) when a private company was running the supply. This prompted Jean-François Julliard of the satirical magazine *Le Canard Enchaîné* to comment: 'This figure has been passed over in silence by most of the media, which, it is true, get a lot of advertising from the water merchants – when they are not directly controlled by them (as in the cases of TF1, M6, Canal+ and L'Express).' The same paper published a large dossier with the title 'Magistrates expose the water spongers. False accounting, concealed profits, a blind eye at the mayor's office... The Île de France audit office explains how Parisians' wallets are being tapped. But water bills are also bumped up in other towns.'[31]

The report of the National Audit Office, published on 20 February 2002, analysed the seven government programmes implemented since 1993 to protect water in Brittany from agricultural pollution, and sharply concluded that the balance sheet was 'quite mediocre, even catastrophic'. The €310 million investment in these schemes, raised from various taxes and consumers, 'worked almost entirely to the farmers' advantage' and did not prevent a worsening of pollution. The Office placed little hope in further programmes scheduled for the 2002–06 period, unless there was a major policy shift; indeed, without a far-reaching reform, the problems of water quality might soon be compounded by the threat of shortages, as catchment areas regularly became unfit for human use, and other regions might experience the same difficulties as Brittany.[32]

According to *Le Canard Enchaîné*, the prefecture and regional council of Brittany filed away for three years the results of a poll conducted in 1998, in which 1,006 Breton households had been asked for their opinion of the quality of the water supply. To the question 'Do you drink tap water?', 53 per cent answered 'Never!' Why not? 'A bad taste' (57.7 per cent); 'fear of diseases' (37.8 per cent); 'its smell' (36 per cent); 'its colour' (23.8 per cent). For 73 per cent of respondents, the blame lay with farming and its string of nitrates, pesticides, hormones, antibiotics and atrazine. In the view of 81 per cent, drinking water in Brittany was a problem 'that needs to be urgently addressed'.[33]

At the end of 2000, the US Environmental Protection Agency published a panel study showing that the herbicide atrazine can seriously disturb children's development, delaying the onset of puberty and causing hypertrophy of the prostate.[34] Worse, its effect on neurotransmitters can definitively alter a child's behaviour. The work of Stephan Müller and Thomas Bucheli, of the Swiss Institute of Environmental Sciences in Dübendorf, shows that European rainwater is so contaminated by pesticides that it would be illegal to offer it for drinking[35] – not that that seems to bother the promoters of Cloud Water, who in late 2000 were marketing as pure and unpolluted a water gathered in nets from the high cumulus of the Auvergne mountains. It is well known, in both Europe and North America, that the pollution emanating from separative rainwater networks is much greater than it used to be thought.

Is the state powerless?

What is the state doing to tackle these dangers to public health? The French case would seem to suggest that it is more or less powerless. In December 1999, the High Council that has overall responsibility for the public sector repeated its request that the government create a regulatory body for the water market. To no avail.

However, in July 2001 environment minister Dominique Voynet left the government after four years in office, having failed to gain parliamentary support for a version ('much watered-down', according to *Libération*[36]) of her plan to revise the 1992 water law. *Le Monde* explained that 'pressure groups had wrecked her project'.[37]

In 2001 Commissariat Générale au Plan – the government's economic advisory committee – published its report on 'the policy of preserving the resource intended for human consumption'. This prompted Dominique Voynet's successor, Yves Cochet, to say: 'It is a big problem that perhaps a third of Breton cantons may no longer be supplied with drinking water', especially as it was clear that the pollution was not just limited to surface water but had penetrated beneath the ground. The same report deplored 'the insufficient means used to make polluters respect legal standards', demanded a reduction of livestock in relevant areas and called for 'ecological conditions' to be attached to farming subsidies, given that 'environmental concerns still feature little in agricultural policy'. The efforts of the previous three decades, it argued, had only limited the damage from pollution but not tackled the root cause. For the treatment of water before it reached the tap did nothing to prevent the degradation of groundwater, which was no longer replenished normally because of the compactness and impermeability of the soil. Each year, declining standards of purity lead to the closure of many catchment areas: 350 in the Seine–Normandie basin between 1989 and 2000, and 55 in the Loire–Bretagne basin in 1997 alone.

It should be noted, however, that the companies which build water denitrification plants often have crossholdings with, or are actually owned by, the multinationals that are flooding the market with fertilizers and pesticides. So, they make money by polluting – and then by 'de-polluting'.

The state's powerless profile is also due to the pressure for commodification that comes from other regulatory bodies, such as the World Trade Organization. The decisions and declarations of intent at the Doha summit in Qatar, in November 2001, gave a big push for water privatization, within the framework of the General Agreement on Trade and Services (GATS). Thus, under the heading 'Trade and Environment', Article 31iii of the final Doha agreement required 'the progressive reduction or, as appropriate, elimination of tariff and non-tariff barriers to environmental goods and services', including water, so that any attempt to control the export of water for commercial purposes could be ruled illegal. Article 32 further seeks to prevent states from using non-tariff barriers, such as environmental protection measures. For the champions of GATS, therefore, water is no longer a social but an economic good – a commodity. The Agreement implies not only loss of control over tariffs, but 'the placing of parliaments under tutelage', as the Geneva deputy Alberto Velasco put it. According to an internal memorandum, in the run-up to the G8 meeting in June 2003, the European Commission was working to include 'water for human use' in the WTO category of environmental services, so that 'European service providers can have real and substantial market access' in seventy-two countries. But the European Commission was not, and is not, proposing to liberalize its own water distribution services.

The issue of the water market is hotly debated in North America, where Canada and its great neighbour are locked in a serious trial of strength. Some would like nothing more than to export water in giant tankers, under the terms of the NAFTA agreement, but despite differences between Ottawa and certain provinces Lloyd Axworthy, Canada's foreign minister, has formally stated that 'water is not simply a commodity' and imposed a moratorium on this kind of negotiation.[38] In retrospect, the period of 'cohabitation' in France between a Socialist government and a Gaullist president offers a striking example of how politicians think and talk about the status of water. In March 1998 Jacques Chirac – whose campaign manager in 2002 was none other than Jérôme Monod, former chief executive of Lyonnaise des Eaux – assured the UNESCO Conference on Water and Sustainable Development that 'water has a price' and stressed that it was necessary to put an end 'to the sterile oppositions between market and state, free and chargeable use, sovereignty over resources and the need for solidarity'. But Prime Minister Lionel Jospin, addressing the same participants at the end of the conference, had a different message: 'You have abandoned an old belief, too long held, that water is a gift from heaven and can only be free. But this economic approach should not be confused with a commercial vision, for water is actually not a product like any other. It cannot enter into a pure market logic, regulated only by the play of supply and demand.' The list of reasons for a new water law – which the Jospin government was unable to enact before its electoral demise – included the need for 'a better balance between local management and delegated management' – that is, between public and private management. It also foresaw the creation of an independent authority – the High Council for Public Water Services – that would have the power of injunction and investigation, and, more important, announced a number of supply and reserve regulations (necessary for major works on water distribution and purification) that would in practice have allowed private groups to build up large liquid assets. Writing on the front page of *Le Monde*, under the heading 'The impossible transparency of water', Benoît Hopquin and Martine Orange asked:

> Is France doomed to remain murky? Dominique Voynet …
> wanted to restore the trust of French people, who are more
> and more suspicious of a new water bill first tabled in 1998. The
> point then was 'to strengthen democracy and transparency in
> the sector'. Two years and fourteen draft bills later, the great
> plan has turned into nothing more than an incomprehensible
> technical document.[39]

But, the authors added, 'since it is a sensitive subject, the parliamentary debate will probably be postponed until after the local elections'. In fact, the bill was never voted on!

The social treatment of water

Water is an inherited common good before it is an economic good. Its economic status is quite special, since its production cost and use value bear no relationship to each other. The use value of water cannot be reduced to its cost of production, and for this reason – argues Jean Margat – waste should and must be kept to a minimum. Recognition of water as an economic good implies that its cost should incorporate not only production factors but also 're-cuperation after use' – that is, repair and restoration enabling water to be preserved and reproduced through the hydrological cycle.

The social dimension cannot be simply brushed aside, especially in the context of North–South relations. It is unrealistic and scarcely imaginable that water should be wholly subject to the laws of the market, with no compensation and, above all, no help for deprived sections of the population. Of course, the market has a role to play in correcting bad habits and extravagant jobs (as in Las Vegas or the luxury hotels and golf courses of certain tourist countries). But will those who can afford it be put off? No. In 1994, when Indonesia suffered a terrible drought, the inhabitants of Jakarta were left without water, but its golf courses – the playground of rich tourists – were never deprived of their daily 1,000 cubic metres.

Similarly, in 1998, in the midst of a three-year drought that dried up the island's whole hydrological system, the government of Cyprus cut its people's water supply by 50 per cent but provided more than enough for the needs of 2 million holidaymakers. More recently, South Korean farmers armed themselves with hoes and pitchforks to prevent lorries from pumping out water for the inhabitants of Seoul and other cities, in the fear that this might leave their crops short of the precious liquid.[40] In 2002, the Indian state of Madhya Pradesh suffered such severe shortages that tankers had to have an armed escort to protect them from attack; in the same year the city of Madras had to assemble a whole fleet of tankers to meet the urgent needs of its inhabitants.

Faced with the kind of vigorous criticism and action that we saw in Cochabamba, Bolivia, the water merchants are trying out new techniques to duck the issue and force people to pay for their services. Again let us take the example of India:

The residents of Bangalore (pop. 6.5 million) are in a fairly privileged position: two-thirds have the benefit of sewers. In some parts of town, however, the water supply is on for only two hours every two days. The poorly maintained public network reports losses of 40 to 50 per cent. In the last few months, the French groups Vivendi and Lyonnaise des Eaux each received a municipal contract to cover an area with a million inhabitants. At the end of a five-year trial period, they will share water distribution throughout the metropolitan area and spread the experiment to other big cities, including the capital, Delhi. Armed with their experience in other developing countries, the two French companies are above all trying to persuade local people to pay a modest price for running water, instead of buying bottled water or using the wells. They are even installing connections in the shanty towns, and relying on local *caïds* to help them make a rupee (€0.20) per 15 litres of water. Once a solid financial base has been achieved, they will be able to make much-needed investment in the supply network and treatment plants.[41]

To put it plainly, people have to get used to paying for water so that it makes a profit for French dealers. Suez's energetic chief executive, Gérard Mestrallet, would hate to be left behind and, after a remarkable public offer of his services to distribute water to everyone as 'a common good', melodramatically launched the slogan 'Water for everyone, fast!' as if it were a new idea. Being the world leader in water distribution and engineering, he even issued an assurance: 'We are not water merchants. We do not sell a product but provide a service.'[42] And soon he was presenting the European commissioner, Romano Prodi, and the big international institutions with an 'Appeal for the real water battle', in which he restated his opposition to privatization of this naturally given good and offered joint action to prevent its becoming 'another source of instability in the world'.[43]

Yet citizens themselves, if united, can effectively counter the traps and manoeuvres of the water merchants. In 1966 the inhabitants of Bevaix, in the Swiss canton of Neuchâtel, successfully thwarted Nestlé's plan to exploit a high-quality local spring. Then in 1996, the Pauserlax company from Chaux-de-Fonds tracked down the high-quality Treytel spring in the same commune and made an application to begin bottling it in 20,000 cubic metre cylinders, deliberately keeping the quantity modest so as not to scare the local population. But people soon realized that the agri-food giant Nestlé was lurking behind the proposal: local associations started to campaign against it, and a hundred people wrote letters opposing privatization of their spring. As the news spread, Nestlé beat a retreat and said that the Treytel water was anyway not up to its requirements!

In fact, the market makes the water problem worse, for the following six reasons:

- the primacy of profitability;
- the role of frenetic competition, even in the frequent cases of agreement and price-fixing among the water giants;
- the global race to build financial and industrial giants, which tends to poison economic and geopolitical struggles between countries for the control of natural resources;
- the role of absolute territorial sovereignty;
- contempt for the principle of a community interest;
- contempt for the principle of fair and reasonable use of the resource – as in the dispute between Turkey and Syria and Iraq, or between Israel and Jordan and the Palestinian territories, not to speak of the wider Middle East.

For the last three of these factors, it is important to underline the responsibilities of nation-states too for the worsening problems.

As we can see, the supply-side thinking of professionals is ineffective and should be counterbalanced by more open and collective management resting on democratic debate. It should be made clear to the water merchants that, on several occasions – most notably at Mar del Plata (1997) and Rio de Janeiro (1992)

– the international community has consecrated a 'universal right of access to drinking water, in sufficient quantity and quality to satisfy essential needs', and that this right is now part of the International Pact on Economic, Social and Cultural Rights.

PART III

The public health problem

9

Water and health

Human beings drink 80 per cent of their diseases.

Medical adage

The number of taps per thousand people will become a better health indicator than the number of hospital beds.

Halfdan Mahler, former director of the WHO

Water is life. No life is possible without it. A human being cannot go without drinking for more than two days, but can go without food for weeks. Even 2 per cent dehydration leads to a 20 per cent loss of physical capabilities. But if a healthy individual must drink 2 litres of water a day to stay alive, someone suffering from malnutrition or living in a tropical climate needs considerably more. In fact, thirst appears as soon as our organism has lost 1 per cent of its fluids, and a risk of death develops once the loss reaches 10 per cent. The mechanisms of intake and elimination ensure that the body's water remains at a constant level: the intake side depends on a sensation of thirst triggered deep inside the brain (subfornical organ) by the hormone angiotensin; elimination takes place by means of the kidneys and skin (perspiration, under the control of the vegetative nervous system).

As a substance indispensable for life and health, water now features among the basic human rights. In 2002, thanks to social mobilizations and struggles, sometimes involving deaths, the UN Committee for Economic, Social and Cultural Rights took the initiative of including water in the general text accompanying the International Pact on Economic, Social and Cultural Rights. The 145 countries that ratified this pact now have an obligation gradually to ensure universal access to safe water, fairly and without discrimination. Undoubtedly this is a major step towards a change in water policies.

The importance of water for health has been noted since time immemorial. In the fourteenth century, for example, the great Arab traveller Ibn Battuta noted:

> The city of Basra lies on the banks of the Euphrates and Tigris. The tides can be felt in the river.... Saltwater prevails over freshwater when the tide is rising, and the opposite is true when it is ebbing. As the people of Basra use this water for their household needs, they say that their water is brackish. This is why Basra's air in unhealthy, and why the yellow, pallid skin of the population has become proverbial.

Many centuries later, following a trip to the Congo, André Gide wrote of a village there that it 'floats in a vast enclosure.... A lifeless branch of the Logone rises almost level with it. Swamps, fever, mosquitoes.' In another village, he noted: 'Strange, incomprehensible disease', and immediately added: 'The water is the colour of a white coffee, but sadly it does not taste like that.'[1]

Water-related illnesses:
like 300 Boeings crashing every day

In 1993 the WHO General Assembly solemnly declared: 'Protecting water is protecting life'! Yet one hospital bed in two around the world is occupied by someone suffering from a water-related illness. According to the UN, 36,000 people die every day from lack of safe drinking water and sanitation, the equivalent of 300 planeloads; it is a terrible figure, quoted so often that it has become almost banal. But the fact is that more than a billion human beings do not have access to safe drinking water, and another 2 million have neither drains for wastewater nor sufficient water for their personal hygiene. The WHO also estimates that 1.5 billion people on Earth are infected with parasites originating in faecal matter. In the context of research into the SARS outbreak in May 2003, the world organization paid special attention to China's 'damp markets', where 'consumers buy rats, tortoises and live snakes, and where the sanitary conditions are often poor';[2] water might thus have made it possible for the virus to jump from animals to humans.

The Ivory Coast national plan for environmental action in 1994 recognized that investment in drains was benefiting only 30 per cent of people in the capital, Abidjan. In Bouaké, the country's second city, there are only a few systems built as part of property development schemes, draining no more than 26 per cent of wastewater. The treatment systems associated with these networks have ceased to function because of lack of maintenance. Throughout the Ivory Coast, people anarchically throw sludge from sewerage ditches into ponds, wasteland and even the street[3] – and, as several thousand CFA francs are needed to build a new ditch, many throw out their sewage directly. The same practice occurs in India. And even Alexandria, Egypt's second-largest city, has no sewerage system. The contrast with the North is certainly striking: whereas in Quebec, for example, the percentage of people connected to a municipal sewerage system soared from a mere 2 per cent in 1980 to 98 per cent in 2000, the figures in the South are derisory by comparison. In March 2003, the NGO Médecins Sans Frontières issued a first-hand report on the cholera epidemic along the Congo river:

The province of North Katanga, in the Democratic Republic of Congo, is favourable terrain for the spread of cholera. The deadly contagious disease flared up this year.... A trip up the Congo makes you understand how the epidemic has spread. On the banks of the river, and of the numerous lakes dotted around the region, fishermen live precariously in temporary camps erected for the fishing season, drinking water contaminated by villagers' faeces and selling infected fish in the nearby markets. With help from the current and dugout canoes, the vibrio ravages village after village along the river. This was how the epidemic started in February 2002. But by late June, at the end of the dry season, the number of cases was rising significantly in the region.

The cholera vibrio causes an intestinal infection with diarrhoea and vomiting, which in a few hours results in severe dehydration. Without proper care, 50 per cent of patients are likely to die. Yet the treatment is simple enough: to rehydrate patients by making them drink or, in severe cases, by attaching them to a drip; the WHO recommends for this a solution containing kitchen salt, bicarbonate of soda and sugar. But the ideal answer, of course, would be to provide safe drinking water and sanitary installations to the whole population. The recent resurgence of cholera in Latin America (400,000 cases), after a century of eclipse, is a sign of the deteriorating quality of water, demographic pressure and official incapacity to meet the people's needs. However, Moscow, which boasts a rather more sophisticated technological environment than that of Latin America, has been recording cases of hepatitis A, dysentery and even malaria; cholera too staged a comeback in the Russian capital and Kazan in August 2001. It would seem that a safe water supply and a properly maintained system of drains are harder for the Russian government to achieve than the development of remote-controlled missiles or chemical weapons. Concerning cholera in Latin America, *Le Monde* editorialized:

Drinking water and sewerage: no more is needed ... to slow its advance. It is a long, painstaking job that the various states have to take on.... It would be necessary to dig wells with motor-driven pumps, to launch health education campaigns on a huge scale, and to try to remedy the unhealthy living conditions.[4]

How much more we know about cholera than we did in 1854, when Dr John Snow halted an epidemic in London's Soho by removing the pump handle from a contaminated well! The developed countries only gradually solved their medical problems linked to the water supply, as we can see from the history of Paris or London, which only reached a population of a million through the provision of safe drinking water and the building of modern sewers. The difficulty for newly emerging countries is that they have to confront hydroecological problems at a time when basic issues of hygiene have not yet been solved. This is due to the colonial legacy and the lack of political will among today's leaders to solve mundane problems that are nevertheless people's main concerns and the key to their well-being.

Only 6 per cent of wastewater is treated in Latin America, and in Asia and Africa the figure is still under 10 per cent. Asit Biswas, president of the Third World Centre for Water Management in Mexico City, argued at the second Asian conference on water and wastewater management (in Tehran, May 2001) that since large cities have the financial and political means to treat water, whereas small communities are powerless to stop the contamination of their surroundings, the real health danger comes from the growing phenomenon of ruralization, as in Morocco or Brazil. What this leaves out of account, however, is that by the year 2025 there will be seventy-five cities in the world with more than 15 million inhabitants, and that of these only Tokyo can be described as wealthy. Water greatly contributes to human dignity, but its lack – like the poverty that usually accompanies it – makes a big dent in basic human values. Whether people have access to safe water or not has been used as a criterion of development, and nearly twenty-five years ago the United Nations Conference on Human Settlements (known as Habitat I) concluded that a water crisis was evident virtually throughout the Third World. It is scarcely surprising, then, that health and water are serious problems, whose fallout affects not only the poor and consumers in general but also the activities of fishing and tourism. In the waters off the island paradise of Penang, in Malaysia, bathing is prohibited as a potentially lethal activity; all the hotels have swimming pools, which means the local population goes short of water. Golf courses also create tensions in places where tourism is a dominant feature: in Morocco and Tunisia, as in Malaysia or Thailand. In the last of these countries, moreover, people who collect rainwater are careful to avoid the first half-hour of a downpour, since car exhaust fumes and industrial pollution give it an acidity equal to that of tomato juice.

The figure for deaths due to water-related illnesses has reached 25 million a year, or a third of all deaths in the Third World. Dirty water decimates populations, mainly through diarrhoea: 4 million children (1.5 million in India alone) succumb to related infections and dehydration. Several billion human beings have contracted other diseases such as malaria, infestation of the small intestine with ascarid or trichocephalus worms, anklylostome infestation of the duodenum, bilharziasis (a disease of the urinary tract prevalent in the Nile valley), trachoma and dengue fever (a disease that develops in dirty water and is carried by the *Aedes aegypti* mosquito, which ravaged Indonesia in May 1998).

In March 2003 the WHO representative in Gambia, Dr James Mwanzi, estimated that malaria caused a 1.3 per cent cut in Africa's annual GNP, and that this would have been 32 per cent higher in 2002 if the disease had been eradicated back in 1960. On the occasion of African Malaria Day 2003, the World Bank put at $12 billion the loss of GDP attributable to its presence. We can see the heavy tribute that the continent has to pay as a result of this mosquito-borne hydric infection – not to speak of the human suffering it inflicts or the children it kills at the rate of one every thirty seconds in Africa.

In late March 2003, following the ravages of the Japhet cyclone at the beginning of the month, the WHO and various NGOs reported high mortality from malaria in Zimbabwe and Mozambique, whose peoples are also threatened with starvation as a result of harvest failure brought on by the disaster. Elsewhere, the massive hydraulic projects in Turkey have led to a resurgence of the disease, posting a serious warning to dam-builders in countries infested with malaria or only recently cleared of it. It is to be hoped that the hill lakes created in the last few years in Algeria and Tunisia will not lead to the return of anophelism.

In June 2002, referring to an outbreak of dengue fever in Rio de Janeiro (the eighth to hit the city in twenty years and by far the most violent), *Newsweek* wrote:

> Few [diseases] are so well suited to the modern urban planet as dengue. Potholes and potted plants, plastic scrap and rubber tires, a ditch or a muddy footprint – *Aedes aegypti* has a million incubators. Now dengue is once again a global scourge, endemic everywhere in the tropics, where more than 2.5 billion people – 40 per cent of the world's population – live. The World Health Organization (WHO) reports that every year 50 million to 100 million people catch dengue, 500,000 are hospitalized for hemorrhagic fever and at last 12,000 die.[5]

We shall have to wait ten years for a vaccine to stamp out this viral disease, and in the meantime the WHO proposes some simpler solutions that are not very attractive to local politicians: ending breakneck urbanization, collecting the rubbish, conserving water in a mains supply rather than open-air reservoirs, and teaching people the secrets, and the rules, of hygiene and the virtues of water.

A giant step: the chlorination of water

The use of local knowledge is indispensable in this connection. Thus, during a terrible yellow fever epidemic in 1940 in the Nuba highlands of Sudan – an epidemic that affected 15,000 people and killed 1,500 – it was noticed that the disease did not spread to the Maro Nuba area, where the local inhabitants kept little terrapins (natural predators of mosquito larvae) in their earthenware jars and water tanks. Similarly, when Guy de Maupassant visited Tunis in 1889, he was struck by its 'unquestionable salubrity', in spite of the open sewers and the pestilential stench coming from its lake. The only explanation he could find was 'the perfect purity of the water', since 'the Zaghouan water, harnessed underground some 80 kilometres from Tunis, reached people's houses without having the least contact with the air, and therefore without gathering any trace of contagion.'

Dirty water and a lack of proper sewers cause the death of 30,000 people every day. Moreover, water contaminated by faecal matter from a polio sufferer can transmit the disease, which has completely disappeared from Europe (according to WHO information in June 2002) but remains present in poor countries where drains, safe drinking water and vaccines are still so hard to come by.

'By now there is a certain awareness, but African governments are good at making fine declarations and not following them up with action', says Pireh Otieno, programme director of the non-governmental African Water Network. In his view, corruption also creates 'stress situations inside countries – for example, when the authorities allocate water to a golf club rather than to local residents. It's a paradox, but in Africa the poor pay more for their water than the rich, who have only to turn their tap.'[6] In 1996 the APEC Study Centre in Melbourne described water pollution as 'the most common environmental problem in Asia':

polluted rivers not only spread diseases but raise the cost of treating water. Nevertheless, although a sewerage system and a clean water supply may not seem affordable, the cost of inaction and general negligence is prohibitive in terms of public health and days off work – as A.H. Khan has demonstrated in a UNICEF study (1997) of certain insalubrious areas of Karachi. The policy review that took place in 1991, on the basis of more than a hundred special studies, showed a 69 per cent reduction in mortality due to water-borne diseases when people have access to safe drinking water and bathroom installations.

In the case of Israel and the occupied Palestinian territories, an article in *Ha'aretz* on the regular summer water shortages emphasized that the water supply is Israel's exclusive responsibility:

> Israel's basic principle regarding the water supply is that every Palestinian must make do with a third or a quarter of what an Israeli consumes. Good management of water in Israel means that citizens do not wash their car and refrain from sprinkling the garden next to their house. To cut the water supply once more to Palestinians means that tens or even hundreds of thousands of people will not drink enough, will make less use of baths and sanitary facilities, and will be more exposed to pollution and disease. Naturally, that is Israel's responsibility.[7]

Chlorination is an extraordinarily useful technique for the disinfection of water – at least in the countries of the South – because of its simplicity and modest cost.

> The Center for Disease Control and Prevention (CDC), in fact, ranks chlorinated water among the greatest public health achievements of the 20th century, right up there with penicillin and vaccines. Thanks to chlorine treatment, the chronic outbreaks of cholera and dysentery that plagued crowded American cities through the 18th and 19th centuries are gone.[8]

It has long been known that, when chlorine acts on water rich in humic matter and organic products, there is a risk of the formation of volatile organic chemicals (VOCs) – especially the hepatoxic chloroform – which the US Environmental Protection Agency and others suspect of being carcinogenic. In the early 1990s, these fears gave the Peruvian government a pretext to end chlorination of water, when its only real concern was to force financial cuts on the Lima municipality; this dealt a severe blow to the health of those too poor to boil their drinking water, at a time when they were still reeling from price increases on the paraffin they use for fuel. In the opinion of the highly respected scientific journal *Nature*, the decision also played an important role in spreading the cholera epidemic that was hitting Latin America at the same time. Meanwhile, accusations were heard in the United States that chlorinated water can cause miscarriages – although today's science is in no position to settle this difficult issue.

In any event, chlorine is close to being a perfect disinfectant that clears pathogenic bacteria from water. It is a cheap and well-tried technique that saves millions of lives, and it should be much more widely used in the South. Yet certain interests have turned chlorine and water purification into veritable instruments of warfare against Third World countries. In the run-up to the second Iraq war, for example, a White House report claimed: 'At Fallujah and three other plants, Iraq now has chlorine production capacity far higher than any civilian need for water treatment, and the evidence indicates that some of its chlorine imports are being diverted for military purposes.'[9] The fact is, however, that neurotoxins such as VX, Sarin or Tabun are much more effective, and that ever since the First World War military experts have regarded chlorine (aka Bertholite) as an unreliable substance.

A similar case occurred with the US embargo on drugs and water treatment products for Cuba, under the Cuban Democracy Act of 1992, which led in June–July 1994 to an epidemic of Guillain–Barré syndrome, a frequent complication of infection with the *Campylobacter* found in wastewater.

Water is so linked in the human imagination to purity and health that a French brand of organic milk assures customers that its cows are given 'quality-controlled water', while a number of mineral waters proudly declare themselves 'nitrate-free', as if that was not to be expected for something costing one hundred times more than France's (mostly excellent) tap water. One specimen from an Alpine spring, distributed by a large retail chain, is described with the generic epithets 'pure and limpid' applicable to any drinking water. Is this infantilization, underestimation of people's intelligence, or phobic manipulation to make people purchase bottled water despite its negative impact on their pockets as well as the environment? An almost psychotic obsession with 'pure water' sharpens the appetite of many a charlatan or quack scientist. Take, for example, this publicity gobbledygook that a reader reported to the American Chemical Society weekly:

> Silken hair, softer skin … easier rinsing, more lather… You can get all that with this chemical-free water conditioner. Attach it to your main water inlet … and its magnetic field will change the mineral salt polarity in your water by limiting the formation of sediments, lime build-up and calcium deposits. It won't remove vital elements from your water, but it will help stop their debris blocking your pipes.[10]

The same journal also reported this gem from the *Ladies Home Journal*: 'Keep young for ever, live longer', thanks to the 'Electron Water/Air Machine', which works by 'breaking water's chemical bonds that are so solid (104°) they can spread diseases however pure the liquid. Nutriments and electrons cannot enter the cells.'[11] Truly grotesque!

Bottled water: a godsend for business

Reflecting in the eighteenth century on the question of value, Adam Smith said that water, the element of life, costs nothing whereas diamonds, which are useless for life, are worth a huge amount of money. Today's water merchants certainly do not share that view: they see the vital liquid as the stuff of a new El Dorado. In the United States sales of bottled water have trebled since 1985.[12] Or, to be more precise, whereas Americans drank 1.5 billion litres of bottled water in 1977, the figure has skyrocketed in the past twenty years to 12.6 billion litres. Coca-Cola has profited from this bonanza by marketing its Dasani, while Pepsi sells America's leading brand, Aquafina, and even special savoury snacks, 'to give consumers a thirst'.[13] In California, to the great displeasure of industry, the government published a bill in April 2003 that will require controls on bottled water at least as stringent as those on tap water. On the Australian market, where as much as 400 million litres of bottled water was being consumed by 1999, Coca-Cola has introduced its own Pump brand.[14] We should note, however, that 1 litre of bottled water is sold for the same price as 1,000 litres of tap water and ten thousand litres of irrigation water.[15] Danone is the world's second largest producer of bottled water (Volvic, Badoit, etc.). Nestlé's aggressive marketing of Aquarel, in Belgium, for example, included the offer of a free bottle to all families on 21 April 2001, with the obvious aim of gaining their loyalty and weaning them off tap water.[16] In the same country, some water merchants target offices and civil service departments with 'classical and designer fountains' and 'crystalline water from a Belgian spring' – offering to throw in a GPS system for good measure. Clearly, water holds out the prospect of windfall profits in these times when there is so much doubt about the quality of our food and drink. But the ecological and economic costs are probably very high: has not Coca-Cola bought two aquifers in Amazonia? Nor should we lose sight of the energy costs (transport, bottle plastic, household refuse, etc.) associated with bottled water. In April 2002 *Nature* revealed that the Norwalk-like virus (NLV), which is known to cause gastroenteritis, had been found in eleven bottles belonging to twenty-nine leading European brands of mineral water. When the satirical paper *Le Canard Enchaîné* questioned the Danone group (Evian, Volvic, Badoit) and the Nestlé group (Perrier, Vittel, Quézac, Contrexéville, San Pellegrino, Hépar) about these findings, they refused to comment.[17] As to the French Bottled Water Industry Federation, it claims that 'for twenty years there has been no evidence of infections due to the consumption of mineral water', and that only 'traces of viruses' have been discovered. Yet do such traces not indicate the presence of faecal contamination? As *Le Canard Enchaîné* points out, 'European regulations ban treatment to disinfect mineral water, the aim of this being to find ultra-pure underground water to pump up.'

The ravages of publicity

As France, after Italy, is the world's second largest consumer of bottled water, its producers compete with one another in ingenuity, efforts and research – Nestlé even having a subsidiary 'Water Institute' – and use insertions in free newspapers to attract new customers.[18] They promote the bottle as a protective shield against all kinds of pollution, especially nitrates, and each brand name pitches in with its special flavour and exotic promise. Contrexéville – which occupies the 'slimmer's companion' niche – markets Eaux plus Beauté containing guava extracts and Eaux plus Tonus with ginseng. Water may be perfumed with lavender or elder and given an extravagant colour such as 'fleshy pink', 'lagoon blue' or 'tropical green', in the case of Perrier's Fluo. There is even a Cloud Juice from Australia, consisting of '4,875 drops of rainwater'. Real snob appeal, if you can get hold of it. The aggressive publicity hype plays on themes of ageing and obesity, youth, fitness and beauty – while nothing remotely comparable is done for ordinary tap water. But it is all worthwhile for those seeking short-term

profits. According to survey figures published in May 2003 by the
Centre d'Information des entreprises d'eau et d'assanissement, 64
per cent of respondents considered French tap water 'good'; this
was 6 per cent less than a year before, and among the sceptics 73
per cent never drank anything other than bottled water.

Faced with the craze for 'health products' and the growing
market for bottled water (120 billion bottles sold worldwide in
2002), US corporations have decided to produce and market what
they pompously call 'purified water', which is not a natural product but simply tap water treated by reverse osmosis. This process
eliminates all salts and trace elements – and, in fact, has become
one of the most reliable desalination techniques for the processing
of seawater and brackish water. The lack of salts means that such
'purified water' is not recommended for human consumption, and
so producers add salts of dubious origin and then use the purity
image to sell the result for a higher price than spring water. In
France, the health ministry ensures that the term 'mineral water' is
used only for water with a stable chemical composition beneficial
to human health. Producers of 'spring water' are not allowed to
make such claims: its salt content actually varies from one spring
to the next, and its production is regulated by local by-laws.

The passion for bottled water has also reached the countries
of the South. In Tunisia, where a number of brands fight it out
with television ads for a middle-class public, 247 million litres
ended up in (often uncovered) rubbish bins in 2001; plastic bottles,
which attract vermin, are carried by the wind in the streets of
the modern city as well as the medina, disfiguring the beaches,
countryside and olive groves, and polluting and scarring whole
districts. In Egypt, which has major problems with drinking water
and sanitation, Nestlé brashly markets its 'Pure Life' brand, no
less, using English rather than Arabic to target affluent layers
of the population who can alone afford to buy it. As for Aqua,
promoted as 'natural water' and authorized by the Egyptian health

ministry, its publicity states that it conforms to the standards of the US Food and Drugs Administration.

Sunita Narai, director of the Delhi-based Centre for Science and Environment (CSE), notes that the spread of bottled brands in India 'has accustomed people to paying for the water they drink'. And she adds: 'People daily spend more money on the water they drink than on milk.' Between July and December 2002, the CSE analysed the quality of seventeen kinds of bottled water in and around the capital, marketed by local firms or multinationals such as Coca-Cola (Kinley brand) and Pepsico (Aquafina). Its findings are enough to make one's hair stand on end.[19] With the exception of Evian, which is imported from France, all the waters in question contained a horrifying cocktail of pesticide residues, at levels much higher – in some cases three or four hundred times higher – than the maximum permitted in the European Union. The substances included organochlorides such as HCH (lindane) and DDT known for their persistence in the environment, but also, more disturbing still, neurotoxic organophosphates such as malathion and chlorpyfiros (which Coca-Cola's Kinley brand contained at 109 times the EU's permitted maximum).[20]

Sellers of mineral water have certainly found it hard to swallow the study by Heinz Valtin, published in the *American Journal of Psychology*, which dismantles as 'lacking any rigorous proof' the claim that 'at least eight glasses of water should be drunk each day' to maintain good health, and which names as one of those responsible for spreading this idea Lise Bankir, a research director at Inserm, the French National Health and Medical Research Institute.[21] The satirical magazine *Le Canard Enchaîné* comments, in its inimitable style: 'It is, of course, a coincidence if [as *Le Canard* has pointed out] this researcher is a member of the Evian Water Centre.... As transparent as rock water?' This raises the whole issue of expert knowledge and scientific reliability in this vital area of research, for consumers find themselves torn between the views of not such independent academics or even crooks using a pseudo-scientific language. In fact, Dr Valtin and other experts have pointed out that, especially among athletes, the consumption of too much water leads to a condition known as hyponatremia, a major dilution of sodium in the blood that can result in convulsions, respiratory difficulty and even death.[22]

A lifestyle in question

At a time when more than a billion people do not have access to safe drinking water, the obscene mania for bottled water, which brings in billions to a get-rich-quick industry and floods the world with moronic publicity, is proof of the sickness of our societies, particularly when we consider that in Arizona the pumping of groundwater has caused the Santa Cruz river to dry up, and that in Florida dangerous gaping holes have opened up.[23] The effects of this constant pumping can be rapid and dramatic, but may also, for example, lead gradually and imperceptibly to a fall in the population of birds, butterflies, fish and trees. And, as Rachel Carson reminds us, 'our fate is indissolubly linked to that of animals'.[24]

A European household consumes 150 litres of water a day (3 litres for drinking and eating), whereas an Indian counterpart has to make do with 25 litres a day. An American household, however, consumes a grand total of 3,000 litres a day, one reason for this being that the preparation of 'French fries' central to the fast food industry requires huge amounts of water.

The quality of water will be an acute question in the future, in the main urban centres around the world. For urbanization considerably increases the consumption of water, as the case of the United States eloquently shows: in 1900 an American household used 10 cubic metres of water a year, but today the figure has risen to 200 cubic metres. Why? In 1900 most people lived in a rural setting, where wells and public standpipes served most needs, and running water was common only in the large cities.

The urbanization process, going hand in hand with the rise of the motor car and the industrialization of agriculture to feed the new cities, has led to unprecedented levels of pollution on the planet.

I 0

Pollution in many different forms

> What would the idea of purity mean without clear,
> limpid water, without that beautiful pleonasm
> which speaks to us of pure water?
>
> *Gaston Bachelard*

In today's world the real problem is competition for water among different sectors of activity: agriculture, industry, cities, tourism... Thus, the average factory producing chips and wafers for household appliances and the electronics industry uses enough water every day to fill twenty-four swimming pools, with a level of purity two thousand times that of drinking water. The absence of any dust is especially important for microsoldering work on silicon wafers and printed circuits, as a single fleck can prevent the flow of current. Only water is capable of such perfect dust removal. In 1993, a total of 900 factories of this type existed in the world, 350 of them in the United States. Since then another 24 have been planned or built in the USA, and since 1997 Intel, for example, has been building one every nine months.[1]

Resource competition

In the state of Wyoming, the extraction of natural gas (methane) is seriously disturbing the flow of water for agriculture and livestock farming. Since the gas lies close to the surface in the Rockies, imprisoned in coal beneath enormous aquifers, the surrounding water has first to be pumped out. In the Powder River basin, for instance, drills will pump out more water than New York uses in thirty months. In the right place, it will certainly come as a godsend for cattle-breeders – although, if it is too salty, it could ruin pastureland, lower the groundwater level, cause wells in the area to empty (as has already happened on some farms), and dry up the watering holes of local wildlife. Worse still, gas escaping from the coal has made some watercourses sparkle as if they were carrying champagne – a highly inflammable kind, of course. One can imagine the bitterness of the conflict among stock-breeders, farmers and environmentalists, on the one hand, and the gas companies on the other, especially as the Stock Raising Homestead Act of 1916 assigned ownership of the subsoil not to the farmers but to the federal authorities. Some counties have already banned the corporations from drilling within their jurisdiction, but their orders are being challenged in the courts. As for the Bush administration, which is entirely in the pockets of these corporations,[2] it is set to approve the record drilling of 39,000 wells on federal land to extract gas over an area of nearly 10 million acres.

Each year, throughout the world, 69 per cent of freshwater use is accounted for by agriculture, 23 per cent by industry and 8 per cent by domestic consumption. But there are major differences between the continents: whereas agriculture consumes 33 per cent in Europe, the corresponding figures for Africa and Asia are 88 per cent and 86 per cent, respectively. 'Everything can wait, except for agriculture', said Jawaharlal Nehru in 1948, at the time of India's independence. As for industry, its share of water consumption is 54 per cent in Europe but only 5 per cent and 8 per cent, respectively, for the other two continents; while the domestic shares are 13 per cent, 7 per cent and 6 per cent, respectively. In Chile, the Atacama desert is the driest region in the world, yet nearby water is being diverted from domestic use to mining activities; the resulting shortages have been so severe that in 1999 it was necessary to ration electricity (itself now privatized) by cutting the supply for two hours a day, at a cost of $100 million a month to the affected companies.[3]

Judging by what historians say, the Green Revolution was a veritable 'water orgy':[4] four to seven times more water was needed per hectare to triple or quadruple output. The Green Revolution involved two serious mistakes: it assumed that the sources of groundwater were inexhaustible; and it greatly underestimated the cost of drainage.

Today, in India, prawn farming requires fifty times more water than rice cultivation, and the intensive pumping associated with it has resulted in subsidence and real earthquakes. It means that rice-growing has become unprofitable, although it is a vital cereal – which, according to Hindu tradition, was given to man by Vishnu – and accompanies Indians even after death, when a little is sprinkled on their funeral pyre.

At the same time, whereas 1,000 litres of water are required to produce 1 kilo of bread, a huge quantity (180 litres) is needed for the production of one battery egg, and similar levels of waste are to be found in so-called industrial agriculture.[5] (Switzerland has banned industrial poultry farming since 1991, because of its environmental drawbacks and the poor flavour of the product.) In Brazil one glass of orange juice uses up twenty-two glasses of water, and in the United States 1 litre of juice requires 1,000 litres of irrigation water. This example shows the aberrations inherent in agribusiness, since juice produced in Brazil crosses the 12,000 kilometres separating it from the European market, concentrated at 8 per cent of its original mass and frozen at −18°C.[6] How much water and energy are wasted on a beverage most of whose vitamin C is unlikely to survive all the manipulation and travelling to which it is subjected!

The revival of EU water directives in 1989 was largely due to Dutch, German and Danish concern over the eutrophication of the North Sea. And yet, by failing to question agricultural policy in general, they tend to underestimate the role of agriculture as the underlying cause of this eutrophication, and in the end the two directives (on urban wastewater and agricultural nitrates) have been brought to bear mainly on consumers of drinking water and sanitation. The World Wide Fund for Nature (WWF) and Bird Life International state, in a report, that the intensive cultivation of olive trees, encouraged by EU subsidies in Italy, Spain, Portugal and Greece, is causing soil erosion, water shortages, desertification and loss of habitat. Huge plantations have been replacing the traditional family units − hence the destruction of habitat and arable land, and the more frequent use of irrigation and toxic agricultural substances in areas where water is already in short supply. In the view of Richard Perkins, of the WWF, 'European Union subsidies for olive-growing are ruining the Mediterranean environment'.[7]

The watchword 'save water'

Recent studies have shown that, when the cotton plant is given only 75 per cent of its water requirement, it continues to provide more than 90 per cent of its maximum yield, and that drip irrigation makes it possible to supply only 50 per cent of the requirement without a significant loss of output. This is interesting for the farmer, even if he has to make an investment in this kind of irrigation.[8] At a meeting in Cairo in early May 2003, representatives of countries bordering the Nile set themselves the aim of improving the productivity of water in agriculture and decided to make investments in the way it is managed. World food security is a major issue for many nations: the erosion of arable land, the growth of cities and water shortage will probably lead to radically new crop choices in the next few decades. At the same time, it will be necessary to increase the efficiency of irrigation in many countries, since 70 per cent of crops are completely dependent on irrigation water, yet only 37 per cent of it is actually absorbed by them (the rest being lost).[9]

In some countries, a major loss of earnings may be incurred as soon as there is a fluctuation in rainfall. In Tunisia, for example, a 100 mm rainwater shortfall translates into a loss of 11 million quintals of wheat and a considerable fall in olive production. Officially, the grain harvest for 2001–02 was the weakest recorded for fifty-five years, following a drought that affected 75 per cent of the 3.7 million acres under seed.[10] This explains the level of imports and gift aid of cereals and soya oil, especially from the United States. So far as citrus fruit is concerned, although drought was at least partly responsible for lower output in the 2002–03 season in Tunisia, as in the rest of the Mediterranean, the fact remains that the rising salinity of irrigation water in the citrus groves was also to blame for the poor results – a deterioration earlier predicted by Tunisian experts (such as the late lamented Slah Amamou), when they noted with alarm the intensive pumping of water by citrus farmers.[11] Alas, no one paid any heed to their warnings.

We should note that, in the case of Egypt, US aid in the form of wheat has imposed the cultivation of water-thirsty strawberries for export, at the expense of cereals, with the result that in 1994 the country imported 6 million tonnes of wheat but was able to export no more than 7 tonnes of strawberries.[12]

In the oases goats are highly valued, for the simple reason that they only need to drink twice a week yet produce milk, a little manure for subsistence crops, meat for festive occasions, and robust skins that keep water especially refreshing. One finds the same passion for the animal in the Thar desert in India. Nor should we forget to mention the camel – that ship of the desert – and its role in turning the noria to raise water from wells, as well as to send it along the irrigation canals. Moreover, according to desert tradition, when a caravan loses itself in the ergs of the Sahara and is unable to find a source of water, the sacrifice of a camel's life can be its last service, since the animal can go without drinking for four to six weeks and the water stored in its stomach can be used to slake human thirst.

Industrial pollution

Water is especially important in the production of energy, where it is used not only in hydroelectric systems but also for cooling purposes in nuclear and fossil fuel power stations. But industry, households, cities, tourism and the leisure sector place ever greater demands on resources.

Most pollution has its origin in industry, even if a few cleaner water-saving procedures are beginning to see the light of day. Let us first look at the different actual uses. Industry makes abundant use of steam; it also enlists the water for cleaning, air conditioning, cooling and transportation. The oil-refining, food-processing, metalworking, chemical and paper pulp industries consume huge quantities of water. Here are a few revealing figures:

- 13,000 litres of water are needed to produce one of the six-inch silicon wafers that are part of an electronic device.
- 400,000 litres of water are necessary to produce one car.
- 750,000 litres of water are consumed in the production of one tonne of newsprint.

- 8 tonnes of water are required to produce one tonne of end
  product in the processing of tar sands and oil shales, like those
  in Morocco and Canada.
- Mining operations, and especially the extraction of gold,
  consume huge quantities of water. Jewellery manufacture in
  general relies very heavily on water.

Of course, most of this water is seriously contaminated by heavy
metals, solvents, fats or polychloride biphenyls (insulating and
cooling materials used in condensers and transformers), often to
such a degree that any later salvaging is impossible. The reader
may recall the disaster that struck Andalusia in May 1998, when 5
million cubic metres of wastewater rich in heavy metals escaped
from closed mines into the environment, even affecting the bird
reserve of La Doñona at the mouth of the Guadalquivir. So, when
pollution is being discussed, we should not lose sight of industry's
toxic contribution. The situation is all the more worrying in that
global relocation, driven by low wages and lax environmental controls, tends to take place in poor countries where water resources
are already emaciated and polluted by organic matter, and where
ideas of recycling and waste processing are a sick joke. It should be
borne in mind that between 1950 and 1990 industry in the United
States reduced its water consumption by a third, while increasing
its output four times over, and that visible progress has also been
achieved in this respect in Sweden and Germany, among others.
Nevertheless, experts are predicting that the industrial use of
water will double by the year 2025. In China the production of a
tonne of steel requires 23 to 56 cubic metres of water, whereas the
average in the USA, Japan and Germany is around 6 cubic metres.
There is therefore much scope for water saving in countries of the
South that have embarked on industrialization. The balance sheet
is still thoroughly depressing in the poorest countries: each year,
India's fourteen main rivers carry no less than 50 million cubic

metres of untreated wastewater towards the sea; nearly 40,000 kilometres of Chinese river are so polluted that fish can no longer live in them; and 1,200 factories in São Paulo discharge 1,000 tonnes of wastewater daily into the Tiete river.

All this confirms Yves Lacoste's prediction of a 'clash of problems' in the South – that is, an explosive combination of the usual ills of underdevelopment with those of industrial pollution, as in the electronics industry and fine chemicals (e.g. in Morocco, Malaysia and Thailand) or the production of dyes for jeans (in Tunisia and Mexico) and of T-shirts in India. In late March 2003, in the Brazilian state of Minas Gerais, an illegal waste silo exploded and released a huge amount of caustic soda into two rivers, eliminating the supply of drinking water for half a million people. Not so long ago, chemical pollution was seen as the 'curse of the rich' and opposed to biological pollution as the 'curse of the poor'. But, although that idea remains true in global terms, it is tending to break down as certain emergent countries industrialize and the state withdraws from public services in the North. Thus, we can read in the Montreal newspaper *Le Devoir*: 'Within the space of five years, the city authorities issued six hundred warnings for people to boil tap water before drinking it.' In France, too, water contamination incidents have gradually become part of daily life, whether in Britanny or the South West and the Gers, most notably the commune of Mauberguet.[13] In this part of the country drinking water is contaminated with the pesticide atrazine, while elsewhere a recent dossier[14] has emphasized the scale of nitrate pollution and the sense of exasperation felt by local communities – a fury which, in Lamballe, brought farmers into unprecedented open conflict with ecologists and others concerned with water quality, demonstrating the divergence of interests and the clear-cut perceptions of how water is and should be managed in France. The difficulty of finding a balance points to future battles over the quality of life and raises the challenging issue of democratic management. Catherine Coroller has emphasized that it will take years to decontaminate Breton rivers of their nitrates,[15] while the strapline of an article by Benoît Hopquin already speaks volumes: 'Departmental public health committees are accused of turning a blind eye to the farmers' tricks'.[16] In May 2001, the French press reported a survey finding that 69 per cent of the population was satisfied with its tap water, but *Le Canard Enchaîné* tempered the good news with the observation that 'the survey in question was commissioned and paid for by the Water Information Centre, an association ... cobbled together in April 1995 by the water distribution companies. The purpose at that time was to calm the grumbling of consumers unhappy with their soaring water bills.' To this end, the Centre had 'called on the services of doctors who, for a consideration, wrote dozens of pamphlets on the relative dangers of nitrates, lead and pesticides in tap water'.[17]

A study by the Rennes-based École Nationale de Santé Publique has shown that some French people continue to drink and cook with well water; indeed, at Ille-et-Vilaine three-quarters of well owners do not think it necessary to analyse the quality of their water. When tests were performed, however, it turned out that in 90 per cent of cases the well water was not fit to drink because of high levels of faecal coliform and streptococcal contamination, which had caused gastric disorders, allergies and salmonella poisoning among 17 per cent of users. More disturbing still was the seepage of this water into the public supply as a result of inadequate checks by local mayors. 'Privately owned wells are thus a real menace to the quality of the water supply', in the view of René Seux, director of the laboratory that conducted the tests.[18] In a report published on 18 February 2003, the French Environment Institute (IFEN) in Orleans stated that rivers and groundwater were still widely contaminated with agricultural pesticides: only 5 per cent of samples from watercourses were of a sufficiently high quality to permit the risk-free development of aquatic life and the use of untreated drinking water. In 40 per cent of cases, the presence of pesticides indicated an 'average', 'below-average' or 'poor' quality, requiring special treatment to make the water drinkable. No fewer than 148 pesticides were found in 320 samples of surface water, and 62 in 292 samples of groundwater. Not surprisingly, analyses confirmed the massive presence, in both surface and groundwater, of triazines, due to be prohibited in June 2003; unfortunately, it will take many years before they are removed from the environment in France.

In its 2003 report the IFEN also gave a more specific verdict on the drinking water supply: 56 per cent of the 828 places monitored between 1998 and 2000 offered 'good suitability for the production of drinking water' and required no special treatment for pesticides; 3 per cent, however, presented concentrations of substances higher than 2 micrograms per litre of water, which made them unsuitable for the production of drinking water. Nor was groundwater spared. Measurements showed the presence of pesticides at 78 per cent of sample locations in the Rhin–Meuse, Artois–Picardie, Seine–Normandie and Rhône–Méditerranée basins; 45 per cent were contaminated to a degree that made it necessary to treat the groundwater to make it fit for human consumption. We should note that the study did not include the Loire–Bretagne basin, where the water is very poor because of the use of liquid porcine manure and agrichemical applications. These results rest upon 440,000 analyses made at a total of 2,988 places between the years 1999 and 2000. Pesticides were present at 90 per cent of river and 58 percent of groundwater measurements. The IFEN conclusion that substances which have been prohibited for a number of years – such as lindane, dinoterb and dinoseb – are still present in water is a confirmation of the very long elimination periods predicted by chemists and toxicologists for this type of compound. The risks linked to pesticides (various cancers, disorders of the male reproductive and endocrine systems) are sufficiently serious for

320 substances used in pesticide production to have been with-drawn from the French market in 2003. France is set to strengthen its diagnosis of water quality by the year 2004, and indeed an EU directive enjoins member-states to achieve a 'good ecological status for surface water' by 2015. As we can see, water quality is no longer a matter of concern only in the countries of the South – even if we have to keep a sense of proportion in comparing the measures implemented here and in the South.

Chemical pollution remains the chief worry in the industrial-ized countries, as biological pollution is under better control. We should not, however, overlook pathogens such as *E. coli* and *Crypto-sporidium*, or algae toxins such as microcystine, which damages chromosomes and leads to abnormally small brains in laboratory animals.[19] As to the *Pfiesteria piscida* microbe, which has been found in many watercourses in Maryland, it has made 1,800 people ill and caused loss of memory and confusion, as well as piling up hecatombs of fish.[20]

A May 1996 report of the American Academy of Microbiology stated that 'the distribution of safe water to the home can no longer be taken for granted, not even in the United States or Western Europe', and warned of a looming crisis in all spheres of water-borne disease. Experts have identified strains of parasites such as *Cryptosporidium*, *Giardia* and *Ciclospora* that show signs of resistance to the usual disinfectants, which is all the more serious because the ageing of the population, together with the increased incidence of cancers and sexually transmitted diseases, means that the number of immunodeficient individuals has been growing in the rich coun-tries of the world.[21] According to an American study published in 1998, more than 90 per cent of European watercourses have high levels of nitrates, mostly due to fertilizer use and intensive farm-ing. Worse, 5 per cent of these rivers have nitrate concentrations at least two hundred times above the level naturally occurring there. According to the National Audubon Society in Washington

DC, which has surveyed more than 150 countries with wells polluted by fertilizer nitrates, three-quarters of Poland's rivers have such a high level of pollution that they are no longer suitable for industrial purposes. In Europe as a whole, half the lakes suffer from eutrophication, and the state of the groundwater is growing worse. Studies show that 60 per cent of Spain's running water is unfit for consumption, and the environment minister has admitted that this has become a national priority, yet municipal authorities show little interest because it is not likely to win them votes. Loss of water from the public supply is also a major problem in Spain, as is the pollution of waterbeds by fertilizer from irrigated land and by untreated wastewater. In the view of Pedro Arrojo, an expert in water economics at the University of Saragossa, the last few decades have seen a considerable deterioration in the state of rivers, aquifers and wetlands. In Spain today one finds rivers turned into sewers and banks into rubbish dumps, dried-up river beds, and groundwater contaminated through overuse or in the course of salinization.[22] In the United States, 40 per cent of surface water is unsuitable for either fishing or bathing, while 48 per cent of lakes are undergoing eutrophication; 360 different chemical compounds have been identified in the Great Lakes, tumours and lesions are common in their fish, and birds that feed on them display a number of reproductive disorders. Seven of the ten most highly prized fish in Lake Ontario have all but disappeared, and the beluga is severely endangered by pollution of the Saint Lawrence river. In Quebec, the Indian population suffers from Minamata-type neurological diseases, as the fish that is part of their staple diet absorb the mercury from wastewater discharged by pulp factories.[23] Moreover, it is now known that effluent from these factories contains hormonal disrupters such as genistein, an isoflavonoid of plant origin, which can alter the level of sexual hormones and has been shown to alter the reproductive capacity of fish in nearby waters. Such phenomena might also pose a threat to human health and reproduction, and in any event the creeping effect on the fish population would undermine the main source of food for these Indians.[24]

Unsustainable development

Widespread perchlorate contamination of privately owned wells, aquifers and subsoil has recently been discovered in the American Southwest, probably originating in fertilizer (of which the USA uses 54 million tonnes a year) but also in military installations and the industries that use it as an oxydizing agent. There is no federal safety standard with regard to the perchlorate compound, but for drinking water the State of California has set an upper limit of 18 parts per billion that the Environmental Protection Agency considers too high. By preventing the fixation of iodine, the substance affects the thyroid gland and its production of hormones, resulting in mental retardation in the fetus and newborn infant as well as thyroid tumours. Since a number of crops, such as lettuce, store this compound in concentrated form, the population may be exposed to it not only through water contamination but also through various foodstuffs.[25] Eventually, in June 2001, the prime ministers of Ontario and Quebec, together with the governors of eight US states bordering the Great Lakes, addressed the gravity of the threat by signing an agreement to protect the world's largest reserve of freshwater by means of a stricter regulatory framework.

Following a typhoon that ravaged reservoirs in pig and turkey farms in the Southwest, there was much talk of the contamination of the groundwater – and therefore of the water supply.[26] But the chronic pollution due to industrial farming can be devastating for whole ecosystems. Beaches in Brittany are being thoroughly disfigured by algae invasions, and in the Gulf of Mexico a hypoxic zone 20 metres deep has been stripped of all life by nitrates and phosphates that the Mississippi and Atchafalaya have brought from upriver farms. Between 1983 and 1993, this 'dead' area (now 1 per cent of the whole gulf) doubled in size – largely as a result of the Mississippi floods of 1993 that poured into it thousands of tonnes of polluted sediment. Salvation can lie only in reduced use of chemical fertilizer and liquid manure and a switch to more soil-friendly farming practices. But agribusiness has little inclination to do this so long as environmental damage remains only a negative cost external to its budget.

In fact, industrial pollution raises the problem of our whole way of life. Apart from industrial farming, a host of other things – from televisions to cars and walkmen – carry an environmental cost that is expressed in water contamination by heavy metals, solvents, resins, pigments, monomers and plastics. The same is true of intensive agriculture and indoor rearing, which involve the discharge of nitrates, pesticides, fertilizer, antibiotic residue and organic matter into watercourses. The disposal of polluting substances places huge strain on the capacity of the world's waterways for elimination and self-purification. Engineers use a golden rule that 'dilution is the way to remove pollution', but it would seem that this formula is becoming meaningless. For, if 450 cubic km of wastewater are discharged annually into rivers, lakes and other receptacles, 6,000 cubic km will be needed to dilute it before it can be used again – that is, two-thirds of the total available freshwater; the UN Food and Agriculture Organization calculates that, by the middle of the century, the steady content of all the world's rivers would only just be enough to effect the dilution and transportation of our noxious discharges. Thus, in 1998 Egypt generated 85 million cubic metres of wastewater; 65 per cent of the urban population and 10 per cent of the rural population were connected to the drainage system, and drinking water was available to 95 per cent of the former and 89 per cent of the latter. It was predicted that in 2002 the average Egyptian would daily consume 290 litres of drinking water and generate 150 litres of wastewater, and that by 2007 these figures would have risen to 336 litres and 234 litres, respectively.[27] The Egyptian press is currently filled with expressions of anger, indignation and revolt in the face of repeated flooding due to wastewater and the dysfunctional irrigation system, and readers regularly write in to denounce the negligence of those responsible for these matters.

The per capita demand for water will increase with economic development, industrialization and greater prosperity, as these generate a demand for water-intensive animal protein such as beef and poultry meat. The production of these foods in turn requires larger quantities of grain and cereals (maize, barley, soya, etc.) to yield the same number of calories as before for human consumption. A growing population therefore means more irrigation and more dams, hence increased pollution from animal excreta, pesticides, fertilizer, cattle and poultry antibiotics, salinized soil, and so on.

Such a way of life is clearly unsustainable. It is also profoundly unjust, for it currently embraces only an eighth of humanity and remains out of reach for the great majority (however familiar it is to them from television, cinema and advertising). Moreover, although the whole of humanity will have to suffer the environmental consequences, only the richest sectors will have the means to protect themselves. What is necessary is that these sectors should begin to learn a degree of frugality.

PART IV

Ethics, solidarity and development

The question of dams

What makes the desert beautiful, said the little prince,
is that a well lies hidden in it somewhere.

Antoine de Saint-Exupéry

Oh Dnieprogress, oh autumn rain
Oh great dam of our hopes

Louis Aragon

The world has 40,000 dams greater than 15 metres in height,
most of them built around the middle of the twentieth century.
In all, some 45,000 such dams were constructed in the course of
the century – an average of more than one a day! In the 1930s the
Hoover dam on the Tennessee river was a source of great national
pride, as was the Aswan dam for Nasser's Egypt in the late 1960s.
Lenin, in 1921, famously defined socialism as 'electrification plus
soviets', and in the years to come Soviet cinema would celebrate
the heroes building dams on the Volga and spread the cult worship
to the countries of the South. Non-Marxists shared these views:
Nehru, for instance, went out of his way to point out that India
had built a 5.4 km long dam in 1650 BC,[1] and described dams
in general as 'the temples of modern India' – a view which, as

Arundhati Roy tells us, found its way into the country's school manuals. In India, as in most countries of the South, dams have become an article of faith indissolubly bound up with nationalism; to cast doubt on their utility is almost tantamount to sedition. Today, nearly a half of the world's watercourses are endowed with at least one dam. This passion – driven by technology and an urge to master nature – stems from a logic that is at first sight impeccable: the water stored behind the dams makes it possible to electrify the country, to regulate the flow of water, to spread irrigation projects and to increase agricultural output.

Leader's pride and white elephants

Yet, although these projects ensure a regular supply of water, they still endanger aquatic ecosystems, fauna and flora, by impeding the cyclical flooding of lowland and swamps, blocking canals and altering currents in rivers, deltas and wetlands. The classical example is the construction of the first Aswan dam in Egypt, which between 1898 and 1902 cut off hippopotamuses and crocodiles from the northern Nile. The disappearance of papyrus reeds and other Nilotic flora radically changed vegetation in the lower course of the river,[2] and, last but not least, the process uprooted a total of 40–80 million people. Local inhabitants are always promised the moon in the early days, but in the end find themselves facing hopeless situations and having to fight back against repression. In Brazil, for example, a powerful movement has grown up among those affected by dam operations that not only swallow up billions of dollars but turn out to have disastrous consequences. The costs – including special studies and consultations with foreign experts – most often exceed estimates, and sometimes a civil war might mean that the project never sees the light of day and becomes yet another 'white elephant'. A perfect example of this is the huge Jonglei navigational canal in Sudan, a project which began in 1978 but was never completed, after work on it came to a standstill in 1984, largely as a result of civil strife. For this Herculean project, planned to be 360 kilometres long, 28–50 metres wide and 4–7 metres deep, the French Compagnie des Constructions Internationales (CCI) had imported a massive German-built 'spade-wheel' previously used to dig the 101 km canal between the Indus and the Jhelum in Pakistan. By diverting the water of the White Nile from the great marshlands of the Sudd,³ the Jonglei canal was supposed to solve many problems of irrigation and drinking water, in a country which, paradoxically, is short of water despite the huge hydroelectric potential of the Nile and its tributaries. Alas, the finance and organization were always inadequate, largely because of shortcomings at a political level. In 1994, following the ceasefire signed between Khartoum and rebels on 15 October 1992, the Sudanese president undertook to see the project through to completion.

Rajiv Gandhi, the former prime minister of India, once pointed out that only 65 of the 246 major irrigation projects launched in 1951 had been fully accomplished by 1986, and that the country derived few benefits from those started after 1970. His bitter but lucid comment was: 'For sixteen years we have poured out money. The people have got nothing back, no irrigation, no water, no increase in production, no help in their daily life.'⁴ The reason why this is so often the case is that bureaucrats and technicians base themselves mainly on political considerations external to the region in question: the needs of the local population rarely feature at all. Yet it is well known that indigenous peoples are especially vulnerable to the effects of these hydraulic projects. Having different values and cultures, they yearn for control over their own environment in the hope of resisting the threats to their way of life; the Yavapai Indian tribe – to take but one example – waged a protracted struggle against the construction of the Orme dam in Arizona. Loss of their water robs them of their historic identity and well-being, for in their eyes water is either a common good, or an ancestral legacy, or private property. The World Commission on Dams (WCD), an independent body set up in 1997, now openly recognizes these violations of peoples' rights, accepting that many projects disturb the lives and future production of people living downriver.

Some of these dams, of course, are erected to the glory of the Leader, as in Tunisia under Bourguiba, where mass production was diligently carried out by successive prime ministers.[5] Elsewhere the very name of the project may be highly eloquent: Lake Nasser, behind the Aswan dam in Egypt; or the Assad dam and lake in Syria, the Talal dam in Jordan (named after the father of the late King Hussein) or the Atatürk dam on the Euphrates in Turkey (42 billion cubic metres). The leader cult has also blossomed in China, where the Gezhouba dam project was hurriedly launched in 1970 to coincide with the seventieth birthday of the Great Helmsman Mao Zedong, only to be later completely revised and spread over eighteen long and costly years, instead of the original five.[6] In India, the Delhi bi-monthly *India Today* coined the indignant formula: 'Promise a dam, win an election',[7] referring to some three hundred unfinished irrigation projects due to a minister or deputy minister who had wanted to see his name on the foundation stone. Meanwhile, more than 65,000 Indian villages live without water resources, and by the year 2005 the towns will no longer be in a position to provide more than two bucketfuls per day. 'These projects are deliberately excessive,' the magazine concludes, 'and this is what keeps the bribes coming in.' Not all the criticisms are fairly balanced, it must be said. For example, it may be tactically useful in Egypt to criticize the Aswan dam, but for all its negative aspects it has averted many a crisis and kept the country supplied during some really major droughts. It has also made river communication with Sudan easier and brought electricity to the farthest corners of Egypt, while the fish in Lake Nasser have made it possible to raise protein intake for ordinary people. Nevertheless, some parts of the project have not fulfilled their economic promise and are now in the course of sedimentation. Because of the scale of water retention, evaporation remains one of their most serious defects.

Some dams have caused grave ecological disturbances: those on the Indus, in Pakistan, prevent water from reaching the delta, leading to the destruction of mangrove swamps, sea encroachment into farmland, population displacement, famine and social disorders.[8] Moreover, the decomposition of vegetable matter behind the dams provides a breeding ground for microbes and increases atmospheric acidity to a degree that is structurally damaging. The microbes in question metabolize heavy metals such as mercury and introduce them into the food chain. By eating contaminated fish, animals and humans then begin to suffer from serious neurological disorders, as has often happened in Brazil and Canada. The social disturbances, too, are very often disastrous: uprooted populations are not always rehoused or given the land promised them in compensation – which leads to flight from the countryside, the spread of shanty towns and misery of all kinds.

In Africa the Diama dam on the Senegal, designed to prevent the intrusion of salt water, has spawned a whole class of absentee farmers, a bourgeoisie originating in Dakar with the means to buy pumps to irrigate rice fields by using local manpower. The beautiful town of Djenné in Mali, a UN world heritage site famed for its mosque[9] and mud buildings, lives only by the grace of the Bani river, whose flooding during the rainy season permits market-gardening, fishing and farming. This being so, one can understand the fears of the local population at the approaching end of the Talo dam project, begun in 1998 despite their opposition – especially as they know that the Sélengué and Manantali dams led to soil infertility and the appearance of 'unknown diseases'.[10]

The government is promising pumps to irrigate the fields with water from the Bani, and stresses that the dam will permit controlled flooding of Djenné throughout the year, instead of the thin line of water that currently comes from it during the dry season. Askia Muhamed, press attaché at the president's office, explains the official position as follows: 'Mali cannot feed itself with the means it has at its disposal. The priority is development. It cannot be stopped, even to save the national heritage.'[11] Strange rhetoric! How many crimes are committed in the name of development, while the authorities close their eyes to the catastrophic dredging for gold in the Falémé river, a tributary of the Senegal! To complete the picture, we should also mention that, on 2 April 2003, the Mali Council of Ministers decided to press ahead with development plans in the Niafunké lake area, 'to improve control over the water, to raise agricultural output, to increase producers' incomes, and to reduce poverty'.

Dams arouse people's passions

The dam issue is also raising questions in Europe. In the Adour-Garonne basin in south-west France, plans for some twenty new dams have run into problems because of lack of coordination; and, according to Friends of the Earth, some have even been destroyed on tributaries of the Loire to clear the way for salmon migration. In Portugal, on 8 February 2002, the continent's largest lake was created when the gates of the giant Alqueva dam closed in the Alentejo. For the prime minister, the coming into service of the dam 'has ended the political neglect of a region weighed down by depopulation, desertification and relative poverty', and, in an allusion to the origins of the project way back in 1957, under the Salazar dictatorship, he added that 'Alqueva is not a myth but a reality' – a reality that has anyway taken forty-five years to come into being. The original aim of the project had been to supply a new industrial town with energy, but for the moment the official line is that it will allow irrigation of south-western Alentejo, one of the driest and poorest regions in Western Europe. As we see, it is politicians who take the decisions, and when they leave power their dams change or come to serve a quite different purpose. One negative effect of Alqueva is that, when the waters behind the dam reach their maximum height of 152 metres, they will engulf the village of Luz and a number of cave paintings; the displaced villagers are refusing to live in the buildings set aside for them on the shores of the lake. So, China evidently does not have a monopoly on this kind of cultural and human disaster. The Portuguese government is hoping to irrigate 110,000 hectares of land. Environmentalists, for their part, are demanding that the water level should not exceed 139 metres – a maximum that would reduce the area to be submerged and save 400,000 trees, whereas the authorities envisage the felling of a million.[12]

Asia has the dubious privilege of hosting some fifty giant dam projects, including those on the Mekong, the Bakun in Malaysia, the San Roque in the Philippines, the Pak Mong (a tributary of the Mekong) in Thailand, the Man Theun 2 in Laos and the Three Gorges in China.[13] The World Bank has ingloriously, and quite shamelessly, withdrawn from the Narmada dam project in India,[14] which it had fiercely defended for years on end, and it is now keeping a respectable distance from the Three Gorges. Seeing water as a Trojan horse, the Bank seeks to act as an intermediary in water-related disputes between countries of the South, promoting market solutions and unfettered international trade as a universal panacea. On 26 June 2001, in Geneva, its then chairman James Wolfensohn opened a session of the International Consortium for Cooperation on the Nile (ICCON) to discuss the role of cooperation in the development of water resources, the fight against poverty and the furtherance of economic integration.[15]

International financial bodies have always played a major strategic role in the global promotion of giant dam projects, conferring on them a legitimacy that has persuaded governments of developing countries to support them. Yet the financial contribution of these bodies has usually not risen above 15 per cent of the total cost. Some of the dams are true pharaonic projects, and the full scale of their human and ecological impact is often difficult to predict.

Work on the Three Gorges dam in China is scheduled to end in 2009. The project was originally conceived in 1919, the first sketch left the drawing board in 1944, a detailed plan saw the light of day in 1955, and the first work began at the end of 1992. Costs have already overshot the budget by 44 per cent. A lake 660 kilometres long will come into being and a flooded area of 632 square kilometres will swallow up twenty prefectures in the 'province-city' of Chongqing. The lake will bury for ever millennia-old towns along the Yangtse–Kiang: Fengdu, Wanxian, Fengjie (considered 'the peak of poetic perfection' since the Tang era, 618–907 AD) and Baidicheng (much celebrated by the great poet Li Bai, 701–763 AD), as well as 4,500 villages and 162 archaeological sites. The lake/reservoir began to fill up in June 2003. The hydroelectric dam will be the largest in the world, comprising 26 generators, with a total power of 18.2 million kW and an annual capacity of 84.7 billion kWh. The project will eventually displace between 1.3 and 1.9 million people: in China, as elsewhere, it is the poor and the environment that pay the heaviest tribute for these disproportionate ambitions of the current authorities, and of the wider national pride, even if – as Friends of the Earth and the International River Network claim – this means trampling on human rights, silencing all protest and repressing all opposition. According to the same NGOs, the French Alstom and BNP–Paribas groups are participating in the massive construction work, with the benefit of guarantees from the French government's export-credit agency, COFACE, but Brazilian, Canadian, Swedish and Swiss firms are also involved. The flooding of once densely populated areas will probably lead to serious water pollution. Some 1,300 mines, 300,000 square metres of latrines and 3 million tonnes of domestic and industrial waste, as well as abattoirs, cemeteries and 4,000 hospitals will be covered by the rising waters. In November 2002, the authorities launched a huge clean-up operation upstream, but will the Party bureaucracy and corrupt local officials allow things to be satisfactorily completed? For the displaced populations, the main hope must be to avoid a repetition of the mistakes made in the construction of the Xinanjiang dam, during the Great Leap Forward in 1958, when people were pressured to leave and to 'take with them more good ideology and less old furniture'. Significantly, perhaps, the new Chinese president Hu Jintao – who took office in March 2003 – obtained an engineering degree in 1965 from the hydroelectricity department of the Qinghu Polytechnic University in Beijing.

Meanwhile, the Farraka dam on the Ganges has become a bone of contention between Bangladesh and India that ensures the port of Calcutta is kept open. The problem is that sedimentation is clogging and choking the port, and a new port has therefore had to be built at Haldia on the Bay of Bengal. So, what is the point of continuing to divert the waters of the Ganges, if the port of Calcutta no longer needs to be protected from the sediment carried down by the river? The development of Bangladesh is being obstructed by the cycle of drought and flooding, and some channels of the Ganges are so dry that saltwater is breaking into the wells and adding to the tragedy of arsenic contamination.

In the Philippines, the San Roque dam will be one of the largest in Asia, 0.2 km high by 1.2 km long. It will make life more difficult for the Ibaloy indigenous communities in the Cordillera, who were already badly wronged in 1956 and 1960 by the construction of the Agno 1 and Agno 2 dams. A consortium of banks and investors will provide the finance, the leading force being the Export–Import

Bank of Japan, which approved the project in spite of intense local opposition and international pressure from environmentalists and human rights campaigners. After a meeting in late 2000 with the mining companies that stand to gain most from the project, a leader of the Cordillera People's Alliance sharply expressed the general view: 'Where are we supposed to go, now that our land has been sold? If the mining operations erode the soil, if we are forbidden to set foot on our own lands, and if the building of mega-dams takes away our livelihood, where are we supposed to go? A place to live is a right, not a privilege!'[16]

Faced with the ordeal of being uprooted, local peoples eventually turn to the courts to protect them. Thus, Agence France-Presse recently reported: 'On 5 September 2002, nearly four thousand Indonesians lodged a novel complaint against Japan before the Tokyo district court, to demand compensation after the construction of a dam funded out of lavish Japanese development aid.'[17]

Projects for dams and major irrigation works may also give rise to corruption and serious malpractice with public money, as many NGOs have reported in connection with the Three Gorges. The journalist Dai Qing's book on the issue, *Yangtse! Yangtse!*, published in February 1989, is highly embarrassing to the ruling Communist Party, and has subsequently been banned. In a speech at a North–South conference on sustainable development, held in Berne in May 1998, the author repeated his charges of corruption against Chinese bureaucrats, stating that the authorities gag journalists and lie about the number of people rehoused; any criticism is 'suicidal', because the project is being used 'to vaunt what the new China is capable of achieving' and 'enthusiasm for the dam becomes a way of expressing loyalty to the central authorities, the manes of Mao Zedong, Zhou Enlai and revolutionaries as well as the Chinese people.' Dai Qing also pointed out that peasants are the first victims of such projects and pay the harshest tribute: those displaced by the Sanmenxia Three Gate Project in 1994, for example, live today in abject poverty; and their opposition has deep roots in the fact that displacement robs them of the chance 'to be buried in the family cemetery alongside generations of ancestors'. According to the organization Reporters without Borders, another journalist, Gao Qinrong, who worked for the official Chinese press agency Xinha, was sentenced to thirteen years' imprisonment for investigating the treatment meted out to the peasantry in these areas. The authorities especially blamed him for his reports on the failure of the irrigation project in Yuncheng (Shanxi province), whose 60,000 reservoirs, built in six months, they had presented as 'a triumph over nature in this arid region', but which, as Gao Qinrong showed, were not connected to any water taps or any conduit to fields used for farming. In an article that appeared on 27 May 1998 in *Neibu Cankao Xiaoxi*, a journal reserved for Communist Party cadres, he claimed that the whole project had served only to glorify certain local leaders, regardless of the real interests of the farmers. After receiving the prison sentence, he defended himself in a letter to the Chinese Communist Party leadership: 'The struggle against corruption is a decision of the Central Committee. As a Party member and a journalist, I thought it was my duty to report the people's grievances.' The result: Gao Qinrong is unjustly languishing in a Chinese jail.

All around the world, obsolete dams are an environmental and aesthetic headache for people in charge. What is to be done with thousands of tonnes of toxic sediment? Where should the rubble be stored? How should the site be restored to some other use? Even the task of demolition costs a fortune. In the United States, which has no fewer than 95,000 such structures, laborious efforts are sometimes made, with varying degrees of success, to turn them into leisure spaces, fishing areas, and so on.

There are also tragedies. On 28 April 1895, France was the scene of the terrible collapse of the Bouzey dam, near Épinal, when the villages of Bouzey and Sanchey lost a fifth of their inhabitants. In

1959 the Malpasset dam, on the Reynan above Fréjus, gave way and killed 400 people. Worse was to come in China, in 1975, when 20,000 souls perished as a result of the collapse of a dam in the middle of Hunan province. Then, on 4 June 2002, the Zeizoun dam in Syria burst with the loss of at least twenty lives, causing the shadowy and tyrannical regime of Bashar al-Assad to ask the UN for emergency aid to restore the electricity, water and telephone supplies; a total of 20,000 acres was under water, and the wheat, barley and beet crops were destroyed. Local people claimed that the authorities had made light of cracks that appeared on the surface of the structure, and that this had worsened the eventual disaster. In Tunisia the new Hima dam is a stone's throw from a quarry where several charges of dynamite are exploded every day. One journalist wondered: 'What impact will the explosions have on this dam of the future that was completed nearly a year ago?'[18] And this confirmed the 'constant, systematic incapacity to evaluate the negative impact of dams', noted by the World Commission on Dams. Feasibility studies are thus far from identifying all aspects or taking account of all the risk factors.

Furthermore, dams are not the panacea for underdevelopment that some see in them, and indeed they often given rise to heated debate. The Pak Moon dam in Thailand, completed in 1994 with World Bank funding at a time of seemingly firm demand for energy, operates at only 40 per cent of capacity and has never fulfilled the hopes invested in it. Badly designed, located near the ecologically sensitive confluence of the Mekong and Moon, the dam has severely undermined the halieutic wealth that provides a livelihood for thousands of people, especially as the fish ladder built by the World Bank has never functioned. The affected villagers have repeatedly sought compensation for their loss of earnings and demanded that the sluice gates be left open all the time to allow the ecosystem to recover. They protest against the violation of their economic, social and cultural rights (for example, the dam has made impossible a number of religious celebrations), in breach of the UN Convention signed by Thailand in 1999. But successive governments have refused to meet their demands, although numerous studies have shown that the cost of the project has largely outweighed the expected benefits. The new prime minister elected in late 2002 claims to be a 'champion of the poor', but the Pak Moon dam has called his bluff.[19] For the moment, what we see are a series of politicians' gestures. In mid-November 2002 the head of government ostentatiously convened a four-hour meeting, broadcast live on television, during which he listened in the manner of a feudal lord to the arguments of technicians, academics and thirty villagers. He also declared his intention to visit the area before announcing his decision.

The late lamented Anil Agarwal argued in favour of small-scale local projects, on the grounds that they would reduce the massive evaporation associated with large dams. He asked: 'Does a large dam with a catchment area of a million hectares harvest more water than a million microstructures with a catchment area of one hectare each?' In fact, his proposed alternative has now been approved by the World Commission on Dams, which questions the efficiency of large structures in many countries and, in particular, deplores the fact they are able to capture resources at the expense of small decentralized structures. One of the most negative aspects of large dams has been the devaluing of traditional irrigation practices. Thus, in the same spirit as Agarwal, Arundhati Roy notes in her *The Cost of Living*[20] that India's technocrats, in the name of the 'mission of electrification', have not only built 'new dams and irrigation schemes' but have also taken 'control of small, traditional water-harvesting systems that had been managed for thousands of years and allowed them to atrophy.' Europe is now encouraging small-scale hydroelectrical projects, because they help the fight against the greenhouse effect, as well as preserving environments (migrating fish, reserved flows, etc.) and the diversity of river use (energy, fishing, sports, heritage value, etc.).

For all the 'rural electrification' rhetoric in India, centralized electrification has benefited towns and industry far more than the countryside. This is particularly unjust because the natural capital invested in it comes from the countryside and the forests and ends up sustaining the growth of urban industry and the comfort of city elites. In fact, agriculture has been undervalued or even scorned in comparison with industrial 'modernity', which is seen as embodying the future and adding real value to the economy.

This injustice is fuelled not only by powerful local coalitions of technocrats but also by international interest groups making ideological use of dams and centralized electrification. Then there are the multilateral development agencies, the multinational corporations such as Bechtel, ABB and Enron (which have made huge profits from building dams and providing services and advice in the energy sector), and the exporters of power stations such as General Electric, Westinghouse, Siemens and Alstom.

Roy calculates that, over the last fifty years, large dams have displaced 33 million people in India – 60 per cent of them untouchables and members of ethnic minorities. In neither the Philippines, Laos, Thailand nor India is there a rehousing policy for these 'environmental refugees'. She argues that since independence in 1947 dams have carried a number of huge environmental costs: the disappearance of forest, the destruction of fishing grounds, the emergence of new flood-prone regions and natural disasters due to irrigation, and – most disturbing of all – the fact that at the beginning of the twenty-first century not one of India's rivers contains water fit to be drunk. But there are more insidious and staggering effects than those. Rammed into river valleys 'that nature never intended for them', dams stuffed with water deform the earth's crust and periodically send out seismic waves. The fantastic liquid mass even has an effect, albeit minimal, on the speed of the earth's rotation, while sea levels are three centimetres lower than they would be if all the rivers poured out their full contents. (This does have another, more positive side, of course, in that it mitigates the effects of rising ocean levels due to global warming.)

In the face of such facts, we need to keep a cool head and, above all, to grasp the great disparities that they conceal. At present, the developed countries use nearly 70 per cent of their hydroelectric potential, whereas the corresponding figure for developing countries is 15 per cent and for Africa a mere 3 per cent. Ethiopia and Norway have practically the same hydroelectric potential, yet in 1995 the former produced 2,000 Wh/year and the latter 112,676 Wh/year. In 1995 Asia had an annual hydroelectric output of 33 TWh/year, Africa 67 TWh/year and the NAFTA countries 653 TWh/year. Without electricity, you cannot obtain safe water or achieve proper levels of agricultural output. If you want to put an end to – or at least limit – deforestation, greenhouse gas emissions and water-borne diseases, electricity is an indispensable condition. In this regard, it may be that small power stations are a good option, especially in terms of the irrigation that is so vital for agriculture in many countries around the world. Be that as it may, in March 2003 the Third World Water Forum, in Kyoto, was so riven with contradictions that it dared not take a clear position on the dam issue. Its final declaration, neither chalk nor cheese, recognized 'the role of hydroelectric energy as a source of clean, renewable energy', but added that 'it should be used in a way that is environmentally sustainable and socially acceptable'. One might have expected that a gathering of 10,000 delegates and a hundred or so ministers would issue a statement showing a greater sense of responsibility, as well as an unequivocal condemnation of certain pharaonic projects.

For the United Nations, the world water crises could be brought under control if the rich countries made an additional financial contribution of $100 billion. During one panel discussion at the Forum, the well-known expert Peter Gleick said that an extra $10 billion a year would be enough, provided that it was earmarked for a lot of small-scale projects in Africa, Asia and Latin America. In short, there will be no salvation without cooperation and solidarity. Meanwhile, the Pentagon is spending $1 billion a day.

12

Water and development ethics

Come on, give him something to drink, my father said.

Victor Hugo

The starting point has to be an order of priorities. First come solidarity and the renunciation of egotistic positions, since water and the water cycle are the common denominator joining together human beings on Earth.

Solidarity with regard to water can have a number of un-expected beneficial effects. Thus, the twinning of the village of Krakeroy in Norway with a small town in Latin America to which the Scandinavians send aid has kept the community safe from the death squads, because of the international spotlight that would be trained on any crimes.

The Paris city councillor Lucien Finel made a plea for solidarity at a conference in 1997:

In France, particularly in Paris, we spend a fortune not on making water more drinkable (which it has been in Paris for a long time) but on improving its taste and quality, through re-search costing tens of millions on the amount of chlorine to add or the quality of the water supply – whereas people are dying of thirst in Sahel Africa, and international health problems are of concern to us all.

On the quality of the environment, he concluded: 'We should take care to avoid a certain kind of waste, out of respect for the millions of human beings for whom survival is a problem of considerably greater magnitude separating them from our own demands for environmental safety standards.'[1]

To manage the distribution of water locally, nationally and even internationally, and to avoid the outbreak of conflicts over water, it is necessary to promote a water ethics that goes far beyond empty rhetoric and fosters contractual and managerial transparency. For, as things stand, contracts are not usually made public – as the examples of Budapest or Coimbatore and Tirupur (India) show. The latter led environmental writer and activist Vandana Shiva to say: 'Business that can only be carried out behind closed doors, under secrecy, does not promote freedom. It extinguishes both freedom and democracy',[2] because it takes no account of the opinion and consent of ordinary citizens. The World Bank – whose investments in water amount to 14 per cent of all its loans – does not accept either that the terms of its main loans in this sector should be made public. Given the general philosophy of this institution, we may suppose that its 'structural adjustment loans' are meant to include the water privatization and 'full cost recovery' that are so harmful to popular layers. Similarly, in spite of efforts to maintain secrecy, a document of the Directorate General Trade of the European Commission, obtained on 25 February 2003, proves that the EU has asked a number of African countries (Botswana, Kenya, Lesotho, Madagascar, Mauritius, Morocco, Mozambique, Namibia, Nigeria, Senegal, South Africa, Tanzania, Tunisia and Zimbabwe) to open their markets to European water corporations.[3] The EU knows perfectly well that privatization threatens the provision of basic services in Europe, so how could it be less dangerous in the much poorer countries of Africa? In fact, everyone knows that only a public service has the three qualities of universality, equal access and unbroken service.

Water is also crucial for the practice of 'active subsidiarity' in local decision-making, when citizens express themselves and decisions are taken higher up. Water is a vital necessity for human beings – and indeed for the whole of the biosphere. It might therefore be elevated to the level of a right (as we already find in the draft constitution of South Africa) or a 'heritage property' of humanity. The French water law of 3 January 1992 states that it 'forms part of the common heritage of the nation', and that it should be developed in the general interest. On the question of whether there is a human right of access to water, the Quebecois legal expert Sylvie Paquerot starts from the principle of 'equal human dignity' inscribed in the preamble to the Universal Declaration of Human Rights and reaffirmed by the Vienna Conference of 1993, when it qualified such rights as intrinsic and therefore 'inalienable and universal'. She writes:

> If access to water is an essential condition for human dignity, then there certainly does exist a right of access to water. And, like all other human rights, it is universal because intrinsic in all human beings; it is also interdependent and indivisible with the other rights essential to human dignity. Lastly, it is inalienable: that is, it cannot be taken away from us, nor can we be forced to give it up.[4] The real issue, therefore, is whether or not the existence of this right is recognized, first of all politically, then in formal legal terms.[5]

And she continues:

> Although access to drinking water is, with a few rare exceptions, not explicitly defined as a human right in the general instruments of positive law ..., many consider it to be implicit and deduce it, in particular, from the right to life, the right to health, the right to an adequate standard of living, the right to be free of hunger or the right to housing, all inscribed in the Pacts or the Universal Declaration.

We must therefore develop for ourselves a 'water ethics' capable of really making things move, far beyond such anodyne concepts as 'sharing' or 'stakeholders'. The aim must be to empower those who are thirsty, the poorest marginalized layers, to express themselves and take decisions, in a way that allows an ethics of global solidarity to emerge. Some encouraging signs are already visible: in New Zealand, for example, the local government minister declared to parliament in January 2002 that 'access to water is not a commodity but a fundamental human right', and in Switzerland the Federal Council has asked the government to support a treaty that 'makes access to clean drinking water a human right'.[6] Similarly, the UN secretary-general considers that access to water is a human right, as does the director-general of the World Health Organization (WHO).

In the wake of meetings all over Africa, the WHO mentions among the factors making for the sustainability of water supply and sanitation projects: (a) community involvement at all levels of the planning, design, implementation, management and running of projects, with due account taken of the differences between men and women; (b) community self-improvement; and (c) better management of information. Yet doubts are certainly permissible about the capacity to meet these conditions in some developing countries, where government respect for the population and a democratic culture are not yet sufficiently implanted. The hope there lies with the NGOs and international pressure.

Water is an ideal issue on which to campaign for 'reverse' (bottom-up) globalization, as against the globalization decided in the secrecy of apparatuses and hushed boardrooms for which even national governments count as little. We saw an example of the latter at the Second Water Forum in The Hague, in March 2000, when 106 ministers sat attentively listening to the ukases handed down by a few bosses of water multinationals, who had proclaimed themselves great authorities on the subject. The positions taken on that occasion led the NGOs in attendance to speak out loud and clear on 21 March 2000:

> We strongly insist that a clean, healthy environment and access to basic water and sanitation are universal rights, and cannot therefore be negotiated as commodities. Thus, water and water services must be removed from the General Agreement on Trade and Services and the agenda of the World Trade Organization. We also consider that food and water insecurity is intrinsically linked to the current unfair global trade system, embodied in the WTO rules. Access to information, as a prerequisite for participation in decision-making processes, is a fundamental right. Legal and institutional mechanisms must be put in place for the empowerment of communities to participate at all levels. Access to justice must be guaranteed. The key to the sustainable provision of water for life is the maintenance and protection of the ecological integrity of all ecosystems. We call for the adoption and implementation of a restoration agenda for the rehabilitation of degraded ecosystems. We urge a substantial increase in the levels of spending for clean water and sanitation for poor people and communities. Debt cancellation is essential for water security in poor countries. We strongly demand that water and sanitation services are under the control of the local communities and that the benefits stay within the communities. We also demand that the management of these services be participatory and transparent. We reject privatization, other than in accordance with these principles.[7]

In the final declaration of the Hague Forum, however, representatives of the World Water Council, together with ministers present at the gathering and spokesmen for the big corporations, refused to consider access to water as a human right. They simply stated that it was a vital necessity, so that the supply of water ceased to be an obligation for the state and access to water was no longer guaranteed for all.

13

Reasons for hope?

Man, drink water
To make yourself beautiful
And look at the sky
To become big.

Tuareg proverb

The fact remains that, despite the autism of certain politicians, experts and water merchants, objective reasons exist for a cautious optimism.

1. New advances in relation to water are coming more and more from such countries as Brazil, India and China, rather than the Western countries. South–South cooperation is therefore likely to be established on a wider scale, even if a certain know-how is still, internationally, in the hands of the multinational corporations.

2. From the Vatican through certain thinkers and intellectuals to UN commissions and NGOs, water is now seen as a common good of humanity that cannot be treated as a mere commodity on which to turn a profit.

3. The cost of desalination – and especially the nanofiltration

process – has been falling appreciably (from 75 to 70 euro cents per cubic metre in 2001), even if solutions still have to be found for the large amount of salt that it generates.

4. Biotechnology is the source of some hope, in so far as anti-pest techniques such as the development of plants with a low water requirement are capable of reducing overall levels of water consumption and agrichemical pollution.

5. An ethics of solidarity is slowly emerging to replace super-annuated concepts such as the law of the jungle.

6. Sustainable practices are becoming more widely known, and a short-term perspective is less and less the one that people have in mind.

7. World Water Day, first celebrated on 20 March 1992, has increased awareness of water as a decisive strategic issue for the future.

8. The many international conferences are starting to bear fruit, slowly and sometimes with difficulty, and civil society asserts its presence in relation to them by organizing counter-conferences free of all lobbying (in 2003, Florence versus Kyoto).

9. Faced with the activity of think-tanks such as the Global Water Partnership (GWP) and the World Water Council (which is virtually an offshoot of the World Bank and the multinationals[1]), we can only hope that a more unified, more homogenous leadership will develop in a sector currently fragmented among the WHO, WMO, FAO, UNESCO and a host of other organizations. The main hope lies with the organization and struggles of civil society: the new awareness and education of consumers, legal actions against multinationals, lobbying of elected representatives and public authorities, and enlistment of experts familiar with the mysteries of the multinationals.

It is estimated that $36 billion is needed to procure safe drinking water and adequate sanitation for the whole of humanity: that is, the equivalent of 4 per cent of worldwide military and weapons expenditure. The language of the Millennium Development Goal, with its aim of halving the percentage of people without access to safe drinking water and sanitation by the year 2015, falls far short of what is required. The truth is that the universal provision of water depends on the priorities that humanity sets itself, for what we do with our water ultimately reflects our deepest values. The water cycle binds us all together within the global village, up to and including the whole biosphere.

Anil Agarwal once said: 'Water is the ultimate depository for all man's sins. All the waste that he produces finds its way there in the end. The more a society commits sins against water, the more it is impervious and indifferent to it, and the worse the state of the streams, the rivers and the lakes.'

We can increase the amount of water available to meet our needs, so long as we do not lose sight of the basic fact that water resources are finite – and, above all, so long as we learn to use them more sensibly with the help of traditional knowledge, reduce the extent of losses through leakage and evaporation, and grow plants that are suited to the local soil and climate.

Education is crucially important to instil a proper respect for water and an understanding of its exceptional importance for life. It is necessary to encourage moves towards a new society, a society that is much more sparing with water and appreciates how precious a resource it really is. It must be used more advisedly and with a greater sense of responsibility towards future generations and those who do not have enough today. More particularly:

- We must rethink our lifestyles and become more frugal, in ways that avoid wasting water and reduce pollution – in short, that apply the principles of ecodevelopment formulated by Ignacy Sachs. It is also necessary for people to recognize that water has a number of different functions.

- The traditional knowledge that has had considerable success, from Rajasthan to Niger, needs to be more widely used.
- Mechanisms should be put in place for the peaceful resolution of disputes concerning waters that supply several communities and/or countries. To this end, the international community should establish an international water court, which should include, along with professional judges, people drawn from the ranks of farmers and other users, representatives of different cultures, women and special envoys from the Water Court in Valencia, Spain (who could help with the centuries of experience acquired by this highly original institution).
- The management of water resources must be made transparent and democratic, and a war should be waged against negligence and bureaucracy. In short, an appeal needs to be made for 'active subsidiarity'.
- Consumerist lifestyles that waste and pollute water resources need to be revised: we must realize that they can never be extended to the whole of humanity without causing serious environmental, political and social-economic imbalances, especially as the climate crisis beating down on us gives the lie to the 'Promethean illusion of man's superior capacity' to dominate everything, and shakes people's faith in technocratic solutions.
- Work needs to be done to promote an ethics of water management and distribution that allows us all to live in peace and cooperation with one another.

The water issue, itself part and parcel of the major ecological disturbances now affecting humanity, poses key questions for 'our economic system, our energy supply, our modes of production, our means of transport, our collective organization, our social behaviour and our individual lifestyles'.[2]

Our very survival on Earth depends on a straight answer to these questions, without the usual politician's manoeuvres.

Notes

Chapter 1

1. Kazimierz Michalowski, *L'Art de l'Égypte*, Paris: Citadelles & Mazenod, 1994.
2. Robert Collins, *The Nile*, New Haven: Yale University Press, 2003.
3. Ahmed Shawki (1868–1932): Egyptian poet, dramatist and politician, driving force behind the renewal of Arabic poetry, exiled to Andalusia during the First World War. After his return, venerated as the 'prince of poets' at the 1927 festival of poetry. Studied law in Montpellier and Paris.
4. *Géo* 282, August 2002.
5. In the Koran, the sun sets in a 'boiling spring' (Sura XVIII, v. 86, in the French translation of J. Berque).
6. Mark Kurlansky, *Salt: A World History*, Princeton NJ: Princeton University Press, 2002.
7. WHO, *Water and Sanitation in Islam*, Regional Office for Eastern Mediterranean, WHO, Alexandria, 1996.
8. Agung Ruliyantoj, 'La lente mort d'un peuple: les derniers chasseurs-cueilleurs de Sumatra', *Courrier International* 609, 4–10 July 2002, pp. 42–3.
9. Stephen S. Hall, 'Lost discoveries: the non-western roots of science', *New York Times*, 1 December 2002.
10. The water in this well plays a vital role in the case of war or siege, as the life of any warrior is safe if he manages to enter the holy area.
11. Ali Chenoufi writes in *La Revue IBLA* [published by the Arabic Literary Institute, Tunis] 146, 1980/1982: 'The Omayyads had hunting scenes

depicted on the walls of their palaces, as well as bathing scenes featuring not only men and animals but also naked women.' A bathing miniature of the Abassid grand caliph Al Maamun, son of Harun er-Rashid, has come down to us from sixteenth-century Iran. Valère-Marie Marchand, *Les ouvriers du signe. Calligraphie en culture musulmane*, Courbevoie: ACR Éditions, 2002.

12. Alexandre Papadopoulo, *Islam and Muslim Art*, London: Thames & Hudson, 1980.

13. This practice was the theme of Anat Zuria's film *Untouchable Wives*, which received a special mention at the 2003 Biarritz Festival.

14. *Water and Sanitation in Islam*.

15. *L'Éternité n'est pas de trop*, Paris: Albin Michel, 2002. An English version, translated by Timothy Bent, exists as *Green Mountain, White Cloud*, London: St Martin's Press, 2004.

16. Guy de Maupassant, *Écrits sur le maghreb*, Paris: Minerve, 1988.

17. In fact Egyptians rarely say 'the Nile' but call the river *ba'hr* – that is, 'sea' or 'ocean'.

18. The much longer Hari Rud, which flows for 1,100 km through Iran, Afghanistan and Turkmenistan, is eventually swallowed up in the immensity of the Kara Kum desert.

19. Quoted from *Le Petit Journal des Grandes Expositions* 346, 2002.

20. Joseph Ki-Zerbo, 'L'environnement dans la culture africaine. Les rapports entre les Africains et la Nature', *Les Cahiers du cycle postgrade en sciences de l'environnement* 1, EPFL, Lausanne, 1996.

21. Ibid.

22. Curve joining the points that receive the same quantity of rainfall for a period under consideration.

23. Ki-Zerbo, 'L'environnement dans la culture africaine'.

24. Pierre Merlin, *Espoir pour l'Afrique noire*, Paris: Présence africaine, 1991 (quoted in 'Éthique négro-africaine et Technoscience moderne. Défi pour de nouvelles orientations dans l'Afrique contemporaine', thesis presented by On'Okundji Okavu Ekanga to the philosophy faculty, Université Jean Moulin Lyon III, December 1996).

25. In 2002 the Reno Sparks Indian Colony in Nevada called on the justice minister in Washington to ban the digging of a clay mine on their territory for the production of cat litter, as such operations seriously threatened the quality of water on the reservation. 'Cat-litter firm digs in over mine plan', *International Herald Tribune*, 2–3 November 2002.

26. *Los Angeles Times*, 8 May 1999.

27. In November 1990, following a visit to Saddam Hussein's Al Qadissiya palace in Baghdad, the Cuban diplomat Alcibiades Hidalgo spoke of 'inner patios with magnificent fountains'. *Le Monde*, 11 March 2003.

28. 'Tolède XII–XIIIe siècle', *Autrement* 5, February 1995.

186 *Water under Threat*

29. Roger Garaudy, *Mosquées, miroir de l'Islam*, Paris: Éditions du Jaguar, 1985.
30. William Dalrymple, 'Le labyrinthe musulman de l'Inde du Sud', *Courrier International* 628, 14–20 November 2002, p. 77.
31. André Gide, *Retour de l'URSS*, Paris: Gallimard, 1936.
32. '"Carp" Diem', *Newsweek*, 14 October 2002.
33. *Courrier International* 616, August 2002.

Chapter 2

1. Philip Ball, *Life's Matrix: A Biography of Water*, New York: Farrar, Straus & Giroux, 2000.
2. 'Making water move without gravity', *New York Times* online, 26 January 2001.
3. With the well-known anomaly, at 4°c, of the specific mass through which the gram weight is defined.
4. This water content has not escaped the sagacity of military men. According to the journal *Air et Cosmos* (quoted in *Le Monde*, 12 September 2002), the Americans have an E (electromagnetic) bomb which acts 'like a microwave oven' and 'at a temperature of 45°c induces the activity of water molecules composing human cells, with the associated effects of cooking and burning'.
5. *Science*, vol. 295, no. 99, 2002.
6. Maureen Rouhi, 'Computations: from water to ice', *Chemical & Engineering News*, 1 April 2002.
7. Matthew L. Wald, 'Nevada states case against waste dump in mountain', *New York Times*, 3 December 2002.
8. *Disc. Faraday Soc.*, vol. 42, no. 109, 1966.
9. Louis Wassermann, 'Revisiting chemistry's infamous detour', *Chemistry*, 125 years issue, 2001, p. 45.
10. Jim Kling, 'Splitting water with a lanthanum-modified catalyst', *Chemistry Org.*, American Chemical Society, 24 February 2003.
11. Jeremy Rifkin, *The Hydrogen Economy: The Creation of the Worldwide Energy Web and the Redistribution of Power on Earth*, Cambridge: Polity Press, 2002.
12. Diane Raines, *Water Wars: Drought, Flood, Folly and the Politics of Thirst*, New York: Riverhead, 2002.

Chapter 3

1. *Foreign Affairs*, vol. 78, no. 2, March–April 1999.
2. 'China approves massive diversion of water', *Environmental Science & Technology*, 1 March 2003, p. 90A.

3. Igor Shiklomanov, 'Prospective de l'eau à l'horizon 2025', in *Les clefs du XXIe siècle*, Paris: Le Seuil/Éditions UNESCO, 2000.
4. The Beirut daily *L'Orient-Le Jour* reported on 20 June 2001 that Iran and Kuwait had agreed to build a 550 km aqueduct from the Karkeh dam in Iran to the ultra-rich emirate, after what Tehran's vice-minister responsible for water, Gholamreza Manouchehri, called a 'critical threshold' had been reached. Are these political-religious games, involving a front against Wahabi Saudi Arabia? Only time will tell.
5. *New York Times*, 30 March 2003.
6. *Le Monde Diplomatique*, May 2002.
7. Jean Despois, *L'Afrique du Nord*, Paris: Presses Universitaires de France, 1958.
8. A Tunisian proverb, mainly referring to grains, says: 'March rains, pure gold.'
9. Eric Roose, 'Le zaï: un labeur de termites et de paysans en zone soudano-sahélienne', *La Revue durable*, pilot issue, June 2002, pp. 22–3.
10. The Société Nationale des Eaux de Niger supplied water too rich in fluoride in the Maradi region, as a result of which 500 children were handicapped for life by osteo-dental fluorosis.
11. Michael Tobias, 'Desert survival by the book', *New Scientist*, 17 December 1988.
12. Judith A. Carney, *Black Rice: The African Origins of Rice Cultivation in the Americas*, Boston MA: Harvard University Press, 2001.
13. André Gide, *Le retour du Tchad*, Paris: Gallimard, 1928.

Chapter 4

1. 'US proposes global water security alliance to counter crises', *Agence France-Presse*, 10 April 2000.
2. Colin Powell, 'Aid for the enterprise', *Washington Post*, 10 June 2003.
3. *Al Wafd* (Cairo), 7 May 2003.
4. See Jean Poncet, 'À propos de Ibn Khaldoun', *La Pensée*, February 1967.
5. André Aymard and Jeannine Auboyer, *L'Orient et la Grèce antique*, Paris: Presses Universitaires de France, 1953.
6. Kazimierz Michalowski, *L'Art de l'Égypte*, Paris: Citadelles & Mazenod, 1994.
7. *Courrier International* 606, 13–19 June 2002, p. 41.
8. In Muslim countries prayers for rain are a common practice, and in spring 2002 the Tunisian and Algerian governments officially carried out the relevant ceremonies. In Senegal, where it is believed that tam-tams may hinder the arrival of rain, the authorities banned their use because of the terrible drought of 2002. On 11 August 2003, according to Reuters,

'Pope John Paul II prayed to God for rainfall to ease the extreme heat and the forest fires.'

9. Thomas Fuller, 'Jakarta lays the groundwork for clean water', *International Herald Tribune*, 27 March 2000.

Chapter 5

1. Robin Wright, 'Bush's Mexico trip will aim to launch new era in relations', *Los Angeles Times*, 12 February 2001.

2. Tom Clancy, *Op Center 4: Acts of War*, Berkeley: Berkeley Publishing Group, 1997.

3. Quoted from Arundhati Roy, 'The Ordinary Person's Guide to Empire', *Guardian*, 2 April 2003.

4. The Khabur, the main tributary of the Euphrates in Syria, has been dry for five years. As its groundwater is in Turkey, the two countries hold each other responsible for the situation, but it would seem that persistent drought is as much to blame as the uncontrolled drilling.

5. Charles Lane, 'High court to hear Md-Va water case', *Washington Post*, 29 April 2003.

6. *Le Monde*, 10 April 2001.

7. *Pour la Science* 308, June 2003.

8. Vanessa Dougnac, 'La bataille de l'eau', *Le Point* 1573, 8 November 2002.

9. Michael Wines, 'For a sickening encounter, just turn on a tap in Karachi', *New York Times/Le Monde*, 3–4 November 2002.

10. Françoise Chipaux, 'Au Pakistan, la sécheresse accentue la déroute économique', *Le Monde*, 16 May 2001.

11. On account of the exceptional drought of 1999, however, Israel has failed to meet its commitments and cut the agreed quota by 60 per cent.

12. *Le Monde*, 24 April 2001.

13. *Courrier International* 550, May 2001.

14. *Al Ahram*, 31 May 2001.

15. *Al Liwa* (Beirut), 20 June 2001.

16. *New York Times*, 28 December 1999.

17. 'The bulldozer war', *Le Monde Diplomatique*, English edition, May 2002.

18. 'Les Palestiniens assiégés: Israël contre Israël', *Le Monde Diplomatique*, January 2002.

Chapter 6

1. Mohamed Larbi Bouguerra, 'Une guerre à nulle autre pareille', *Le Monde Diplomatique*, July 1992.

2. *Los Angeles Times*, 30 April 1998.

3. *San Francisco Chronicle*, 7 September 1998.
4. Bab El Oued: literally, 'gate of the *oued*' (an intermittent watercourse).
5. Hugues Le Masson, 'Le marché de l'eau dans les pays en développement', *Revue des Ingénieurs (Mines)* 386, June 2000, pp. 20–21.
6. *Le Monde*, 2–3 September 2001.
7. 'Pénurie d'eau', *Le Monde*, 2–3 September 2001.
8. *Le Monde*, 22 September 2001.
9. *Le Monde*, 8 February 2002.
10. *Liberté*, 12 February 2002.
11. *Le Monde*, 29 May 2002.
12. *Le Monde*, 31 May 2002.
13. In her haste to get some water, one young girl was run over on 7 June 2002 by a water-tanker in Algiers.
14. 'Halte aux fuites d'eau potable', *Le Matin* (Algiers), 8 January 2003.
15. *L'Humanité-Hebdo*, 1–2 June 2002.
16. *Jeune Afrique l'Intelligent* 2157, 13–19 May 2002, p. 86.
17. In Bermuda a law obliges every homeowner to instal 1.5 square metres of roof per occupant to catch rainfall in a tank.
18. *Le Matin*, 8 January 2003.
19. Literally, 'those who hold up walls': the unemployed.
20. Robert Belleret, 'Algériens, solidaires dans le drame', *Le Monde*, 7 June 2003.
21. *Essabah*, 26 July 2001.
22. *La Presse de Tunisie*, 1 November 2001.
23. 'Stratégie vitale', *La Presse de Tunisie*, 23 October 2001.
24. *Le Monde*, 19 April 2003.
25. *Al Wafd*, 7 May 2003.
26. *Al Ahali*, 30 April 2003.
27. Quoted by Pierre Cornut, in a doctoral thesis presented at the Université Libre de Bruxelles, 1999.

Chapter 7

1. *Courrier International* 505, July 2000, p. 30.
2. Pierre Cornut, doctoral thesis, Université Libre de Bruxelles, 1999.
3. The Tuaregs in Algeria, Libya, Burkina Faso, Mali and Niger have also been severely affected: the droughts of 1973 and 1984 decimated their herds, and a rebellion from 1990 to 1995 led to thousands of deaths and the poisoning of many of their wells.
4. Reproduced in *International Herald Tribune*, 5 March 2002.
5. Peter H. Gleick, 'Preparing for a drought', *New York Times*, 4 March 2002.

6. *New York Times*, 3 May 2002.

7. Anil Agarwal and Sunita Narai, *Dying Wisdom: Rise, Fall and Potential of India's Traditional Water-Harvesting Systems*, Delhi: CSE, 1996; author's translation.

8. 'Nor any drop to drink', *The Economist*, 24 August 2002.

9. Ashok Sharma, *Catch Water* 1, February 1999.

10. *Le Monde*, 14 November 1998.

11. Associated Press despatch, in *New York Times* online, 1 July 2000.

12. Testimony given by Leila Shahid at the Sorbonne, 26 November 2002.

13. Testimony of people close to him, in *Israël, Palestine. Le livre noir*, Paris: La Découverte, 2002.

14. *Jeune Afrique l'Intelligent* 2179, 14–20 October 2002.

15. Pierre Le Roy, 'Nul besoin d'une seconde planète pour nourrir le monde', *Le Monde*, 29 April 2003.

Chapter 8

1. Sandra Postel, 'Water shortages loom; technology, creative approaches offer solutions', *Environmental Science and Technology*, 1 October 1999, p. 398A.

2. *New York Times*, 23 November 2002.

3. *Privatization News*, January 1999.

4. *Cahiers du MURS* 34, fourth quarter of 1997, Part 3, p. 56.

5. Patrick Point, 'L'économie de l'eau face aux enjeux mondiaux', *Revue des Deux Mondes*, September 2000, pp. 9–19.

6. *Courrier International* 645, March 2003.

7. *Le Devoir* (Montreal), 1 June 2000.

8. *Chemical & Engineering News*, 13 March 2000, p. 29.

9. Janice Long, 'Herbicides foul drinking water', *Chemical & Engineering News*, 24 October 1994, p. 29.

10. Bette Hilleman, 'Rules in the fast lane', *Chemical & Engineering News*, 13 March 2000, p. 9.

11. Chuck Fox, 'Arsenic and old laws', *New York Times*, 22 March 2001; see also Douglas Jehl, 'EPA to abandon new arsenic limits for water supply', *New York Times*, 21 March 2001.

12. *L'Express*, 12 September 2002.

13. See the editorial 'Everglades in peril', *New York Times*, 21 April 2003.

14. The idea for the film probably came from a number of tragedies that rocked the nation: in Woburn (Massachusetts), McFarland (California) and elsewhere. See Mohamed Larbi Bouguerra, *La Pollution invisible*,

Paris: Presses Universitaires de France, 1997.

15. *New York Times,* 14 November 1998.

16. Peter Y. Hong, 'Stockton puts water services in private hands', *Los Angeles Times,* 21 February 2003.

17. *Water Privatization: A Broken Promise,* available online at www.citizen.org/cmep/water/.

18. Christopher Sheil, *Water's Fall,* Sydney: Pluto Press, 2000.

19. Pierre Cornut, doctoral thesis, Université Libre de Bruxelles, 1999.

20. *Ecologist,* July–August 2000, p. 51.

21. *Le Figaro Économie,* 9 March 2001.

22. Nicolas Beau, 'Henri Proglio, l'as du cash flotte', *Le Canard Enchaîné,* 30 May 2003.

23. In a recent film, *The Navigators,* Ken Loach portrays the dramas accompanying privatization of the railways in Britain.

24. Pierre Cornut, *Histoire d'eau: Les enjeux de l'eau potable du XXIe siècle en Europe Occidentale,* Brussels: Luc Pire, 2003.

25. Paul Blustein, 'Lesotho bribery charges read like "Who's who of dam builders",' *International Herald Tribune,* 14–15 August 1999.

26. Susan Rose-Ackerman, 'The political economy of corruption: causes and consequences', *Public Policy for the Private Sector,* Note 74, Washington DC: World Bank, April 1996.

27. Antoine Bigo, 'Riche de son pétrole et de son eau douce, le Sud argentin attise les convoitises', *Libération,* 4 March 2003.

28. Manuel de la Fuente, Ana Maria Seifert and Frida Villareal, 'Bolivie: l'enjeu de l'eau', *Le Devoir* (Montreal), 17 July 2000, p. A6.

29. In 1997, the mayor of Angoulême was sentenced to two years' imprisonment for corruption involving a water multinational. Directors of the Générale des Eaux were found guilty of corrupting the mayor of Saint-Denis in the island of Réunion.

30. Jean-François Julliard, 'Ces maires qui partent en guerre contre "la bande à Bonne eau"', *Le Canard Enchaîné,* 20 September 2000.

31. *Le Canard Enchaîné,* 16 February 2000.

32. *Le Monde,* 21 February 2002.

33. *Le Canard Enchaîné,* 20 January 2001.

34. *Chemical & Engineering News,* 18 December 2000, p. 14.

35. Fred Pearce and Debora Mackenzie, ''It's raining pesticides: The water falling from our skies is unfit to drink', *New Scientist,* 3 April 1999.

36. *Libération,* 27 June 2001.

37. *Le Monde,* 28 June 2001.

38. Anthony de Palma, 'Free trade in fresh water? Canada says no to US companies', *New York Times,* 7 March 1999.

39. *Le Monde,* 12–13 November 2000.

40. Maude Barlow, *Black Gold: The Global Water Crisis and the Commodification*

of the World's Water Supply, San Francisco: IFG, June 1999.

41. *Le Monde*, 24 February 2001.
42. *Le Monde*, 26 October 2001.
43. *Le Monde*, 19 February 2002.

Chapter 9

1. André Gide, *Voyage au Congo*, Paris: Gallimard, 1927.
2. Geoff Dyer, 'Virus: Sleuths seek clues about Sars origins', *Financial Times*, 2 May 2003.
3. Auguste César Zeboua, final dissertation, Senghor University, Alexandria, May 2003.
4. *Le Monde*, 28–29 April 1991.
5. 'The bug is back', *Newsweek International*, 17 June 2002.
6. Emmanuelle Marendaz, 'L'Afrique craint les guerres de l'eau au prochain millénaire', *Le Temps* (Switzerland), 7 June 1999.
7. Quoted from *Essabah* (Tunisia), 28 June 2000.
8. Christopher Wanjek, *Washington Post*, 12 March 2002.
9. *New York Times*, 13 September 2002.
10. *Chemical & Engineering News*, 2 September 2002.
11. *Chemical & Engineering News*, 14 October 2002.
12. *Journal du Dimanche*, 21 January 2001.
13. Ibid.
14. Michelle Hamer, 'Insatiable thirst for water creates a boom for bottlers', *The Age*, 4 February 2001.
15. Michel Beuret, Jean-Philippe Buchs and Cathy Macherel, 'L'eau, nerf de la guerre', *L'Hebdo*, 22 March 2001.
16. *Le Soir*, 19 April 2001.
17. *Le Canard Enchaîné*, 24 April 2002.
18. See, for example, *À nous Paris* 171, 24 February–2 March 2003.
19. 'Pesticide residues in bottled water', *Down to Earth*, vol. 11, no. 18, 15 February 2003.
20. PepsiCo and Coca-Cola denied these facts and demanded that they be examined by the five leading Indian specialists, claiming that 'these allegations are politically motivated'. See Edward Luce, 'Pepsi and Coca-Cola deny pesticide claims', *Financial Times*, 6 August 2003, p. 6.
21. *Le Canard Enchaîné*, 29 January 2003.
22. Gina Kolota, 'New advice to runners: Don't drink too much water, *International Herald Tribune*, 8 May 2003.
23. Robert Glennon, *Water Follies: Groundwater Pumping and the Fate of America's Fresh Waters*, New York: Island Press, 2002.
24. Rachel Carson, *Silent Spring*, Boston MA: Houghton-Mifflin, 1962.

Chapter 10

1. Jan Mazurak, *Making Microchips: Policy, Globalization and Economic Restructuring in the Semiconductor Industry*, Cambridge MA: MIT Press, 1999.

2. Blaine Harden and Douglas Jehl, 'Pumps extract gas and ranchers' anger', *New York Times*, 12–13 January 2003.

3. Gérard Moatti, *Les Echos*, 29 April 1999.

4. Mohamed Larbi Bouguerra, *La recherché contre le tiers-monde*, Paris: Presses Universitaires de France, 1993.

5. See the special issue 'Facing the Farm Crisis', *Ecologist*, vol. 30, no. 4, June 2000.

6. I am grateful to Suren Erkman for this example.

7. 'EU policies on olive farming: unsustainable on all counts', *Environmental Science & Technology*, 1 September 2001, p. 360A.

8. *Science et Vie*, June 2000, p. 150.

9. J.W. Maurits la Rivière, 'Threats to the world's water', *Scientific American*, September 1989, pp. 48–55.

10. Reuters despatch, 'Drought cuts Tunisia's cereal crop to 0.49 mn T', 13 September 2002.

11. *Essabah*, 23 December 2002.

12. Youssef Al Akid, reading notes, *Akhbar Al Adab* (Cairo), 24 May 2003, p.30.

13. The mayor of Mauberguet at the time was none other than Jean Glavany, minister of agriculture in the Socialist government of Lionel Jospin.

14. *Le Monde*, 20 April 2001.

15. Ibid.

16. Ibid.

17. *Le Canard Enchaîné*, 23 May 2001.

18. *Le Canard Enchaîné*, 4 July 2001.

19. 'Melbourne tests for algae toxins in drinking water', *Orlando Sentinel*, 9 June 2001; and 'Algae poisons lurk in Florida drinking water', *Orlando Sentinel*, 27 May 2001.

20. *Washington Post*, 4 April 2001, p. B03.

21. Vincent Kiernan, in *New Scientist*, 1 June 1996, p. 19.

22. *Courrier International* 518, October 2000.

23. In May 2001 the Supreme Court of the State of Maine handed down a verdict in favour of three papermakers who had contested the water rights of the Penobscot and Passamaquoddy Indian tribes (*USA Today*, 4 May 2001, p. 6A). In Quebec, in 1997, the Cree tribe was more successful in blocking the James river dam, thanks largely to international support, but a new project costing $13 billion has been scheduled for the Churchill river. Another battle in prospect.

24. Yannis Kiparissis, Richard Hughes, Chris Metcalfe and Thomas Ternes,

'Identification of the isoflavonoid genistein in bleached kraft mill effluent', *Environmental Science and Technology*, 15 June 2001, pp. 2423–7.

25. Rebecca Renner, 'Study finding perchlorate in fertilizer rattles industry', *Environmental Science and Technology*, 1 October 1999, pp. 394–5.

26. *New York Times*, 18 October 1999.

27. *Al Ahram*, 10 April 1998.

Chapter 11

1. Michel Serres, ed., *Éléments d'histoire des sciences*, Paris: Bordas, 1989.

2. Kazimierz Michalowski, *L'Art de l'Égypte*, Paris: Citadelles & Mazenod, 1994.

3. From the Arabic word for 'barrier'.

4. John Madeley, *Food for All: The Need for a New Agriculture*, London: Zed Books, 2002. It should be remembered that these dams were wanted by politicians in Gandhi's own Congress Party.

5. This dam programme is not about to come to a halt. On 18 May 2002, the pro-government *Presse de Tunisie* reported that the Arab Fund for Economic and Social Development (AFESD) would contribute 154 million dinars to the construction of six dams.

6. Patrick McCully, *Silenced Rivers*, London: Zed Books, 1996.

7. *Courrier International* 400, July 1998.

8. Erik Eckholm, 'Where a river is diverted, a sea rushes in downstream', *New York Times–Le Monde*, 12 May 2003.

9. As Amadou Hampâté Ba, the renowned Malian writer, said with reference to the mosques of Djenné and Timbuktu: 'In Africa, Islam is the water: it takes its colours from the surrounding land.'

10. Boubacar Diarra, Senghor University, Alexandria.

11. *National Geographic*, June 2001.

12. 'Portugal turning 1950s lake plan into reality', *International Herald Tribune*, 9 February 2002.

13. Construction work on the Yangtse project, which is supposed eventually to divert 44.8 billion cubic metres of water to the arid north of China, at an estimated cost of $59 billion, began on Friday, 27 December 2002.

14. Fred Pearce, 'And the waters rushed in ...', *New Scientist*, 1 May 1999, p. 55.

15. *Financial Times*, 25 June 2001.

16. *Archipel* (journal of the European Civic Forum), December 2000, pp. 5–6.

17. *La Libre Belgique*, 6 September 2002.

18. Salem Trabelsi, 'El H'ma: un barrage et une biodiversité à préserver', *La Presse de Tunisie*, 14 February 2003.

19. Amy Kazmin, 'Dam dispute poses test for Thai premier', *Financial Times*, 23 December 2002.
20. 'The Greater Common Good', in Arundhati Roy, *The Cost of Living*, New York: Modern Library, 1999.

Chapter 12

1. *Cahiers du MURS* 34, fourth quarter, 1997.
2. *Agribusiness Examiner* 247, 13 May 2003.
3. Luc Coppjeans, Africa-Europe Faith and Justice Network (AEFJN), Brussels, 26 February 2003.
4. This corresponds to the ruling of the Canadian Supreme Court on the ancestral rights of indigenous peoples.
5. Sylvie Paquerot, communication to the Oh! Festival in Créteil, May 2002.
6. H. Smets, *Le droit à l'eau*, Paris: Académie de l'eau, 2002.
7. 'NGO Major Group Statement to the Ministerial Conference', 21 March 2000, The Hague.

Chapter 13

1. Chaired in 2001 by Egypt's minister of water resources and irrigation Mahmoud Abu Zeid (who backed the controversial Zoshki irrigation project in the Libyan desert), the World Water Council has as one of its governors Jérôme Monod, former director of the Lyonnaise water multinational and political adviser to President Jacques Chirac. Since the 1970s Mr Monod has been constantly at Chirac's side, and was his principal private secretary when the present head of state was prime minister. *Le Monde*, 23–24 June 2002.
2. Jean-Paul Besset, 'Faire face à l'aggression climatique', *Le Monde*, 9 August 2003.

Further reading

Bachelard, Gaston, *L'Eau et les rêves*, Paris: José Corti, 1991; *Water and Dreams: An Essay on the Imagination of Matter*, Dallas: Pegasus Foundation, 1983.

Ball, Philip, *Life's Matrix: A Biography of Water*, New York: Farrar, Straus & Giroux, 2000.

Barlow, Maude, *Blue Gold: The Global Water Crisis and the Commodification of the World's Water Supply*, San Francisco: IFG, 1999.

Barraqué, Bernard (ed.), *Les Politiques de l'eau en Europe*, Paris: La Découverte, 1995.

Bougerra, Mohamed Larbi (ed.), *Sept propositions pour la gouvernance de l'eau*, Alliance pour un monde responsable, pluriel et solidaire, Paris-Lausanne: Fondation Charles-Léopold Mayer pour le progress de l'homme, 2000. An English translation, 'Brief of proposals relating to the question of water supply', is available online at www.geocities.com/allianceaumondial/htdocs/proposal.htm.

Caïs, Marie-France, Marie-José del Rey and Jean-Pierre Ribaut, *L'Eau et la vie. Enjeux, perspectives et visions interculturelles*, Paris: Charles-Léopold Mayer, 1999.

Commissariat Général au Plan, *Rapport sur l'eau*, September 2001.

La Conquête de l'eau, Ciedel/Solagral, Paris: Charles-Léopold Mayer, 1995.

Cornut, Pierre: *Histoire d'eau*, Brussels: Luc Pire, 2003.

El Ayeb, Habib: *L'Eau au Proche-Orient: la guerre n'aura pas lieu*, Paris: Karthala, 1998, in collaboration with CEDEJ, Cairo.

Institut Français de l'Environnement, *Les Pesticides dans l'eau*, Orleans: Collection Études et Travaux No. 19, October 1998.

Farruqui, Naser I., Asit K. Biswas and Murad J. Bino (eds): *Water Management in Islam*, Tokyo: United Nations University Press, 2001.

Petrella, Riccardo, *The Water Manifesto: Arguments for a World Water Contract*, London: Zed Books, 2001.

Pringle, Laurence, *Rivers and Lakes*, Amsterdam: Time-Life, 1990.

Rose-Ackerman, Susan, *The Political Economy of Corruption: Causes and Consequences*, World Bank public policy for the private sector, note no. 74, Washington DC: World Bank, 1996.

Shiklomanov, Igor, *World Water Resources at the Beginning of the 21st Century*, Cambridge: Cambridge University Press, 2003.

Index

Mars, planet, 38; climatic cycle, 41
Marx, Karl, 59
Maspéro, François, 78
Maupassant, Guy de, 26–7, 132
Mauritania, –Senegal water dispute, 67
Maya civilization, disappearance, 17–18
McNaughton, John, 66
Médecins Sans Frontières, 127
Mecca, Zemzem well, 19
media, water crisis rhetoric, 9
Mekong river, 72, 170; dams, 165
Merlin, Pierre, 31
Mestrallet, Gérard, 119
Mexico, 149; drought, 97; Mexico City, 17; presidential campaign 2000, 60; ruralization, 129; –US water dispute, 66
Michalowski, Kazimierz, 59
microsoldering, water need, 142
'Millenium Challenge Account', 59
Millenium Development Goals, 182
Miller, Arthur, 104
Milwaukee, USA, 101
Minc Alain, 97
mining, 148
Mississippi river, 1993 floods, 155
Mogae, Festus, 60
Mohammed, the Prophet, 16, 20
Moisie river, Quebec, 11
Monod, Jérôme, 116
Mont Djurdjura bottled water, Algeria, 80
Moon river, 170
Morocco, 107, 148–9; dam construction, 78; Dayat Aoua lake, 76; High Atlas water struggles, 85; ocean humidity, 54; tourism, 130
Moscow, water-borne illness, 128
Mozambique: malaria, 131; privatization, 110
Müller, Stephan, 114
Muhamed, Askia, 164
Musi river, India, 34
Mwanzi, James, 130

N'Dow, Wally, 65
Nablus, 93
Nacer, Rostomi Hadj, 79
Naceri, Mohamed, 92
Nadeau, Barbie, 35
Nader, Ralph, 106
Namibia, 73; –Lesotho water dispute, 67
Naraj, Sunita, 139
NASA, US space agency, 41
Nasser, Gamal, 58, 159
National Audubon Society, USA, 152
natural gas extraction, 143
Nature, 41, 134
Nehru, Jawaharlal, 143, 159
Nestlé, 120, 137–8; Aquarel water brand, 136
Netherlands, 46, 100; external water dependence, 72
Nevada, US state, 43
New York, 143; water shortage, 76; water supply, 105
New Zealand, 178
Newton, Isaac, 12
Niger, 4, 52, 54; drought, 90; Keita district, 55; river, 55; water cost, 56
Nile river, 12–14, 26, 34, 59, 72, 130, 146; delta marshlands, 62; pollution, 85; White, 161
Nommo, spirit, 28
North American Free Trade Area (NAFTA), 116, 173
North Battleford, Saskatchewan, 102
North Sea, eutrophication, 145
North–South conference, Berne 1998, 168
North-West water company, UK, 98
Norwalk-like virus (NLV), 136
Norway: hydroelectric potential, 173; Krakeroy town, 175
Nu, divinity, 14

'occult precipitation', 54
oceans, climatic effect, 39
Odysseus, 14
OECD countries, per capita; water consumption, 5

Index

207

About this series

'Communities in the South are facing great difficulties in coping with global trends. I hope this brave new series will throw much needed light on the issues ahead and help us choose the right options.'

MARTIN KHOR, *Director,*
Third World Network, Penang

'There is no more important campaign than our struggle to bring the global economy under democratic control. But the issues are fearsomely complex. This Global Issues series is a valuable resource for the committed campaigner and the educated citizen.'

BARRY COATES,
Director, Oxfam New Zealand

'Zed Books has long provided an inspiring list about the issues that touch and change people's lives. The Global Issues series is another dimension of Zed's fine record, allowing access to a range of subjects and authors that, to my knowledge, very few publishers have tried. I strongly recommend these new, powerful titles and this exciting series.'

JOHN PILGER, *author*

'We are all part of a generation that actually has the means to eliminate extreme poverty world-wide. Our task is to harness the forces of globalization for the benefit of working people, their families and their communities – that is our collective duty. The Global Issues series makes a powerful contribution to the global campaign for justice, sustainable and equitable development, and peaceful progress.'

GLENYS KINNOCK, *MEP*

The Global Issues series

Already available

Peter Robbins, *Stolen Fruit: The Tropical Commodities Disaster*

Toby Shelley, *Oil: Politics, Poverty and the Planet*

Vandana Shiva, *Protect or Plunder? Understanding Intellectual Property Rights*

Toby Shelley, *Nanotechnology: New Promises, New Dangers*

Harry Shutt, *A New Democracy: Alternatives to a Bankrupt World Order*

David Sogge, *Give and Take: What's the Matter with Foreign Aid?*

Vivien Stern, *Creating Criminals: Prisons and People in a Market Society*

Paul Todd and Jonathan Bloch, *Global Intelligence: The World's Secret Services Today*

In preparation

Liz Kelly, *Violence against Women*

Alan Marshall, *A New Nuclear Age? The Case for Nuclear Power Revisited*

Roger Moody, *Digging the Dirt: The Modern World of Global Mining*

Edgar Pieterse, *City Futures: Confronting the Crisis of Urban Development*

Peter M. Rosset, *Food is Not Just Another Commodity: Why the WTO Should Get Out of Agriculture*

For full details of this list and Zed's other subject and general catalogues, please write to: The Marketing Department, Zed Books, 7 Cynthia Street, London NI 9JF, UK or email Sales@zedbooks.net

Visit our website at: www.zedbooks.co.uk

Participating organizations

Both ENDS A service and advocacy organization which collaborates with environment and indigenous organizations, both in the South and in the North, with the aim of helping to create and sustain a vigilant and effective environmental movement.

Nieuwe Keizersgracht 45, 1018 VC Amsterdam, The Netherlands
Phone: +31 20 623 0823   Fax: +31 20 620 8049
Email: info@bothends.org   Website: www.bothends.org

Catholic Institute for International Relations (CIIR) CIIR aims to contribute to the eradication of poverty through a programme that combines advocacy at national and international level with community-based development.

Unit 3, Canonbury Yard, 190a New North Road, London N1 7BJ, UK
Phone +44 (0)20 7354 0883   Fax +44 (0)20 7359 0017
Email: ciir@ciir.org   Website: www.ciir.org

Corner House The Corner House is a UK-based research and solidarity group working on social and environmental justice issues in North and South.

PO Box 3137, Station Road, Sturminster Newton, Dorset DT10 1YJ, UK
Tel.: +44 (0)1258 473795   Fax: +44 (0)1258 473748
Email: cornerhouse@gn.apc.org   Website: www.cornerhouse.icaap.org

Council on International and Public Affairs (CIPA) CIPA is a human rights research, education and advocacy group, with a particular focus on economic and social rights in the USA and elsewhere around the world. Emphasis in recent years has been given to resistance to corporate domination.

777 United Nations Plaza, Suite 3C, New York, NY 10017, USA
Tel. +1 212 972 9877   Fax +1 212 972 9878
Email: cipany@igc.org   Website: www.cipa-apex.org

Dag Hammarskjöld Foundation The Dag Hammarskjöld Foundation, established 1962, organises seminars and workshops on social, economic and cultural issues facing developing countries with a particular focus on alternative and innovative solutions. Results are published in its journal *Develpment Dialogue.*

Övre Slottsgatan 2, 753 10 Uppsala, Sweden.
Tel.: +46 18 102772   Fax: +46 18 122072
Email: secretariat@dhf.uu.se   Website: www.dhf.uu.se

Development GAP The Development Group for Alternative Policies is a Non-Profit Development Resource Organization working with popular organizations in the South and their Northern partners in support of a development that is truly sustainable and that advances social justice.

927 15th Street NW, 4th Floor, Washington, DC, 20005, USA
Tel.: +1 202 898 1566   Fax: +1 202 898 1612
E-mail: dgap@igc.org   Website: www.developmentgap.org

Focus on the Global South Focus is dedicated to regional and global policy analysis and advocacy work. It works to strengthen the capacity of organizations of the poor and marginalized people of the South and to better analyse and understand the impacts of the globalization process on their daily lives.

C/o CUSRI, Chulalongkorn University, Bangkok 10330, Thailand
Tel.: +66 2 218 7363 Fax: +66 2 255 9976
Email: Admin@focusweb.org   Website: www.focusweb.org

IBON IBON Foundation is a research, education and information institution that provides publications and services on socio-economic issues as support to advocacy in the Philippines and abroad. Through its research and databank, formal and non-formal education programmes, media work and international networking, IBON aims to build the capacity of both Philippine and international organizations.

Room 303 SCC Bldg, 4427 Int. Old Sta. Mesa, Manila 1008, Philippines
Phone +632 7132729   Fax +632 7160108
Email: editors@ibon.org   Website: www.ibon.org

Inter Pares Inter Pares, a Canadian social justice organization, has been active since 1975 in building relationships with Third World development groups and providing support for community-based development programmes. Inter Pares is also involved in education and advocacy in Canada, promoting understanding about the causes, effects and solutions to poverty.

221 Laurier Avenue East, Ottawa, Ontario, K1N 6P1 Canada
Phone +1 613 563 4801   Fax +1 613 594 4704
Email: info@interpares.ca   Website: www.interpares.ca

Public Interest Research Centre PIRC is a research and campaigning group based in Delhi which seeks to serve the information needs of activists and organizations working on macro-economic issues concerning finance, trade and development.

142 Maitri Apartments, Plot No. 28, Patparganj, Delhi 110092, India
Phone: +91 11 2221081/2432054   Fax: +91 11 2224233
Email: kaval@nde.vsnl.net.in

Third World Network TWN is an international network of groups and individuals involved in efforts to bring about a greater articulation of the needs and rights of peoples in the Third World; a fair distribution of the world's resources; and forms of development which are ecologically sustainable and fulfil human needs. Its international secretariat is based in Penang, Malaysia.

121-S Jalan Utama, 10450 Penang, Malaysia
Tel.: +60 4 226 6159   Fax: +60 4 226 4505
Email: twnet@po.jaring.my   Website: www.twnside.org.sg

Third World Network–Africa TWN–Africa is engaged in research and advocacy on economic, environmental and gender issues. In relation to its current particular interest in globalization and Africa, its work focuses on trade and investment, the extractive sectors and gender and economic reform.

2 Ollenu Street, East Legon, PO Box AN19452, Accra-North, Ghana.
Tel.: +233 21 511189/503669/500419   Fax: +233 21 511188
Email: twnafrica@ghana.com

World Development Movement (WDM) The World Development Movement campaigns to tackle the causes of poverty and injustice. It is a democratic membership movement that works with partners in the South to cancel unpayable debt and break the ties of IMF conditionality, for fairer trade and investment rules, and for strong international rules on multinationals.

25 Beehive Place, London SW9 7QR, UK
Tel.: +44 (0)20 7737 6215   Fax: +44 (0)20 7274 8232
Email: wdm@wdm.org.uk   Website: www.wdm.org.uk

This book is also available in the following countries

CARIBBEAN

Arawak Publications
17 Kensington Crescent
Apt 5
Kingston 5, Jamaica
Tel: 876 960 7538
Fax: 876 960 9219

EGYPT

MERIC
2 Bahgat Ali Street,
Tower D/Apt. 24
Zamalek, Cairo
Tel: 20 2 735 3818/3824
Fax: 20 2 736 9355

FIJI

University Book Centre,
University of South Pacific
Suva
Tel: 679 313 900
Fax: 679 303 265

GUYANA

Austin's Book Services
190 Church St
Cummingsburg
Georgetown
austins@guyana.net.gy
Tel: 592 227 7395
Fax: 592 227 7396

IRAN

Book City
743 North Hafez Avenue
15977 Tehran
Tel: 98 21 889 7875
Fax: 98 21 889 7785
bookcity@neda.net

MAURITIUS

Editions Le Printemps
4 Club Rd, Vacoas

NAMIBIA

Book Den
PO Box 3469, Shop 4
Frans Indongo Gardens
Windhoek
Tel: 264 61 239976
Fax: 264 61 234248

NEPAL

Everest Media Services,
GPO Box 5443
Dillibazar
Putalisadak Chowk
Kathmandu
Tel: 977 1 416026
Fax: 977 1 250176

NIGERIA

Mosuro Publishers
52 Magazine Road
Jericho, Ibadan
Tel: 234 2 241 3375
Fax: 234 2 241 3374

PAKISTAN

Vanguard Books
45 The Mall, Lahore
Tel: 92 42 735 5079
Fax: 92 42 735 5197

PAPUA NEW GUINEA

Unisearch PNG Pty Ltd
Box 320, University
National Capital District
Tel: 675 326 0130
Fax: 675 326 0127

RWANDA

Librairie Ikirezi
PO Box 443, Kigali
Tel/Fax: 250 71314

SUDAN

The Nile Bookshop
New Extension Street 41
PO Box 8036, Khartoum
Tel: 249 11 463 749

UGANDA

Aristoc Booklex Ltd
PO Box 5130, Kampala Rd
Diamond Trust Building
Kampala
Tel/Fax: 256 41 254867

ZAMBIA

UNZA Press
PO Box 32379, Lusaka
Tel: 260 1 290409
Fax: 260 1 253952